Entwined

Cherie Colyer

AN EMBRACE NOVEL

OMNIFIC PUBLISHING
LOS ANGELES

Omnific Publishing
1901 Avenue of the Stars, 2nd floor
Los Angeles, CA 90067
www.omnificpublishing.com

First Omnific eBook edition, April 2015
First Omnific trade paperback edition, April 2015

The characters and events in this book are fictitious.
Any similarity to real persons, living or dead,
is coincidental and not intended by the author.

Library of Congress Cataloguing-in-Publication Data

Colyer, Cherie.
  Entwined / Cherie Colyer – 1st ed.
  ISBN: 978-1-623421-96-0
  1. Witchcraft — Fiction. 2. Paranormal — Fiction.
  3. Romance — Fiction. 4. Magic — Fiction. I. Title

10 9 8 7 6 5 4 3 2 1

Cover Design by Micha Stone and Amy Brokaw
Interior Book Design by Coreen Montagna

Printed in the United States of America

This one is for my readers.
You helped make this book possible,
and I'm so very grateful to you.

Chapter 1

Digging Up the Past

The third grave on the left belonged to Vladimir Godspeed. He died in 1666. Not that I could easily tell that from the worn etching on his tombstone. It's just that I'd been staring at the block letters long enough to figure it out. To say I wasn't happy to be standing next to his grave was an understatement. What made me even less happy was the countless number of shades that lingered in this graveyard. At least, that's what Josh Corey, my good friend, called spirits that took up residence in cemeteries. Never before had I seen so many lost souls. And even though Josh had assured me that shades were nothing more than vapor, they still creeped me out.

A low moan from somewhere off in the distance had me turning to my left with a jerk. The beam of my flashlight stretched outward, illuminating rows of decaying tombstones that seemed to never end. Everything else was lost in the black abyss that was just before nine on a cold February evening in Massachusetts. I wanted to go home, but I wasn't calling the shots.

A demon was.

Caden leaned on a spade with a lit cigarette in his mouth as he watched the hellfire he'd created melt the last of winter's snow from the base of the headstone.

It was his fault I was outside, miles away from my date, freezing my butt off. That's the problem with being in a demon's debt; he can, and most likely will, come to collect at the worst possible times. Caden always did.

"Can you please hurry up?" I whined. My words came out in a puff of white fog.

"The ground's frozen." Caden looked at me through strands of dark hair. "So unless you're going to do the digging, we're waiting until it thaws."

A six-foot shade slithered up to me, stopping inches from my nose. Startled, I screamed, scaring it and me.

Caden shook his head. "If you're nervous to be out here, why don't you cast that calming spell you're so fond of? You'll be too relaxed to care if the dead rise."

"Because I'd rather have my wits about me." I stomped my feet to get feeling back in my toes. Had I known I'd be standing around outside, I'd have worn my fuzzy boots. "This could have waited until morning," I complained for probably the fifth time. "Why are we here again?"

"I told you, to tame death." Caden dropped his cigarette on the ground and snuffed it out with the sole of his shoe.

"Like you can't do that any time of day." He was a crossroad demon with hell's powers at his fingertips. There wasn't much he couldn't do, for a price.

His eyes flashed red—a warning that his patience wore thin. I pressed my lips together to keep from saying anything else.

Caden and I had a working relationship, thanks to the deal I had made with him last December. In the ten weeks since then, I'd removed devil's shoestring from around the windows and doors of three of his clients' homes. I repaired a long scratch in the black paint of his Subaru. And I did a séance so that Caden could talk to the spirit of his old friend Emily Brontë. Caden had sworn he had important information for her, which he didn't. Not unless you counted pointing out to the famous writer that he'd told her she didn't need to make a deal for her work to become a part of history.

Lately, I got the impression Caden sat up at night thinking of things for me to do. To make matters worse, every time he came to call, I was hanging out with my boyfriend, Isaac Addington. I didn't have to read minds to know that Isaac had just about had it with Caden's interruptions or that Isaac spent his nights dreaming up ways to send Caden back to hell permanently. Still, the deal I'd made with Caden was simple: he'd brought my little brother back from the edge of death, and in exchange I became his Beck-and-Call Witch. That meant I did as he requested when he requested, no questions asked.

Only nineteen years, nine months, and two weeks to go. Not that I was counting or anything.

My gaze fell on the shovel, and his last comment sank in.

"Wait! I am not raising the dead. Oh, no-no-no." I paced a few steps away from him. "Definitely not. You agreed that you wouldn't ask me to do anything that would taint my soul, and I'm sure bringing the dead back to life is a form of dark magic."

"Our deal included subclause twenty-three A — to paraphrase, I wouldn't ask you to *kill* on my behalf. Nothing was said about tainting your soul. Do you want to read the contract?"

My forearms burned as if someone had sprinkled hot ashes over my skin. I yanked the sleeve of my jacket up as far as it would go. Glowing red letters covered my arm.

I screamed, rubbing at the writing. Halfway down my wrist, I saw the words *Subclause 23a: Client shall not be asked to take the life of another human being.* "Okay, okay! Get it off me!"

The writing faded along with the pain.

"You can relax." Caden pierced the ground in front of the tombstone with the shovel. "Besides being gross and a hassle to deal with, zombies are too hard to shove back into the grave." His dark gaze met mine. "You'd be surprised how hard it is to kill something that is already dead. Therefore, we aren't raising anyone."

I yanked my sleeve back down. "You could have just said that."

"And you could stop acting as if you don't like our little getaways. Unfortunately, we don't always get what we want." He rested the sole of his boot on the top of the shovel and paused. "Do you think you can summon the tin box that's buried about two feet down? You'd save us time."

"I have to be able to see the item I want to teleport." Being under pressure helped too.

"Have you ever tried?" Caden leaned on the spade, an eyebrow raised in challenge.

"Yes." I kicked the shovel out from under him.

He didn't even stumble. "Maybe you just need practice."

I frowned. I wasn't in the mood to have a creature from hell give me magic lessons.

To show him that I knew my limitations when it came to the powers, I held my hand in front of me, palm up. "Tin box."

Nothing.

"Caden's tin box." I jerked my hand for emphasis. Caden rolled his eyes. "Caden's stupid tin box!"

If there really was a box buried there, it remained under the soil. "Told you, I have to be able to see what I'm summoning."

He snatched the shovel from the grass. "It didn't work because you didn't believe it would."

The six-foot shade came back, this time stopping a few feet to Caden's right. It watched him dig. I glared at it, silently telling it to keep its distance, as if that would really work. I adjusted my knit hat to cover my ears better. "Will you hurry up so that you can get me back to the game before it's over?"

"You don't even like basketball." Caden tossed a shovelful of dirt aside.

He only knew that because of the faraway, lost expression I got whenever he talked sports while we drove to our different destinations. "I like the company."

He glanced up from his work. "Want to know what I think?"

"No."

The sound of metal hitting tin spared me his reply. He knelt and pulled a rusty container the size of a small clutch from inside the hole he'd dug. He lifted the lid and removed a five-inch length of chain. The beam from my flashlight reflected off the intricate silver links.

"You dragged me out here to retrieve a bracelet?" It looked expensive, like something you'd get at Tiffany's.

His mouth tugged upward into a devilish smile. "This isn't a bracelet, nor is it an ordinary piece of jewelry."

It appeared ordinary enough to me. "What's it do?"

He dropped the chain back into the box, slipped it inside his jacket pocket, and stood. "You're on a need-to-know basis, and you don't need to know."

"Seriously?" When he nodded, I asked, "How did you know where to find it?"

"Because I was the one who buried it." He picked up the spade and began to fill the hole. "Are you done with your questions?"

"No." I tried to grab the box out of his pocket and missed.

"Need I remind you our contract states *no questions asked?*"

"That only applies when you ask me to use my powers." So far, all I'd been tasked with was holding the flashlight. Had I not been so annoyed with him, I would have used my powers to create better light to work by. "Why dig it up now in the middle of the night like thieves? Unless it's not yours."

"It's mine." A shovelful of dirt went into the hole.

"Then why the cloak and dagger?"

"Because I'm not the only one interested in it." More dirt went in the hole.

"Who else wants it?"

Caden sighed and stepped on the loose dirt to mat it down. "Need-to-know basis, Madison."

The dulcet taste of my magic morphed to copper as my curiosity turned into frustration. I zapped him with a gossamer bolt of energy.

His brow furrowed. "Did you just assault me with magic?"

"Trust me; if I assault you, it will be with something bigger and more powerful than that." I folded my arms over my chest to keep from doing it again, because I wanted to, and I was pretty sure Caden wouldn't tolerate a second attack. "Why am I here? You obviously didn't need me to retrieve the chain."

He stomped once more on the freshly disturbed soil. "I need you to make it so that no one knows we were here."

My mouth fell open. "You want me to make the grass grow?"

"Grow and then die — it's sort of brown." He leaned against Vladimir's headstone and indicated with a nod for me to get to work.

"This could have waited until *after* the basketball game, and don't try to deny it." I waved my hand over the gravesite, pushing out a little magic. The new grass — more brown than green — knitted together perfectly with its surroundings. "Happy?"

He studied the gravesite. "Yeah. That's good."

We headed back to the car. Frozen grass crunched under our shoes.

"Caden, promise me that the next time you need me to zap something for you, you'll wait to get me until I'm alone."

"Oh, come on!" He gave me a sideways glance. "Admit it. I'm much more exciting than Witch Boy."

"Are not." I skirted around a shade that drifted in my path. "I'm serious. This is the fifth time you've interrupted me and Isaac."

"I know."

I grabbed his wrist to get him to slow his pace. "You're doing it to piss Isaac off, aren't you?"

"Not really, but I do enjoy that little side perk of our relationship. Did you see his face?" Caden stopped walking to look at me — mouth pulled down into a stern scowl and eyes narrowed in hatred to mock Isaac — then he burst out laughing. "For a moment, I was afraid he'd explode. Was that potent stench of steel coming from him?"

"You know it was, and you should stop provoking him."

"Like I said before, where's the fun in that?"

I stalked ahead of him. For a creature that had been around for centuries, he had the maturity level of a six-year-old. He popped the trunk and dropped the shovel inside.

I tossed the flashlight in next to it. "Are all demons as childish as you?"

"You have to enjoy the little things in life: pissing off a witch, the company of a pretty girl, and French fries."

"Don't forget ice cream — it's one of man's finer delicacies," a deep voice said from behind us. Caden froze, hands on the open trunk. "And then there's greed, deception, and hatred, but humans don't have the corner on that market. Do they?"

The guy looked to be in his early twenties. He was husky with broad shoulders, russet brown hair, and the type of smirk that screamed trouble. His angled nose and high cheekbones were a little too perfect, causing me to wonder if he was Fae and donning a glamour to hide his true appearance.

Caden slammed his trunk shut. "What do you want, Derek?"

"World peace." Derek pulled a pack of cigarettes out of his coat and held it out to us, which made me rule out the possibility of him being Fae. Faeries didn't smoke. When neither Caden nor I accepted his offer, Derek shrugged and tapped out a cigarette. The pack went back into his pocket. "Aren't you going to introduce me to your friend?"

"No." Caden turned and nudged me backward toward the passenger side of the car.

Derek stepped closer. "What are you doing here, Caden?"

Digging for treasure, I thought snarkily.

Derek's gaze snapped to me. Caden cursed. Over his shoulder I saw Derek's lips curl around the cigarette hanging from his mouth. The tip glowed, lighting without the need of a match or a lighter. His eyes flashed red like Caden's often did. And, like Caden, he could apparently read minds.

"You're a demon," I said before I could stop myself.

Derek spared me another brief smirk before holding up his hand and wiggling his fingers. "Give me the binding chain. I'll give it to Alistair, and if you're lucky, he'll forget about you for a decade or so."

"It wasn't here," Caden said with cool indifference.

He's not lying. All we got for our trouble was a rusty old tin...

Caden nonchalantly stomped on my foot, effectively cutting off the rest of my thoughts. To keep my mind off his trinket, I studied Derek. He had shifty eyes the color of storm clouds and a stance that made me think he hoped Caden would make a move to fight him.

Derek twirled the cigarette between his thumb and index finger with bored interest. "He doesn't trust you, Caden."

"You wouldn't be here if he did." Caden frowned. "You've become the perfect servant, haven't you?"

Derek blew a thin line of smoke in Caden's face. "I prefer to look at it as self-preservation."

"You would," Caden grumbled.

"That's her, isn't it?" Derek's scrutinizing gaze traveled the length of my body. I felt exposed, like he could see through my jacket and clothes, right down to my birthday suit. "The witch that has the boss excited."

I forced myself to drag my attention away from Derek. "Caden, what's he talking about?"

"Nothing." Caden pushed me closer to the passenger door. "Get in."

"He didn't tell you, did he?" Derek took a long pull on the cigarette, clearly enjoying catching us off guard.

"Tell me what?" I swatted Caden's hands off my shoulders.

It was Derek who answered. "The boss nearly pissed his pants when your contract reached his desk."

"What?" I croaked at the same time Caden rounded on Derek, but not before I saw his irises go from warm brown to fire-engine red.

"Her contract is within hell's guidelines," Caden said, "and Alistair knows it. He's just mad that he didn't make the deal himself."

I took that to mean this boss wasn't happy I wasn't in *his* debt, and for once I was thankful that Caden had dotted every I and crossed every T in our contract, leaving no room for any mistakes on what had been agreed to.

Derek snorted. "No, Brother, he's happy to finally have something to hold over your head. You messed up, and you know it."

Caden didn't reply to Derek. Instead, he turned his disapproving gaze to me. "Get. In. The. Car."

I did. It was better to get a ride home with the angry demon I knew than the menacing one who'd shown up out of nowhere. Caden had just slid into the driver's seat when Derek yelled, "You have less than two weeks to bring him what he wants, or he will kill you and everyone you call a friend."

Caden rolled down the window and stuck his arm out, flipping Derek the bird as we peeled away.

Chapter 2

Demon Trouble

Caden wouldn't tell me why his boss had any emotion whatsoever when it came to my contract. Although I suspected it was because I got to keep my soul. Typically a deal with a crossroad demon cost people that plus years off their life. He wouldn't discuss his brother either, and I had a ton of questions about their relationship. Like why did they hate each other? How had they both ended up in hell? Did Derek hope to be assigned to Caden's crossroad? And if he was, would that mean my contract transferred to him? Then there was the binding chain. What was it, and why did Caden's boss want it?

Caden either ignored my request to be driven back to school so that I could meet up with my friends, or he wasn't really listening to me. I peppered him with questions as he drove me home. He spoke a total of five words: "Need-to-know basis, Madison."

It was infuriating. The guy could read minds. He had to know his silence was maddening and making me want to search for answers on my own. He didn't seem to care, though.

I called Isaac to let him know I was home. I could tell by his pause and then the monotone "Thanks for letting me know" that he wasn't happy I didn't come back to the game. I decided talking about my evening could wait until morning.

Isaac picked me up at nine a.m. on Sunday.

"Good morning." I climbed into his dark green Jeep Rubicon and leaned over the center console to give him a kiss.

His smile reached his velvet brown eyes. "Coffee?"

"Definitely." The stronger the better; I hadn't gotten a lot of sleep, and what I did get was restless and filled with creatures that should only exist in nightmares. I reminded myself that I was going to enjoy the morning. I breathed in deeply to clear my mind. There'd be time to stress later. "It's a beautiful day."

The sun shone brightly in the pale blue sky, heating the air to a tolerable forty degrees. I even saw a robin, a sure sign that spring wasn't far away. It was the type of morning that made me want to pretend I didn't have a care in the world—which is what I was going for until I had caffeine in me—so when Isaac asked if I'd mind taking the long way to his house, I rested my hand over his on the stick shift and said no. The long way added another fifteen minutes to the drive, but it took us along the ocean. He cranked the heat and headed toward Main Street.

"We got killed last night," Isaac said, referring to the basketball game I'd missed. He went over the highlights as I relished the warmth of the sun on my face and the feel of his hand under mine. This was how life should be—a boy and a girl enjoying a morning cruise with the radio playing in the background.

"Did you go out afterward?" I asked when he finished. Before Caden had shown up and cut our date short, Isaac and I had planned on going to The Grill to meet up with friends.

"Nah." He downshifted and took a right into the parking lot at the coffee house. We went through the drive-through. "Sarah asked about you, though. I told her you weren't feeling well."

"Good to know." I'd have to remember not to be surprised if she asked me how I was doing. "I had an interesting night."

I filled Isaac in on the events in the graveyard as we drove to his house. He raked his fingers through his short brown hair when I mentioned Vladimir Godspeed's grave.

"Caden's taking advantage of the deal you made with him," he griped. It was what he said each time I told him about the menial tasks Caden had me perform. And while Isaac was probably right, it wasn't like hell had a complaint line. But his interest was piqued when I mentioned the chain Caden had dug up.

His eyes narrowed. "I've never heard of a binding chain."

"Caden didn't want me to know what it was." I took a sip of my pumpkin spice latte and then told him about Derek. By the time I got to their boss, the color had drained from Isaac's face.

He stopped in the left turn lane. The shadow of concern haunted his eyes. "How could you let me ramble on about the game?"

I scrunched up my nose. "I needed a moment of normal."

A few minutes later, we were at his house. Isaac and I descended the curved stone staircase that led to his basement bedroom. One by one, the candles nestled in the small nooks along the rough brick wall lit.

Isaac's room was unconventional. The floor was stone and the walls were brick. A waist-high iron ring wrapped its way around the circular room, and above us, an old-fashioned iron chandelier dangled from the ceiling. His bedroom was a safe haven from the paranormal. Everything had a reason for being there. The iron fixtures made his room unwelcoming to faeries—a creature allergic to the metal. The devil's shoestring above the door kept demons out. And the many wards Isaac had cast ensured that those who did walk down the stairs had no ill intent against him or his coven.

Isaac set his extra-large mocha with a double shot of espresso on the dresser. "Caden must have had one messed up family for both him and his brother to end up in hell."

"Tell me about it." I sent a wave of power into my latte to warm it and then breathed in its spicy goodness while Isaac rifled through his closet.

"I'm not sure what to focus on: the chain, Derek, or Caden's boss."

I'd had last night to think that over. "We don't know if Caden's boss was excited *good* or excited *bad*, and we don't know what the deal is between Derek and Caden. What we do know is they want the chain. Derek called it a binding chain. I'm not sure what that means, but I'll bet it's a talisman, and if it's a talisman—"

"It's been touched by a witch," Isaac and I said in unison.

I placed a bag of banana walnut muffins and my latte next to his drink and knelt down in front of the black sphere chair to get a look at the books haphazardly piled on top of it.

Last night I had scoured the Internet for any reference of binding necklaces, demon artifacts, and one Vladimir Godspeed. My search was fruitless. But Isaac had an extensive library covering the supernatural at his disposal. It was a benefit of having parents that had learned about the powers from their parents. His ancestors passed down grimoires, journals, and books on the obscure from generation to generation, keeping their families' spells and knowledge of the paranormal alive. Isaac had a wealth of information available to him. Unlike me, who had recently discovered the powers and only had a Hello Kitty journal one-fourth full of the spells I'd learned to date.

Isaac dug his late grandfather's grimoire from the back of his closet.

I moved a book on herbs aside and grabbed *Talismans and Amulets* beneath it. "Think this one might have something useful?"

"Maybe."

We sat on the bed with our backs against the wall. I flipped to the index of *Talismans and Amulets* and quickly discovered that I wasn't going to get lucky and actually find "binding chains." The book did have a large section on good luck charms, though. I contemplated making one. Maybe an Irish four-leaf clover would up my chances of finding what I wanted.

I closed the book with a thump.

"Don't give up yet." Vanilla and spearmint—Isaac's powers—saturated the air a moment before his mocha disappeared from the dresser and reappeared in his hand. He looked at me as if to say, *Your turn.*

I raised my eyebrows. "You sure you want me summoning coffee while I'm sitting on your bed?"

My ability to teleport items from one place to another had greatly improved since my night in the cemetery with Josh, but I was far from perfect. More often than I'd like to admit, the thing I tried to retrieve would make it halfway to me before it appeared out of reach and crashed to the floor.

"I have faith in your abilities."

At least one of us did. I sighed. "Just remember this was your idea."

He kissed me, a tender peck on my cheek, and then smiled. "You spill it, you clean it up. But I've noticed a trend with you and that spell. If it's something you really want, it works."

"It is the last week I can get pumpkin spice."

Isaac chuckled and kept reading as if he really wasn't worried that I'd screw up the spell and drench his bed with milk and coffee.

I drew my powers to the surface and focused on my latte. It quaked, making me thankful for the plastic cap that kept the coffee from sloshing over the sides.

"I'm not helping with the mess if you do drop it," Isaac said without looking away from the page he was reading.

"Concentrating here…"

Out of the corner of my eye, I saw him grin. "Get the bag with breakfast in it too, will you?"

"Shh!" I took a deep breath. "Latte!"

My drink vanished. I prayed it didn't reappear out of my reach. A very long second later, I held it tight in my grasp. A smile graced my face as I said, "Muffins." The brown bag didn't so much as twitch, but two large muffins appeared in my free hand.

Isaac set his coffee on the nightstand next to him and took a pastry. "I never doubted you."

His faith in my magic was one of the things I liked about him. It was the reason he pushed me to keep practicing. *"If you believe you can do it, then any spell you cast will work."* If he said it once, he had said it a hundred times.

Maybe Caden had been right, and the reason I couldn't summon the tin from underground was because I questioned my abilities. I brushed the thought aside. He was a demon. The only reason he'd wanted me to get the spell right was to make his life easier.

Isaac held the leather-bound book he'd been reading a few inches above his lap. It drifted upward, floating to a stop when it was chest height between us. A page turned to the next on its own.

We sipped our drinks and ate our breakfast as we flipped through the discolored pages of his grimoire. We must have scanned a few dozen spells when one jumped out at me. I pointed to the curvy writing. *"Potestas* is Latin for power, isn't it?" When Isaac nodded, I went on. *"Transfero Potestas.* Is that the spell your grandfather used to will his powers to you?"

Isaac ran his hand over the page, smoothing it. "Yeah. It's actually a very simple spell."

He wasn't kidding. You didn't even need to be in the same room as the person you were giving your powers to. Just chant the spell three times, finish up with *as I will it, so mote it be,* and voila! Your powers were transferred to another witch. Isaac's grandfather had given his powers to Isaac five years ago before he passed away. At the time, it had made Isaac a very powerful twelve-year-old.

I used a levitation spell to float my empty cup to the trash can. I then spun around so that I sat facing Isaac, legs straight and ankles crossed. "What's it like to have your grandfather's powers flowing through your veins?"

I had half the magic that he had, and there were times I felt as if I could fly. I couldn't imagine being even stronger.

Isaac's hand went to the Green Man charm hidden beneath his sweater. I knew it had been his grandfather's and that Isaac rarely took it off. "At first, it was sort of like chugging too many energy drinks. I felt wired, had a hard time sleeping, blew a lot of things up doing what should have been easy spells. My dad used to say I was like a hundred-twenty-volt appliance plugged into a two-hundred-twenty-volt outlet. I had more power than I knew what to do with. Casting took twice as much concentration, but I learned how to control the added powers and eventually they merged with mine."

"Or you grew into them."

"I suppose." Isaac turned to the next page in the grimoire.

I fell backward on the bed, landing with a soft bounce. "I can't stare at the tiny writing in that book another minute."

As much as I wanted to figure out what Caden and his cronies were up to, between last night and so far today, I'd spent the better part of twelve hours searching for anything that would tell me about the fancy silver chain. I needed a break.

Isaac set the book down next to him and leaned over me. "You know, out of all the people I know who possess the powers, you're the only one who has a knack for finding yourself in the middle of supernatural threats."

I pursed my lips. "That's not true. Your ex-girlfriend royally pissed off the Prince of Fae, and you've told me stories about the things you and your friends did."

He laughed. "I knew telling you about my search for Gloucester's sea serpent was going to come back to bite me."

Isaac had told me that he and two friends had spent an entire summer break trying to find the mysterious creature. Closest they'd come had been some old rope probably lost by sailors back in the early nineteen hundreds and an algae-covered rubber galosh.

He brushed a few strands of hair away from my face. "What do you want to do?"

I propped myself up on my elbows so that I was a breath away from his mouth. "This." My lips skimmed his. "Or this." My hand slid under his shirt.

He glanced at the grimoire still open on the edge of the bed. "What about—"

I placed a finger over his lips to keep him from saying Caden's name. "We deserve a break."

Isaac smiled. "If you insist."

Our lips met. Brief nibbles turned into slow, passionate kisses. I tucked my powers behind the imaginary wall in my mind to keep them from colliding with Isaac's. "Maybe we should become hermits and just stay down here."

It was a nice thought, one I knew was silly and impossible.

Isaac played along, though. "What about food?"

"Your parents keep the fridge stocked. We'll just twitch our noses and have the food come to us."

"That could work." Isaac wrapped an arm around my waist and spun us around so that I lay on top of him. "Let the demons battle it out without us."

"Exactly."

My favorite song blared from my phone, but I let the call go to voice mail. I was taking a break from reality, after all. Whoever wanted me could wait.

Isaac's hands traveled slowly up my waist and over my back. My fingers got lost in his silky hair. The smell of his cologne mixed with the sweet scent of magic. Any moment now and his powers would reach out to mine in a way that allowed them to mingle instead of colliding and shocking us. I waited for it, but then a chime indicated I'd gotten a message.

Isaac moaned. "You better see who it is or they'll just keep texting."

Much to my dismay, I knew he was right. I hopped up to grab my phone from the dresser. "It's probably my dad checking to see if I can watch Chase for a while or Sarah wanting to know how I'm doing."

One glance at my phone and I wished I'd stuck to ignoring it.

Answer the phone. The message was from Caden. Talk about a mood killer.

My fingers flew over the screen as I typed my reply: *Busy here.*

I scowled at the phone, knowing damn well that he wouldn't care. Sure enough, my phone rang.

"What?" I snapped into it. I'd bet money he knew I was with Isaac.

"Good evening to you too." Caden sounded as if he was in his car.

"It was." I lowered myself onto the corner of the bed. Isaac mumbled something that I couldn't hear and grabbed the grimoire. "Caden, you can't possibly need me so soon."

"I don't. I ran into Derek at the hardware store. He's poking around. Asking questions."

"About you or me?" I had played down my concerns about Derek and this boss of theirs so as not to worry Isaac, but I really didn't like the idea of being on a demon's radar.

"Both. Your dad overheard him mention your name to the cashier."

"What?" Caden worked for my dad. How that came about was a long story. Now, however, Caden claimed being a handyman's assistant kept him busy.

Mark Donovan worked at the hardware store. That had to be whom Derek had talked to. My mouth hung open as I tried to digest the news that a demon was stalking me.

"Your dad doesn't know what I am or what you are. Derek won't bother him—"

"How do you know?" My deal with Caden wasn't supposed to put my family in danger. Deals with crossroad demons were strictly between the demon and the person asking for a favor. I scooped my hair away from my face and held it at the back of my head. "If he blackmails my dad into selling his soul—"

"Crossroad demons don't seek out souls. Derek's fishing, trying to find dirt on me." There was a pause. I imagined Caden sweeping a hand through his hair and it falling in a mass of black right back over his eyes. "Look, Madison, the only people that are supposed to know what I am are those who visit my crossroad. You and I have a contract, so of course you know. But your coven…" Another pause. "Derek might approach your friends. He's crafty. He'll find a way to question them without them knowing they're under interrogation.

They can't let him find out they know about your deal, what I am, or that Derek's a demon."

"He can read minds." I pointed out. "How do you expect them to keep all that a secret if he can pluck thoughts right out of their heads?"

"He can't search their minds for information. He'll only know what they're thinking." I heard a door close. Then a hissing sound I assumed was the wind accompanied his next words. "Madison, no amount of power will be able to protect them from hell's fury if he finds out they know the truth. If you have to, make them promise not to think about me or demons or any of it."

A promise like that would mean I was on my own. That I couldn't talk to my best friend about the things going on in my life. That I had to keep secrets from Isaac. My mouth opened and closed like a guppy out of water. I needed my coven, but how was I supposed to keep the people I loved safe and fight demons?

"I've got to go," he said. "Just warn your friends, and they'll be fine."

By the sudden silence coming from the receiver, I knew Caden had hung up.

Isaac glanced up from the grimoire. "What did he want?"

I wouldn't base my relationship with Isaac on secrets—he deserved better than that—so I told him.

He strummed a finger along the edge of the pages, lifting them up and letting them fall, as I repeated everything Caden had said.

"I don't want you to get hurt." I didn't want *anyone* to. "I'll understand if you choose to make that promise."

"Not going to happen." Isaac held the book so that I could see it. Written in calligraphy at the top of the page were the words *Chains that Bind.*

I scooted closer and read the first paragraph. A binding chain was made up of four sections, each spelled under its own blue moon. "What exactly is a blue moon?"

"It's the third of four full moons in a season. It happens once every two and a half to three years."

I quickly did the math in my head. "So it takes twelve years to make one of these things."

"Yep." Isaac turned the book so he could read from it. "Listen to what's needed—blood of a dead witch, bone of a newborn, dirt from the grave of a friend. The list goes on."

I had to read the ingredients myself to make sure I heard him correctly, and they got stranger: water from a glacier heated over the fires of hell, salt from the Mediterranean Sea, the bloom of a *koki'o*.

"What the heck is a *koki'o?*"

He dug his cell phone from his pocket and brought up a search engine. "A very rare tree."

"This is serious magic." Far more complicated than anything I'd ever seen, and I'd read through several of Isaac's books. "Why would your grandfather have a dark spell in his grimoire?"

"He used to call this book a rare and valuable collection, but more than half the spells in it have never been cast by me or him. And it's not the spell that's dark."

"It requires the bone of a newborn!"

"It doesn't say you have to take it from the living."

I shuddered at the thought of exhuming an infant, not at all convinced this talisman wasn't made from dark magic. My finger landed on the notes in the margin. "A binding chain gives its wearer the ability to control another person?"

"Human or otherwise." Isaac pinched the bridge of his nose. I got the impression that, deep down, he did think the spell that created the binding chain was a dark one.

"A demon could control any one of us if he got his hands on the necklace." Maybe even our entire coven. "Caden didn't want Derek to know he had the first piece."

"Of course he didn't. Caden has a witch to do his bidding." When I opened my mouth to correct Isaac, he added, "You have to do what Caden asks, or your brother will have a relapse and die. I know you, Madison; you're not going to let anything happen to Chase."

There were limitations to what I'd do. I wouldn't kill or use dark magic. Subclause 23a or not, Caden knew that.

"You said yourself that a witch is worth a lot in hell," Isaac said, thinking out loud. "So this boss finds out that Caden has a witch in his service. That makes Caden powerful."

"You think his boss wants the chain to even out the playing field?"

"Or up it. Think about it. If he has that chain, he won't need a deal to be made to have control over a witch's actions, and there'd be no limits to what he can make him or her do."

I mulled that over a moment. "He'd target someone who's more powerful than me." That's what I would do if I were an evil, power-hungry demon.

My mind whirled with more questions that it wouldn't allow my mouth to voice. What if Derek was trying to figure out who was in my coven? What if he was looking for a witch whose magic was stronger than mine? An even scarier thought occurred to me: what if their boss *hadn't* sent Derek here? What if Derek just wanted to outdo his brother by finding a witch for himself? Isaac was the strongest member of my coven. My magic was no match for his. But that never mattered, because we were on the same side.

For now.

Isaac laid a crimson ribbon along the grimoire's crease and closed the book. "What I don't get is why Caden just doesn't leave the chain hidden. The guy's smart. Something else is going on if he's willing to look for the piece now, when others are so interested in it."

I got up and paced. I was missing something. Caden owned the chain. He'd hidden it. Isaac was right; why dig it up? "Derek said their boss would kill Caden if he didn't get the chain."

Could he, though? I thought about our trip to Vladimir's gravesite. Caden hadn't been nervous. He hadn't been the one looking over his shoulder at every creak and moan. He'd been his cocky, normal self.

"Why were we there?" I knocked my knuckles against my forehead as I paced.

"I told you, to tame death."

"Omigod, he meant it literally," I stammered.

"Who meant what literally?"

"Caden. He said we were taming death, only I thought he meant *the dead*. What if he meant Death with a capital D, the actual horseman of the Apocalypse? Caden would be invincible." But why now? Why wouldn't he seize this power before? I reached the stairs, pivoted on my heels, and had stalked back to the bed when the realization finally hit me. Maybe Caden only had the one piece. "He needs a witch." That had to be it. "To find the rest of the pieces. Maybe even to raise Death."

Isaac thought so too. I could tell by the way his gaze didn't quite meet mine and his jaw muscle twitched.

Chapter 3

Time with the Dead

I refused to talk about talismans, demons, or anything supernatural after that. Childish of me, probably. But the thought of being dragged into a battle for control between creatures more powerful than me and my friends combined was something that I needed time to digest. It was a problem that would be there in the morning, which was exactly what I told Isaac when I put the grimoire away and insisted on being driven home so that I could do homework. For once, I was thrilled to have an impossible amount of reading to do for English. And, as Mr. Chaplin's assignments usually did, the book put me to sleep in no time.

Unfortunately, it wasn't a peaceful sleep. I dreamed of bizarre rituals under Play-Doh-blue moons, Ferrari-red moons, and even a school-bus-yellow moon that dripped blood. In another dream, a demon whose face I couldn't see forced me to do a spell that killed everyone in my gym class. To add to the already disturbing list of nightmares, Derek tricked my best friend, Kaylee, into giving up her soul in yet another dream.

It wasn't until my dreams turned to Sanctus and the Prince of Fae that my mind relaxed. Reed was a world away, trapped in the faerie realm. I couldn't become mesmerized by his stormy white eyes or hypnotized by his silky voice in a dream. He couldn't mess with my head from a different dimension. In my dream, Reed bowed and peered at me through a curtain of platinum blond hair. I replied with a smile. I don't remember much after that.

I woke with a start at an ungodly hour. My hair stuck to the sweat on my forehead. The memory of a bacca drop lingered on my tongue. Its nutty yet sweet bouquet had me licking my lips.

"Ugh!" I swung my legs over the edge of my mattress and cursed the lingering effect I still had from consuming faerie food more than two months ago. My hands weren't trembling, though, and my stomach didn't ache like it had when Reed was here in my world. I was getting better.

No, I was better. I just hadn't forgotten how good Reed's candy tasted.

It was only 4:48. An hour and a half before my alarm would go off. I curled onto my side, hugging my deep purple comforter. A few minutes later, I squeezed my eyes shut and rolled to my stomach. Then flipped onto my back. When I didn't drift back to sleep, I twisted to my other side, one knee hanging over side of the mattress, and groaned. Too awake to sleep, I threw the covers back and grabbed my phone off the nightstand. My fingers tapped out a quick message to Kaylee as I made my way to the bathroom: *Pick me up?*

A minute went by, giving me time to relieve my bladder.

You do know it's 5 in the MORNING. Right?

I washed my hands and then replied: *Can't sleep. Coffee's on me.*

My teeth were brushed by the time Kaylee replied.

I'm ordering a venti.

10 minutes?

And a muffin.

9 min 50 sec?

Be outside.

I smiled and hurried back to my room to slip into a pair of jeans and a sweater. Downstairs, I scribbled a quick note on a sheet of loose-leaf paper to let Dad know I left early — it went next to the coffeemaker — and I put the birthday card I'd made Chase a few days ago on the table where he ate breakfast. I then grabbed the silk flowers I'd bought Mom and put them in my backpack.

That took about nine minutes. I sat on the front stoop, backpack at my side, swinging my purse between my legs as I waited for Kaylee.

If Mom were here, she'd have some crazy advice that would put things into perspective. She'd say just the right thing, and I'd know what to do. She was great that way.

The sky was a rolling canvas of midnight blue streaked with steel-gray clouds. It reminded me of the dream with the bleeding moon. Searching for the real one in the sky, I found the faint white thumbnail of the waxing moon off to my right just over the roof of my neighbor's garage.

It's uncanny how quiet my block is before dusk. No dogs barking, no sound of rubber on asphalt, no doors slamming. I glanced up the street, hoping to see Kaylee's British green MINI Cooper. A dark reflection in the glass of my dad's pickup truck caught my eye. I jerked my head and looked behind me, expecting to see Dad standing on the porch in his gray sweatpants and black T-shirt, ready to ask if I realized just how early it was, but no one was there. I looked back at the pickup, and the shadow I'd seen was gone. Or maybe it was never there.

I shook my head. "Lack of sleep is making me delusional."

My foot tapped impatiently on the walk. A few minutes later, Kaylee pulled her car to a stop in front of my house.

"Don't say it," she said as I slid into the passenger seat.

I'd been about to tell her she was late. She went on without giving me a chance to reply.

"I had to wash my face, put on makeup, get dressed, stuff my homework into my backpack, leave a note, *and* move my dad's car so that I could get mine out of the driveway." She stopped at the end of my street and looked at me. "Fifteen minutes, that's what we give each other when we call last-minute." She started driving. "You're lucky I got out of bed. It's cold."

It was the end of February. It was always cold this time of year. "Thank you."

"You're welcome." She flipped her shoulder-length brown hair out of her eyes.

"Would you mind if we stopped to see my mom?" I shoved my backpack onto the floor between my feet.

She gave me a sideways glance. "That bad of a night?"

"The worst."

She pursed her lips. "Why not. Besides, what are friends for if not to break into a cemetery before the crack of dawn?" She glanced at me. "I knew you didn't get me out of bed because you had cravings for a latte. Spill."

I blew out a breath and decided to start with my trip to Vladimir's gravesite and worked my way up to Caden's warning. When I finished, I waited for an *Oh my God* or *This can't be happening*. Instead, she nodded as if I had just told her I signed up for the Young Republican committee at school.

"You're taking this well, considering I just told you a *demon* may want to talk to you."

"A what?"

"Kaylee, this is serious!"

"See? I'm a great actress, and I'll warn Josh." She shot me a pleased smile. "Don't look at me like I'm the one who's nuts. Besides, Caden said we'd be fine as long as Derek doesn't find out we know they're demons, right?"

I wasn't sure what type of reaction I'd get out of Kaylee, but I did think there'd be a moment of stunned silence and a monumental amount of panic. "Do you trust Caden?"

"He's warning us to be careful. What's not to trust?" She eased the car to a stop in front of the black iron gates marking the entrance of the cemetery and twisted in her seat to look at me. "I'm not saying Caden isn't up to no good. The whole binding necklace and Death business is something to worry about. But the guy isn't going to tell us to watch our backs and then sic Death on us."

I bounced my head off the back of the seat, trying to take comfort in that thought.

The cemetery was dark, its residents asleep. I used my powers to unlock the gates and then created a dim rod of light to hover above the road in front of us. So as not to attract unwanted attention, Kaylee turned off the car's headlights and followed my magic around the twisting path deeper into the graveyard. We parked not far from where Mom was buried and got out of the car.

Kaylee held out her hand. Blue flames erupted a few inches above her palm, and she used the magical fire as a lantern to guide us.

Moments later, Kaylee crouched next to Mom's grave. "Hi, Mrs. Riley. Your crazy daughter broke in to see you." She dropped her voice to a mock whisper. "I think she's lost it."

"Shut up!" I bumped her with my hip.

I knelt next to Kaylee and used my magic to create a narrow shaft in the ground in front of Mom's tombstone. I then stuck a bright yellow bouquet of daisies in the hole and repeated the process for the next grouping of flowers.

"Has Josh taught you anything fun lately?"

She shrugged. "I can cast a barrier spell."

"That'll come in handy to keep Oreo out of your room."

"It does." She shook her head. "I'm still not sure what possessed my dad to get a cat."

"I'm not sure what possessed your mom to name a tan and white cat Oreo."

We both knew, though, that Mr. Bishop had gotten the cat because Kaylee's mom missed her son, Chris. He was away at college.

Kaylee stood, tugged her jacket's zipper up to her chin, and wandered around the nearby graves. "Josh tried to teach me how to summon my car keys from inside a locked car."

"How'd you do?"

"I have a better chance of becoming Prom Queen."

"Don't you have to be a senior to run?" I asked.

"That's the point. I have no chance at either." Her hand brushed snow from the top of headstones as she walked. After a few seconds, she said, "Josh gave me a leather journal to write down spells, did I tell you that?"

"No." I leaned back on my heels and tried to decide where to put the sixth silk bouquet.

"He started me off with a few simple spells. The chameleon enchantment is fun." She held her hands to the side and closed her eyes. Calla lilies scented the air a moment before her white jacket turned dusty pink. "And I —" She started, jumping a few feet to her left.

"What are you doing?" I said through laughter.

"Something touched me." Kaylee scanned the immediate area, and I found myself doing the same. Nothing was there. "Maybe it was the wind."

Or a grabby shade. Josh could be wrong. Shades could be more than vapor. But I kept that thought to myself.

Kaylee shook her head as if to clear her thoughts. "Anyway, I breathed life into my mom's dead fern. '*In qua spiritus vitae*, as I will it, so mote it be.' That was cool." She bent down and brushed a layer of damp leaves aside. "Hey, I didn't know Shane Lentz was buried here."

I did. He was two rows up and four graves over. He'd passed away last year of leukemia.

With a wave of my hand, I sent the last bunch of maroon daisies sailing toward her and said in way of explanation, "For his grave."

She caught the flowers. "We had several classes together in junior high. He was sweet. He didn't deserve to die so young."

"No one does."

Shane was one of those guys who got along with everyone. Genuinely happy. I used to wonder if his illness made him see life differently than the rest of us. As if he knew his days were numbered and he wasn't going to waste even a minute hating anyone or anything.

While Kaylee made a spot for the flowers near Shane's headstone, I spoke to Mom.

"Hey, Mom. Spring's around the corner." If you could call over three weeks around the corner. "I brought you daisies because I know how much you liked the bright colors. They're silk, but I think they're pretty and they brighten this place up. Chase hasn't done anything witchy since that day he stirred the air, so maybe I imagined it. I mean, it's possible that the wind picked up on its own. Right?" The breeze brushed my cheek as if in agreement. I nodded a that's-that nod. "Dad's good. Caden's still helping him with odd jobs. I swear Caden's made it his mission to do everything within his ability to upset Isaac. What's with guys, anyway? Not that Caden's a guy."

But technically, he *was* a guy — who also happened to be a cross-road demon.

"I could really use your advice." I fluffed the silk bouquet nearest me. "You'd probably tell me something crazy like 'Guys are like chimpanzees; they don't always play nice.'"

"Did you tell her Caden likes you?" Kaylee asked. She stood next to me again.

"He likes what I am. There's a difference."

She planted a fist on her hip. "Who are you trying to fool, me or you? Because I see how he looks at you. Isaac sees it too. That's why he hates the guy."

I got up. To Mom, I said, "We have to get to school. I'll visit again soon."

Kaylee and I headed back to the car.

"The only reason Caden and I do anything together is because I have to do it. Isaac has nothing to worry about."

She opened the driver's side door of the MINI but didn't get in. "I know that, and you know that. But to Isaac, Caden's a threat. Not because he wants to find the pieces to some relic or because his demon brother is in town. Caden's a threat because he's charming, he's available, and he can whisk you away at a moment's notice."

"Kaylee—"

She held up a hand to stop me. "You wouldn't like it if roles were reversed and Isaac was the one running off with a hot female demon."

She was right—I'd hate it—but there wasn't much I could do to change things.

After grabbing breakfast on our way to school, we pulled into the parking spot next to Isaac's Jeep.

Kaylee looked at me, her expression now serious. "I almost forgot, today's still on, right?"

"Everything's set for four."

"What about your dad?"

I smiled. "I have it all under control."

Chapter 4

Rubbity, Scrubbity, Sweepity, Flow

Timing was everything. We couldn't arrive home too early or we'd ruin the surprise, and if we arrived too late, there'd be a bunch of bored first graders to deal with. Isaac and I got to the sitter's at 3:35 p.m., stopped in, chatted until ten to four, and then left with Chase. We took a roundabout route home, parked in the empty driveway, and walked up to a seemingly deserted house. Chase led the way inside.

Had he paid attention, he would have heard the hushed whispers coming from the family room. I noisily closed the front door and dropped my keys on the small table in the foyer.

Isaac said. "What are we going to do?"

"Play cars! I'll get the track out!" Chase rushed down the hall.

Isaac and I quickly caught up. Chase stood just inside the family room with his mouth hanging open. Dad, Kaylee, Tommy Parker, Justin Mahn, Haley Warren, and several other kids from Chase's first grade class jumped out from behind the couch and chair. "Surprise!"

Blue and orange streamers raced across the ceiling, and *Happy Birthday* balloons in a rainbow of primary colors bobbed around the room. Chase got mobbed by his friends.

"Happy birthday, sport." Dad slipped a finger through the loop of the backpack still strapped to Chase's back and lifted it off his shoulders.

Kaylee secured an orange party hat on Chase's head.

Dad clapped his hands together once and cheerfully asked, "Who wants to play Pin the Tail on the Donkey?"

"Me!" Tommy and Chase screamed.

Haley and a cute brunette with a bushy ponytail quickly started to form a line in front of the television. I motioned for Kaylee to join Isaac and me in the kitchen.

"I think he was surprised." Isaac pulled out a chair and sat.

"Thanks for your help." I grabbed the package of party plates from the counter near the sink and opened them.

"No problem." Kaylee plucked a piece of popcorn from the bowl on the table and popped it into her mouth. "Josh wanted me to tell you he checked his father's grimoire. Nothing on binding chains, but he thinks he'll have better luck with the 'secret'"—she made air-quotes—"books his dad keeps hidden in the basement."

"Good." Isaac looked as if he would say more, but I cut him off.

"No witchy demon talk. There are too many ears." I handed Isaac a package of blue napkins and pointed to the table.

Isaac grabbed my hand and pulled me to him. His powers trickled over my skin in a gentle caress. "You can't keep avoiding the subject."

"I'm not avoiding anything."

"Madison—"

"Okay, maybe I am, just a little." I gave his hand a reassuring squeeze. "But not completely. Trust me; I know Caden and Derek, and this business with the binding chain isn't a problem that will go away if I pretend it doesn't exist. Right now, though, I want to get through my brother's seventh birthday party without having to compel someone to forget a conversation they weren't meant to hear."

Isaac wet his lips. I could tell he wanted to argue, but instead he nodded and opened the package of napkins. The doorbell rang.

"That will be the pizza." I grabbed the money Dad had left near the stove, calling, "I got it!" to Dad as I passed the family room.

I swung the door open. A boy in his early teens stared back at me. He wore a white dress shirt and black slacks. His hair was a messy mane of russet brown that fell over half his face. He wasn't holding a pizza.

I glanced down the driveway expecting to see a parent waiting in a car, but there was none. He shoved his hands into his pant pockets and kicked a sock-covered toe against the stoop.

"Where are your shoes and jacket?" The weather was warming, but it wasn't nice enough to be outside without proper protection against the elements.

"This is all I had with me when I woke." Before I could question him, he asked, "Is Kay here?"

I peered up and down the block, still looking for whoever drove him here. "I'm sorry, you have the wrong house. Do you live around—"

"She's here," he insisted. "I can feel her."

My eyes narrowed. "Did you say you can *feel* her?"

He jerked his head, flipping his long bangs out of his eyes. Only, instead of the gesture being smooth and quick, it was uneven and stiff as if his neck wasn't used to sudden movement. With his hair away from his face, I got a good look at him. His skin was ashen, and red circles highlighted ghostly gray eyes. I recognized him too. But he should not—emphasis on *not*—have been standing on my front porch. He should have been at the cemetery buried two rows up and a few graves over from my mom.

"Shane?" I asked, fully expecting him to say no or "Who?" or some other confused response, because even with everything I'd seen and knew about the supernatural world, there was no way this kid could be the boy whose funeral I had attended when I was a sophomore in high school.

He rocked back and forth on his heels. "Hey, Madison. You look older than I remember."

And you're less deceased than I remember. Not to mention creepily normal-looking for a kid who should be covered in decaying flesh. "Um." I pinched myself, thinking this was a dream. Considering the nightmares I'd been having, dreaming now would have been less farfetched than a dead boy standing on my porch. Unfortunately, my wince from the self-inflicted pain registered loud and clear. "How... how are you here?"

"I don't know." His bones creaked when he raised an arm to scratch the back of his head. "One minute I was with my grandmother. She's dead." I pretty much guessed that since he was supposed to be dead too, but I didn't interrupt. "And then the next I'm in a coffin in the middle of the cemetery."

"Six feet underground?"

He shook his head. "Of course not! How would I be here if I was buried alive?"

I wasn't so sure *alive* was the right word to describe someone back from the dead.

"Who else was there?" I asked, because someone would've had to dig him up.

"No one."

"Right." Incredulous, I reached out and poked his arm with my finger to make sure he was really there. He was. Under his shirt, he was skin and bone. And he smelled like the clothes and blankets in my grandma's old hope chest.

"It's messed up, I know. I heard Kaylee's voice. *In qua spiritus* something or other. Grams didn't hear her, which was weird. Usually, she hears everything. Next thing I know, something's pulling me backward—" he placed his hands over his stomach as if the memory brought on a bout of motion sickness "—and then I'm back in my body in a dark box—"

"Your coffin, which was above ground, sitting out in the open for anyone to see?" I asked just be make sure I was getting this correctly.

"Pretty much. Grams said we'd get another chance at living, but I'm pretty sure she meant we'd be reborn as infants."

I jabbed my finger into his shoulder just to make sure the first time wasn't a fluke.

He swatted my hand away. "Stop that!"

"Sorry, it's just…I guess I thought maybe you were a ghost."

"Well, I'm not! And I don't know how or why I'm back, but I do know that I want to talk to Kay-Kay."

Because I wanted to know if Kaylee would actually see him or if she'd tell me that lack of sleep had me talking to my hallucinations, I held up a finger and yelled over my shoulder. "Kay-Kay, can you come here a minute?" I turned back to Shane. "She doesn't like to be called that, by the way." Just in case I wasn't insane, I felt he should know that.

Kaylee poked her head around the corner. "What did you just call me?"

"Come here!" I hissed.

She marched up to me. "You better have a good reason…" Her voice trailed off when she noticed the boy on the porch. "Who's that?"

Her being able to see him was a win-lose situation. Yes, it meant I wouldn't find myself wearing a straitjacket any time soon, but it also confirmed that there was a moving, talking corpse on my front porch.

"Hi, Kaylee." He wet his lips and shifted his weight from one foot to the other. "I like your hair. Makes you look like a movie star."

Kaylee's head tipped to the side. Her long bangs shaded half her face.

"Give her a minute." I leaned on the door and waited. Out of the corner of my eye, I saw Isaac walking toward us. I was sure he planned to help with the pizza that hadn't arrived yet, and I thought it best to let Kaylee figure out who Shane was before anyone else saw him. "It's just a kid from down the block," I told Isaac. *Way* down the block, around several turns, and through cast iron gates. "Can you see if my dad needs help?"

"Sure." He veered into the family room.

Shane leaned in. "Is there a party going on?"

"It's my brother's birthday."

Kaylee's gazed bounced from Shane to me. "It can't be."

"I'm going with it *can*." When she continued to stare at me in disbelief, I added, "You recited a regeneration spell over his grave. Apparently, it revives more than just vegetation."

"It's not supposed to!" Her voice hitched.

There was the shock I'd expected Kaylee to display earlier when I had told her a demon might question her. A small part of me—okay, a big part of me—was happy that I hadn't been the one to cast the spell that invited even more trouble into our lives. "He's here to see you."

Her eyebrows shot up under her bangs. "Why'd he come to find me?"

Shane rubbed his head, looking as confused as I felt. "I don't know, actually. I mean, I probably should go home and let my parents know that I'm not dead anymore—"

"No!" I grabbed his hand and yanked him into the house. The last thing Mr. and Mrs. Lentz needed was for their dead son to show up on their doorstep.

"Why me?" Kaylee repeated.

A hatchback with a pizza delivery sign pulled into the driveway.

"I'm guessing because he feels a sense of loyalty to the one who brought him back to life," I whispered. I'd learned enough about the supernatural world to know bizarre connections were common.

Those with powers were drawn to each other. Crossroad demons had an uncanny ability to know exactly where to find each and every one of their clients. Why shouldn't a zombie be able to track down its maker? "Take Shane upstairs before someone else gets a good look at him. Go!" We didn't need my dad or the pizza guy recognizing him or for Isaac to realize he wasn't human. I grabbed Kaylee's wrist. "Cast the barrier spell to keep him there until after the party."

"Right." She pushed Shane up the stairs.

I could hear Shane asking Kaylee why he couldn't attend the party. The delivery guy walked up. I plastered a smile on my face. "Hi."

I paid the driver and carried two extra-large pizzas into the kitchen. Chase and his friends joined me shortly after that. Excited chitchat filled the room as they settled into chairs. Dad dished out slices to everyone.

Isaac leaned against the cabinet next to me. "Where's that boy and Kaylee?"

"I'm here," she said breathlessly from next to me. "And the boy just wanted to say hi. Madison and I used to babysit him. He left."

I eyed Kaylee with a stern glare to let her know I wasn't happy with lying, and I hoped Isaac didn't get a good look at Shane, because he didn't look that much younger than Kaylee and me.

Dad handed each of us a paper plate with pizza on it. Kaylee didn't seem able to shut up.

"He likes to stop by. We were his favorite sitters." Kaylee jabbed me with her elbow. "Isn't that right, Madison?"

"Ah." *No*, I added silently. I tried to put myself in Kaylee's shoes to figure out why she felt the need to keep Shane a secret from Isaac.

Isaac eyed us suspiciously. "Is everything okay?"

"Yeah." I took a large bite of cheesy goodness to keep from having to say anything else.

Unfortunately, Kaylee's mouth was still on overdrive. "Just girl stuff. Nothing you guys need to worry about."

I pretended I didn't notice Isaac studying us and kept eating. Chase reached into the pizza box in the middle of the table and grabbed himself and Haley another slice. Justin had pizza sauce on his cheek. First graders had it made. No real responsibilities or worries, just friends, food, and playtime. It almost made me want to be a kid again.

As it was, I hadn't even cast a spell, and I had a dead kid in my bedroom. A disbelieving laugh escaped my lips. Isaac continued to watch me, and I debated telling him the truth. I really did. But I think I knew what Kaylee was thinking: he'd tell Josh.

Kaylee hadn't been born with her powers. She'd been given them. And with the powers being addictive, we'd seen others abuse them. Case in point: our old classmate Emma, but she was mean even before acquiring her powers. And our friend Kevin's magic had only run wild because he hadn't known what was happening to him. But Kaylee had me, Josh, and Isaac to help her control the powers she'd been given. She hadn't meant to cast the spell that brought Shane back to life. His being here was a beginner's accident.

Granted, an enormous one. So, Josh might make her promise not to do magic without him, and I knew Kaylee wouldn't want to be put in a position of having to choose between practicing whenever she wanted and making that promise.

"You sure you're okay?" Isaac asked when we'd finished eating.

"Yep." I dropped my plate in the trash can and started to gather the kids' plates. "Should we do cake or presents next?"

A chorus of "Presents!" rang out from Chase and his friends.

"Presents it is." Dad handed out more napkins. He pointed to his cheek when he gave Justin one. "Get your face too."

Chase bounced in his seat from excitement overflow. It was great to see him so happy. I smiled, hoping Mom was looking down on us. But then movement in my peripheral vision caught my attention. A line of cheerfully wrapped presents bobbed through the air in tune to an unsung song.

I gasped and nearly dropped the trash in my hands. A faint sugary-grape scent filled the air, announcing that someone was using powers. Since not one of mine, Kaylee's, or Isaac's smelled like a glass of too-sweet Kool-Aid, I knew Chase had unknowingly cast the spell.

Kaylee craned her neck to look around the corner and choked. The presents paused, spun, and continued their merry trek to the kitchen.

That kicked me into action. I threw the dirty plates into the garbage can and held my hands in front of me in the universal *stop* gesture. Isaac rushed over, let out a boisterous laugh, and pivoted on his heels so that he faced Chase and his friends. "Did everyone wipe their hands?"

Several enthusiastic *yeahs* answered.

"Send the gifts back," he whispered to me. To the partygoers, he said, "And your mouths?"

There was a mix of *yeahs* and shuffling. I imagined Chase and several of his friends hurrying to wipe their mouths.

Back you go, I thought as I sent a small amount of power out. The large red gift bag that led the procession wavered. A long, narrow tube and a box wrapped in racecar wrapping paper crashed into it. I could feel Chase's magic pushing against mine, wanting to ignore my wishes. There was no way I could deny he possessed the powers. Not after this. Problem was, he and Dad didn't know about magic. They didn't know I was a witch, and I wanted to keep it that way for another year or two, even if Chase's powers had other ideas. Isaac's mom had called it "accidental usage" when I'd told her I was pretty sure Chase had stirred the air.

Determination fueled my magic. I pushed out more power and felt the snap of Chase's spell break. Kaylee and I hurried down the hall, quickly snatching the gift bag and tube out of the air and placing them on the newly formed pile in the family room just as the first of the kids rounded the corner behind us. Chase plopped down on the floor between Tommy and Haley. The other kids found seats on the couch and floor. Dad brought up the rear, his camera phone at the ready. I stepped around them and went to stand near Isaac and Kaylee in the doorway.

"I think it's safe to say there are two witches in your family," Kaylee mused.

I leaned my head against the wall as I watched Chase pull a basketball out of the gift bag. "Why's his magic bubbling over?" To my knowledge, I had never made anything fly across the room when I was his age.

"He's living with a practicing witch," Isaac said. "That would stir his powers. Make them rise to the surface, so to speak."

"Like how Madison's powers were drawn to yours?" Kaylee asked.

"Exactly." Isaac then nodded to Chase, who screamed an excited thank you for the Hot Wheel cars Isaac had bought him.

"Great, I can add my brother's magic to the list of things I have to worry about." I dropped my voice to a whisper and said to Kaylee, "Maybe go check on you-know-who."

She nodded. When Isaac looked at her, she mouthed the word *bathroom* and slipped out of sight.

Isaac slid an arm around my back and pulled me closer. "You know, when I was Chase's age, my parents told me about magic and that I was special. Then they made me promise not to tell a soul. My powers made me keep that promise. You could do the same with Chase. Use the old 'with great power comes great responsibility' line. Kids love that. And then you can make him promise not to cast spells when he's around people."

Which would be most of the time. I grinned. "I'm going to love the words *I promise*." Especially when they came out of Chase's mouth.

Isaac gave me a squeeze. "Want to come over to my house after this?"

I glanced up at him. "Tempting, but I have homework." *And a zombie I need to return to the grave.*

"You sure?" Isaac's fingers laced through mine, and he pulled me into the hallway, out of everyone else's sight. Then I felt it—soft as a feather's touch, almost indiscernible at first. His powers wrapped around mine. Every nerve ending in my body became super sensitive. His warm brown gaze fell to my lips. "We could *study* together."

"I'm not interrupting you lovebirds, am I?" Kaylee said from beside us. "Of course I'm not, because Madison's father is in the next room." She looped an arm through each of ours and steered Isaac and me back into the family room.

Kaylee now stood between us, our arms still linked. Isaac smiled at me over her head. "I think we were just reprimanded."

"I'll take a rain check." I already missed his powers mingling with mine.

Chapter 5

Wayward Coffins

Kaylee piled cold pizza and a massive slice of chocolate cake onto a plate.

"What are you doing?" I asked.

She studied the plate, obviously decided there wasn't enough food on it, and added one more square of pizza. "Shane kept complaining he was hungry."

I stared at her, mouth agape. "For pepperoni pizza?"

She shrugged. "We're out of sausage."

"Kaylee." I lowered my voice so that Dad and Chase didn't hear me. "I've seen *Dawn of the Dead*. Zombies eat people!"

She planted a hand on her hip. "That movie also suggests that you have to chop off a zombie's head to kill one. Are you going to do it?"

"No! Of course not, but he can't stay." I bent closer. "The only reason he's being an obedient zombie and staying locked in my room is because you cast the barrier spell. He probably spent the last hour ticked off at us both and trying to decide who to chow down on first. We need to get him back to the cemetery."

"If he lets us." She poured a glass of milk.

I already thought about that. "We'll tell him the spell's temporary. That at the stroke of midnight, he'll be zapped back to the afterlife and that it would be best if his body was in his coffin when it happens."

I would have loved to hear the internal debate that took place behind Kaylee's honey-brown eyes. Her nose crinkled. Her brow furrowed. Her shoulders drooped. Then she nodded, apparently coming to a decision, because she handed me the glass of milk. "Fine. We'll take him back to the cemetery *after* he eats."

"You can't be serious!" When she picked up the loaded plate, I croaked, "We don't even know if he can eat regular food."

"Well, I don't know about you, but I'm not getting in a car with a hungry zombie." She left the kitchen.

When she put it that way, I agreed. I caught up to her on the stairs. "One last meal for the dead guy, but if he tries to eat us, I'm frying him."

Kaylee didn't have a problem with that. "He didn't try to bite me, by the way."

We found Shane sprawled on top of my comforter. His focus was trained on something in his hand until he noticed us walk in. I fought not to let my expression give away that the sight of a zombie on my bed made me want to sterilize the bedding, but it was too late. To cover it, I casually set the glass of milk on my desk and asked, "Did your mom let you put your dirty feet on your bed?"

"Sorry." He swung his legs over the side of the mattress. "She would've killed me" — no pun intended, I assumed — "if I did that at home." His gaze then fixed on Kaylee as he licked his lips. A moment later, he leaped up. I was just about to zap him with a bolt of power when he took the plate from her. "Thanks!"

I realized the thing in his hand was her cell phone. When he handed it to her, I caught a brief glimpse of the screen and the game he'd been playing.

"Kaylee said you'd tell me what's going on as soon as the party was over." He took a seat at my desk.

"Yeah, about that…" I lowered myself onto the bed and rubbed my hands over my thighs.

Kaylee and I took turns explaining it to him.

"So, you're witches?" he asked between bites of pizza. "And I only have a few more hours before I die all over again."

I couldn't look him in the eye when I nodded. I hated lying to him, but I didn't see any other option. He wasn't really alive.

Kaylee sat on my bed with her legs folded in front of her, elbows on her knees, and chin cradled in the palm of her hand. "I still can't believe you're here. The rejuvenation spell isn't supposed to work on people. I'm really sorry, Shane."

"Your spell sucks." The red that rimmed his eyes turned the color of dried blood as fine black veins darkened his features.

Kaylee and I scooted backward. Shane looked a heartbeat away from becoming a monster from the movies.

"Will I be in pain?"

"No, Shane," I managed to say. "Not if you let us use our magic to help you."

He swiped at his eyes, and I realized he was fighting back tears. The dark lines in his face grew faint.

"At least I had a few hours back on earth. Right?" His words lacked any emotion. It broke my heart. He chewed with less enthusiasm for a minute, then said, "This is good. I think I missed food the most."

"He's just like I remember him," Kaylee whispered.

Minus the total lack of color and black veins, she was right. I squeezed my pillow. If Hollywood agreed on one thing, it was that zombies were decaying cannibals with no recollection of who they were. But Shane remembered who he was, and as I noticed from the beginning, he wasn't decaying. "Why isn't he withered and, I don't know, gross-looking?"

"What?" Kaylee asked.

"He's been dead a long time. Shouldn't he be missing chunks of skin or be a shriveled husk of a person?"

Shane took a good look at his hands as if it hadn't occurred to him that he should look worse than he did.

Kaylee had to pick her jaw up off the bed before she asked, "Would you rather have a decomposing body in your room?"

"No." But it would have made it easier on my conscience if we were re-killing and burying a mummified cadaver. "As soon as he's done eating, we have to take him back."

"So soon?" Bits of crust sprayed out of his mouth. "But I want to see my parents."

"No!" Kaylee and I snapped.

"You'll give them a heart attack," I said more gently.

He ate the rest of his dinner in silence. I couldn't help noticing, now that he had food in his stomach, his cheeks appeared to have a slight blush to them. When the last forkful of cake had been washed down with milk, he asked, "Can we at least drive by my house?"

Kaylee and I exchanged looks.

"Yeah," she said.

It was the least we could do.

I distracted my dad and Chase while Kaylee snuck Shane outside. By the time we got to the cemetery, it was dark.

Shane's casket was a bizarre sight. The dark mahogany coffin was half buried smack dab in the center of what should have been an undisturbed grave. The light from my phone gleamed off the cream interior. It appeared as if the coffin had risen on its own, and if magic could bring it to the surface, then magic could rebury it.

I created two glowing balls of amber light so that we could see and strolled around the gravesite, assessing the situation. Truth was, I had no idea how to pull a soul out of a zombie or how to rebury the coffin without heavy equipment. My magical training was geared toward protection spells and making life easier with a few decent party tricks thrown in to keep things fun. I could conjure a magical shield, turn lights on and off with a glance, and make leaves dance in a non-existent breeze, to name just a few things I had mastered. I hadn't learned how to kill the dead, though.

Kaylee tipped her head to the side as she examined the loose soil surrounding the casket. "Maybe we should call Caden. I bet he'll know what to do."

"Yeah, and he'll tell us for the small price of your soul." I set a thick white pillar candle on top of Shane's headstone. "Not going to happen."

We placed a few more candles on the ground around us. The energy from the flames would help fuel our powers.

I blew on the wick of the nearest candle. It flickered to life along with the rest. "Kaylee, whatever you do, don't raise any more dead people."

Crouching to move one of the candles closer to the foot of the coffin, she tossed a handful of dried grass at me. "Ha-ha, very funny."

Up until now, Shane had been watching from the sideline, expression solemn. I couldn't blame him.

"Ready?" I asked.

"Yeah." He frowned but climbed into the casket.

"It will be like falling asleep," Kaylee told him. She had no way of knowing if that was true, but we were trying to make this as easy for him as we could.

"Shane, can I ask you something?" I waited for his nod. "What's it like on the other side?"

I had wanted to ask him that when we were at my house, but it didn't seem right to tell him he only had a few hours to live and then quiz him on the afterlife.

"It's quiet. A little too bright, but I'm guessing the alternative is worse. But my grandma is there, and we run into other souls waiting to be reborn. That's what Grams says happens, eventually."

I liked the idea of souls being reborn.

"Shall we do this?" Kaylee asked from a few feet away.

I nodded.

We'd decided to concentrate on wanting Shane to pass back over to the other side. Kaylee even came up with an incantation. As corny as it sounded, I didn't have anything better, so we used it.

I closed my eyes, pictured Shane at rest, and chanted right along with Kaylee.

"Return from whence you came. As we will it, so mote it be."

We must have said the spell a half-dozen times before I peeked to see if it was working. I discovered my imagination was far better than reality.

"You're that witch who left large gouges in the ground near dear Margaret Delacruz's grave," a gruff voice said from behind us.

Startled, I spun around to find a man sitting on a rectangular headstone to my right. I snatched my cell phone out of my pocket and turned on the flashlight. The guy practically vanished when I shined the beam directly at him.

He raised a hand to shield his translucent eyes. "Do you mind?"

I lowered my phone. "You're…you're a ghost?"

Or did he prefer a politically correct term like *flesh-challenged?*

"Jeremy McGregor." He inclined his head in a formal manner, which was at odds with his mullet haircut and Grateful Dead T-shirt. From the laugh lines near his eyes and the graying of his hair, I guessed he'd been in his fifties or sixties when he died. His gray gaze slid to Kaylee. "I was hoping to have a word with you when you're finished here."

Kaylee looked over her shoulder as if there might be someone else he could be talking to before pointing to herself. "Me?"

Jeremy nodded. "The others are too."

Kaylee and I did a slow turn; the beams from our flashlights cut narrow paths through the night. The usual shades were there, drifting in the distance. We were used to them, yet Kaylee let out a little gasp and elbowed me. My gaze followed hers to an elderly ghost not too far from Jeremy; judging by her apron and skirt, she had died a long time ago. A third ghost with long stringy hair also blinked into view.

Kaylee screamed, pivoted on her heels, and snatched her bag from the grass. I barely managed to catch her arm and stop her from bolting to the car.

"We can't leave Shane and his coffin like this," I pointed out.

"There are ghosts here!"

She tried to tug free of my grip, but I held tight. "We drove in a car with a zombie!"

Shane tapped Kaylee's arm, sending her jumping a foot into the air.

"I don't think they want to hurt you," he said. "Maybe they're drawn to you like I was."

Kaylee let out a whimper but stopped fighting me. None of the spectral beings made a move to come any closer, which seemed to settle her nerves some.

She dropped her bag on the ground. "Fine. Let's just hurry."

She kept shooting our uninvited audience narrow-eyed glares. On someone else, the look she gave may have appeared threatening. But on Kaylee, who had a heart-shaped face and weighed one hundred and five pounds soaking wet, it looked more like a little girl pouting.

Shane lay back down. "Try saying the spell that brought me here backward. That's what they do in my video games."

I shrugged. "It's not that crazy of an idea. We *are* trying to reverse it."

Kaylee brought up the notepad on her phone and typed out the spell. She then read each word from right to left. She even added *as I will it, so mote it be*, which I thought was a nice touch. When she finished, we peered into the casket. A minute passed. Shane remained still.

Kaylee smiled. "It worked!"

"We did it!" I let out a happy giggle. Isaac had been right. If we believed in ourselves, our spells would work. "Do you think he's in a better place?"

"The other side doesn't have pizza." Shane opened his eyes. "Or cake."

Shane jolted upright into a seated position. Kaylee and I started, but our screeches quickly turned to groans of disappointment.

"Why can't anything be easy?" She kicked the side of the coffin, turned, and then let out a surprised yelp when the ghost of the elderly woman materialized in front of her, nose to nose. Kaylee scrambled away.

"Beg your pardon, miss. Didn't mean to frighten you," the ghost said. She craned her neck to look around Kaylee at Shane. "But you can't reverse what you've done with a spell."

Shane turned an odd shade of seafoam green. "I have to die all over again?"

"Not unless someone separates your head from the rest of your body." The woman bared a set of yellowing teeth and drew a line across her neck with her finger.

"What do you know about magic?" I asked.

Her pale gray eyes found me. "I know it takes more than a few words to send the dead away."

"You mean I'm not going to die at the stroke of midnight?" Shane asked.

"Not unless they brought an ax," she replied.

I was sure the only reason Shane didn't demand answers from Kaylee and me was because our mouths hung just as open as his; although, *our* shock was because a ghost had ratted us out, and his was because he'd almost let us send him away.

The ghost smiled sweetly at Kaylee. "Can you get a message to my husband?"

I didn't have the heart to tell the woman that her husband most likely died a century ago.

Kaylee's brow furrowed. "I don't know him."

"Candace Cromwell," Jeremy scolded. "We agreed we'd leave these girls alone until they took care of the boy."

The woman—Candace—*tsk*ed. "I made no such agreement, and the only thing they can do with the boy is offer him a place to take a warm shower and buy him some new clothes. Even I know boys his age don't walk around wearing dress shirts and ties."

"Candace is right." The other woman floated closer. "A witch would have to tap into the dark to send him back, and your powers are fueled by positive emotions. I can feel them."

"Now what?" Kaylee whispered.

"I don't know, but we can't let a zombie roam free."

I pressed my fingers to my temples. Kaylee rubbed the bronze heart pendant on the necklace I'd given her for her birthday and stared at the car. I got the impression she'd do anything if it meant she could go home.

"Fine," I said. "Shane, get out of the coffin so we can bury it."

He didn't have to be told twice.

"You can stay with Kaylee until we figure out what to do."

"No, he can't!" Kaylee waved her hand, letting her magic close the coffin lid.

I shined my light in her eyes. "You're the one with an extra room, so he stays with you. Now help me hide the coffin."

I slid my phone into my back pocket, raised my hands in front of me, and focused on pushing the coffin downward. When that didn't work, I tried to think of it as teleporting the coffin beneath the soil.

"I don't think the face you're making—" Jeremy squinted, forehead creased and nose scrunched "—is helping."

"She's not very good at this," Candace observed.

With a glance, I sent the candle on top of Shane's headstone sailing through her chest. It hit the tombstone behind her. "One more word out of you and I'll see if I have better luck hitting you with an energy ball."

"Testy, aren't you." Candace blinked out of view and reappeared on the other side of the Jeremy.

After Kaylee gave it her best try, Shane said, "Don't you know any vanquishing spells?"

Kaylee's hopeful gaze met mine. "We know one."

I shook my head. "That can send the Fae back to Sanctus. I'm not sure if you've noticed, but this isn't a faerie."

She shrugged. "The rejuvenation spell isn't supposed to work on people either, yet Shane's here."

CHERIE COLYER

"Someone has to be the first to cast new spells," Jeremy said from his perch on the tombstone.

Shane and Candace nodded encouragingly.

I swept my hands through my hair. "I suppose I could change the words a little."

Kaylee smiled. "Now you're talking!"

I tugged at the waist of my jacket and told myself I could do this. It would be my first original spell. I'd call it *Concealing the Evidence of Your Friend's Screw-Up*. With my hands in front of me and my palms facing the coffin, I said, "From here to six feet under—"

Kaylee grabbed my arm. "Wait! Are you sure you want to send it that far down? I mean, we're going to have to figure out a way to, you know." She jerked her head toward Shane.

"Right." I cleared my throat. "From here to one foot under." I ignored Jeremy when he mumbled, "Better…" and kept going. "From time and space and the afterlife, I…" *What?*

"Command this casket to sink back to whence it came," Kaylee said.

I looked at her. "You really like that word, don't you?"

"What? It sounds mysterious."

I repeated what she said. The ground didn't so much as shudder.

Jeremy glided around the grave. "*Whence* doesn't sound mysterious. It sounds old."

"Shut up!" Kaylee turned her back to him. "Madison, maybe we're overthinking this. Most spells don't require an incantation."

She raised her hands and stared at the coffin through narrow slits. "Sink!"

It didn't.

"Descend!" she bellowed.

No change.

"Just vanish already!" She kicked it for emphasis.

It disappeared. Not instantly. It sort of winked in and out of view a few times and then, like a bad firecracker, fizzled out of sight.

I swung my foot and hit wood. "It's not perfect."

"You can say that again." Jeremy lowered himself onto the invisible coffin. With his translucent form and his legs crossed, he looked like a genie. All he needed was a turban and baggie pants.

"It's going to have to do." I waved a hand from left to right, pushing out magic to smooth the loose dirt around the coffin. Then I cast a glamour over the area to hide the hole.

"Aren't you worried someone will walk into it?" Candace asked.

"We'll just have to hope that most people walk around graves, not over them." I paused. "You wouldn't be willing to keep people away, would you?"

Jeremy zoomed off of the coffin and floated in front of me. "For a price."

I should have known they'd want something in return.

"Forget it." No way was I going to make any more deals. I picked up the candle nearest me and blew it out, then muttered, "Like I want to owe a ghost too."

"Not you, her." He indicated to Kaylee with his chin.

"She's not making any deals either." I picked up two more candles. Kaylee and Shane got the rest. "We'll take our chances, and if someone trips over the coffin, then it serves them right for not respecting the dead."

Kaylee, Shane, and I headed toward the car. Jeremy flew in front of us, halting our progress. "I just want to get a message to my granddaughter. She was a baby when I died. Please."

Kaylee crossed her arms over her chest. "You're not going to tell her something hateful, are you? Because trust me when I say she's better off not hearing something about her dead grandfather that's going to scar her emotionally."

Jeremy's features morphed into something darker with each word Kaylee spoke. In the short time it took her to finish speaking, his cheeks became hollow and his eyes sunken. I made a mental note not to insult ghosts as I created a shield that I hoped worked against something that didn't have a corporal form.

My gaze flicked to the other ghosts. They were still a faded version of the people they'd once been, and it didn't seem to concern them that their friend looked like a transparent monster.

"Of course not!" Jeremy spat. "I loved her and her parents." He sounded genuinely taken aback, which was at odds with his new ominous appearance.

Kaylee stared into his beady eyes. "Is this your unfinished business or something? I deliver your message, and you go into the light?"

He nodded vigorously.

After a few seconds of thought, she squared her shoulders. "I'm not going to become the messenger service for the dead, so this deal stays between me and you or it's off."

"Okay." He held out his hand for her to shake.

She hid her hands behind her back. "This agreement is verbal. Take it or leave it."

"Kaylee—" I began.

"It's one message." She glanced at Candace and the other ghost. "Each."

"Thank you." Color, faded as it was, came back to Jeremy's face. "My granddaughter's name is—"

I looped an arm through Kaylee's and steered her around him. "She'll deliver your messages *after* we take care of our zombie problem."

His eyes narrowed. "How do I know you're not trying to trick us?"

As if he couldn't haunt Kaylee and me if we reneged on the agreement. Or maybe he couldn't. Maybe the cast iron fence around cemeteries kept its residents from wandering outside the grounds.

"I promise," Kaylee said so fast I couldn't remind her to choose her words wisely. "As a witch, my promise binds me to my word."

"It does," Candace confirmed. She was clearly the self-proclaimed expert on witches.

"Now what would a group of teens be doing in a cemetery after dark, talking to ghosts?" a deep voice asked.

Jeremy and the women vanished.

I knew that voice. It belonged to the demon I had hoped to never see again. Kaylee, Shane, and I looked to our right. Holding a cigarette in one hand, Derek watched us.

"We were just—" Kaylee started.

"Visiting my mom," I said. "Kaylee and Shane, this is Derek, my dad's handyman's brother."

Kaylee stiffened next to me, thankfully understanding my cryptic warning that this was Caden's brother, the one who couldn't find out that anyone else knew about demons.

I positioned myself between my friends and Derek. "Are you following me?"

Derek took a drag of his cigarette as he eyed Kaylee. He then looked at me. "I was hoping to find Caden. You don't happen to know where he is, do you?"

So he *was* following me, and he'd probably seen my feeble attempt to send Shane's soul back to the afterlife. Which meant he knew I had not only failed to do that, but I couldn't even rebury one little casket. I didn't like him knowing my limitations.

Shortcomings or not, I'd be damned if I cowered in his presence. I raised my chin and stared straight into his espresso-colored eyes. "Caden doesn't check in with me, so leave me and my friends out of your family quarrel."

"I like you." He smirked and jerked his head in Kaylee's direction. "You and your friend here have spunk."

I stepped forward, leaving little space between us. "You're in my way."

He laughed and stepped aside.

"Let's go." I grabbed Kaylee's and Shane's hands.

I could hear Derek's laughter all the way to the car. My heart threatened to pound its way out of my chest, and it was all I could do not to run. When we were safely on the road, I realized Kaylee was mumbling something that sounded an awful lot like "God Bless America."

"Are you singing?"

She shot me a brief glance. "Demon's can read minds, right?"

"Yeah."

"Well, it was either I sing the first song that popped into my head or chant *oh crap, oh crap, oh crap.*"

I bit my bottom lip. "That was actually pretty clever."

"Thanks." She slowed and got in the turn lane.

Shane slumped in the back seat. "You guys keep strange company."

"Says the zombie," I replied.

He huffed. I dug my phone out of my purse.

"Who are you calling?" Kaylee asked.

"Caden. I want to know why his brother is following me." I pulled up his number. My finger hovered over *call.* If I called Caden, he'd insist on coming over, and I really didn't want to see him.

I called my dad instead and told him I was going to spend the night at Kaylee's. We'd get Shane settled into her brother's room, cast a couple of wards to keep her parents from noticing there was a stranger sleeping in their son's room, and throw up the barrier spell to make sure Shane stayed put.

That left us with one very big question: what the hell would we do with him after that?

Chapter 6
Explaining Away the Dead

I called Caden in the morning to tell him that Derek had followed my friends and me. Caden had been more concerned with why we were in a cemetery after dark than with his brother's actions. Since he wasn't talking when it came to his boss or the binding chain, I decided two could play that game and refused to tell him what we were up to. When he pressed, I shot back a snarky "Need-to-know basis, Caden." He hung up on me. Funny how he didn't like being the one left in the dark.

After that, he didn't answer my calls.

"This is a good thing, Madison," Kaylee insisted. "It means he's finally giving you space. Maybe Derek will back off too."

She and I spent three days secretly scouring Josh's and Isaac's books, searching for information on zombies. Because we were also looking for details about the binding chain, the guys didn't question our need to devour the pages of any and every book we could get our hands on.

The first thing Kaylee and I learned was that there wasn't a counterspell to the one she had quoted. That did make sense, once we thought about it. The purpose of the rejuvenation spell was to revive a dead plant, not a human being. And let's face it, if you didn't want the plant to live, all you had to do was stop watering it. Denying Shane sustenance would have been cruel. Not to mention, we didn't want a hungry zombie on our hands.

There was nothing whatsoever in any of the books we'd read on the living dead, and if we believed what we found on the Internet, a witch needed a lot of seriously dark stuff present to accomplish what Kaylee had with a few misdirected words.

Every day Shane asked to see his parents, and every day Kaylee and I came up with an excuse why he couldn't. The barrier spell ensured he remained hidden at least, though I still worried he'd turn bad. Sure, he was friendly now, but what if rare roast beef sandwiches and cola stopped satisfying his increasing hunger? Kaylee felt his appetite was normal for a fifteen-year-old boy, however, stating her brother used to eat them out of house and home at that age too. I hoped she was right.

Then there was Shane's appearance. His skin gained a little more color with each day that passed. The red that rimmed his eyes faded. It was as if his body was getting stronger. Kaylee even started to question what he was.

"Maybe he isn't undead?" she reasoned. "What if the spell brought him back for real?" She paused thoughtfully before adding, "Maybe we should look for a way to integrate him back into his family's lives."

She was dead serious. Like Shane showing up at his parents' front door after all this time wouldn't freak the crap out of them.

Even so, for a moment I thought she could be right. Shane might be human. So far, he was an average teenage boy who was tired of being cooped up in someone else's bedroom. He ate, used the bathroom, and slept just like we did. Thank goodness Kaylee and her brother shared a Jack and Jill bathroom; the adjoining facilities made it easy for Shane to move around unseen. The oblivious ward I found in Isaac's grimoire helped too. Now that it was cast, Kaylee's parents could walk into the bedroom where Shane was and they wouldn't notice his empty pop cans on the dresser, the smell from the glue he used to put together a model Aston Martin, or Shane himself. Plus, it kept them from hearing our voices when we talked to him. We'd even managed to keep his presence a secret from Josh and Isaac. Considering how often Josh was at her house, that was a major feat.

Yet even if we found a way to explain Shane's miraculous return from the dead, we couldn't explain why he hadn't aged. Kaylee gave it her best try — my favorite being that the doctors had frozen him in his sleep until they could find a way to cure him. As much as I wanted to work with her on fine-tuning the perfect alibi for Shane's missing months, a parent would have a ton of questions we couldn't answer.

So, rather than finding a spell that would allow Shane to pick up where he'd left off, our main focus remained on returning his soul to the afterlife where he could rest in peace. We didn't tell Shane that, though. I felt terrible about deceiving him, but until we understood his condition, we didn't have a choice.

Speaking of not having a choice, Kaylee and I had reached a point where we knew we had to see if the guys knew anything about zombies. The tricky part was doing that without them finding out Kaylee had one living in her house. They weren't stupid. We'd have to tread lightly. Thing was, we hit the one day of the year that I found it hard to care about anything.

My mom had been laid to rest seven years ago to the day. Every year since, my two closest friends spent the anniversary night of the funeral at my house. Sarah Johnson, my second oldest friend, always brought baked potato chips and a tube of chocolate chip cookie dough. Kaylee, my oldest and dearest friend, brought chocolate and peanut butter ice cream and a stack of DVDs. We'd flip through old photo albums and watch my mom's favorite chick flicks while gorging on junk food. They made a difficult day bearable.

This year, I wanted to cancel our annual plans. We had a zombie to keep an eye on and a demonic diabolical plan to foil. Kaylee wasn't having it, though.

"We are not breaking tradition." She slung her backpack over her shoulder and waited for Josh to get out of his silver Mustang. Several of our classmates walked by us on their way into school. "We'll move the sleepover to my house." She dropped her voice to a whisper. "So we can keep an eye on you-know-who."

Isaac closed the driver's side door on the Jeep and looked from me to Kaylee. His eyes narrowed. "What's moved to your house?"

"You must be talking about girls' night," Sarah said from behind me. I hadn't seen her walk up.

Kaylee smiled. "Yep. Five o'clock?"

"I'm really not in the mood this year." There was triple emphasis on *really*. I bent close to Kaylee and hissed, "You're supposed to be on my side."

She ignored me.

"No way are we canceling." Sarah looped one arm through mine and another through Kaylee's. "I've been looking forward to it for weeks."

"Me too." I bounced my purse higher on my shoulder. "But there's just so much going on right now. I won't be able to enjoy myself."

Isaac looked at Josh and asked, "What am I missing?"

Josh leaned in close to him. I didn't have to hear him to know what he said. "It's the anniversary of Mrs. Riley's death." He might have added, "Kaylee and Sarah like to make sure Madison isn't sitting home crying." Which I had done the first year, until Kaylee and Sarah showed up with junk food and a stack of DVDs, thanks to a phone call from Dad.

Time does heal some wounds, though, and for the last few years, we had used the day to celebrate the woman who enjoyed quirky love stories, baked potato chips, and raw cookie dough. I was okay with us postponing the event for a week or two.

"Really, I think I need to mix things up this year." I gave Kaylee a meaningful look that said, *How are we going to hide Shane from Sarah if she's sleeping at your house?* Kaylee tilted her head to the side with her mouth forming a line. Her expression replied, *The confusion spell. Duh!*

I shook my head. It was bad enough we had cast it on her parents. I didn't want to cast it on Sarah too.

"How about dinner? The Grill?" Josh suggested. "We can make it a triple date."

Sarah glanced at Kaylee, who gave a half shrug like she didn't hate the idea.

"Okay!" Sarah dug her phone out of her purse. "I'll text Mark to let him know."

It wasn't exactly what I had in mind, but Mark was into zombie movies, and while he and Sarah didn't know about the powers, it would be easy to steer the conversation toward the new living dead movie. Once I was alone with Isaac, I could then ask him if zombies were real. It was a fair question, considering that since I'd met him I had discovered witches, demons, and faeries existed. I'd be able to find out what he knew about the subject.

First period English started with a pop quiz. I felt confident that I had about as good a chance of passing as Kaylee had at keeping Shane a secret for too much longer. Second period Foods was uneventful. The rest of the day was brutal with two more pop quizzes and a test in math. By the time eighth period ended, I felt mentally drained, and I still had a binding chain to worry about and a zombie to deal with.

Isaac thought he had a lead on the chain. That left me on demon duty and Kaylee on zombie detail. I would have said she had the easier task, seeing as all she had to do was pop home and see if Shane needed anything, but she had driven to school with Josh, which meant he was driving her home, and he always stopped in.

I met Isaac at the doors to the student parking lot.

"Who are we going to see?" I asked as we walked to the Jeep.

"Anastasia Ravenwood. She has a store just outside Salem."

"And how is a psychic going to help us?"

There were psychics and palm readers all over Salem. Call me a skeptic, but I'd never thought of them as a reliable source of information.

He opened the passenger door for me. "She's a natural witch who decided to use her powers to help others. She makes all her teas and potions. My mom swears she never would have lived through me being thirteen without Anastasia's calming tea, and I stock up on her cinnamon chews before finals. They not only give me a boost of energy, but the candy really does help me remember what I've read."

"Isn't that cheating?"

"Cinnamon is a natural way to enhance memory, and the elixirs she uses to make the candy can be bought over the counter. She just knows how to combine everything to make it taste good."

"Does she only cater to witches?" With there being so many people in Essex County who possessed the powers, it seemed possible for a person to make a living by selling to them exclusively.

"Nah. Anastasia will tell you that a witch doesn't need her. Most of her customers are human, but she procures rare items for her premiere customers."

I climbed in the Jeep and waited for him to join me. "You mean witches?"

"Witches she *trusts*. Anastasia can tell if a person's soul has been tainted." Isaac backed out of our parking space and followed a red hatchback to the exit. "According to my mom, Anastasia's mother was a psychic and her father possessed the powers. She inherited both of their gifts."

"Double the supernatural ability. That has to come in handy." I tossed my backpack in the back seat and buckled up. "Speaking of your mom, aren't you afraid Anastasia will tell her you stopped by?"

Isaac took a right at the light and blasted the heat. "She didn't tell my parents when I bought the book on Fae or when I went back a few months later asking if she had anything that would banish a faerie."

"Yeah, but you can't put faeries in the same category as a necklace that can control Death."

Isaac stopped at a red light and looked at me. "Faeries are manipulative creatures who steal life from humans. How's that not as dangerous as someone controlling Death or anyone else, for that matter?"

I would have pointed out that not all faeries were malicious, and even though Reed had tried to drag me to the faerie realm, he wasn't purely evil. Vindictive, arrogant, and righteous, yes, but he'd had his reasons — messed up as they were — for targeting me.

I hoped Isaac was right, though, that Anastasia would keep our visit a secret from his parents. I really didn't want them to know I had made a deal with a crossroad demon.

We took MA-128 south. It was cold outside, but with the windows up and the heat on, it was a pleasant ride. I closed my eyes, letting the sun's rays warm my cheeks.

Isaac pulled up to a small cobalt-blue Cape Cod cottage. The weathered sign in the front yard read *Mystic Endeavors*. Brass sun and moon wind chimes sang an enchanting song as we walked up the front steps. Nothing hinted to the owner reading fortunes.

"I thought you said she was a psychic?"

"That part of her business is word of mouth." Bells rang out when Isaac opened the door.

I took a step to enter the small shop, but then paused to examine the large round planter next to the threshold. It was filled with dried flowers and leaves. One of which I recognized.

"You said she's a *natural* witch, right? Her father possessed the powers?"

Isaac nodded.

I ran my fingers over a sprig of devil's shoestring. "You sure about that?"

There was only one reason to have devil's shoestring near the doors and windows of a building, and that was to keep demons out. I'd removed enough from the homes of Caden's clients to know the herb worked.

"I'm positive. You know, Madison, most people want to keep demons out of their homes, regardless if they've made a deal with one or not."

I strolled past him, ignoring the jibe, and thought about the first house that Caden had brought me to. I could still see the young mother sitting at the kitchen table, helping her daughter with homework, and I wondered if Anastasia was the witch who had put up the protection ward there too. Not that it had done the woman a lot of good. Deals with crossroad demons couldn't be broken. One way or another, when a person's debt came due, hell collected.

Isaac followed me inside. "I still think you should plant some around your house."

I sighed. "You know I can't."

Isaac couldn't either. Caden had made sure of that during one of our outings.

"I've seen that look before, Madison," Caden said when he saw me twirling a sprig of dried devil's shoestring between my fingers.

I pulled my attentions away from the dark green leaves and glanced into his eyes. "What look?"

He stuck a cigarette between his lips and inhaled, lighting it effortlessly. "The one mortals get when they realize they can use certain information to their advantage." He paused. "Being at my beck and call means that I can reach you when I need you."

"I know." Boy, did I know. I would have denied that I was thinking of keeping a piece of the plant in my purse so that I'd have some control over when and where Caden could reach me—at least then he'd have to call before he dropped in—but there was no point in lying when he could pick thoughts out of my mind.

Caden nodded as he took a drag of the cigarette. He blew a thin line of smoke out of the side of his mouth, away from me. "You'll learn things from me that you won't find in books. I want you to promise never to use these things against me and never to let your friends do so." When I said nothing, he added, "Promise or I'll find a reason to drag you away from your friends and family every single day until you do."

I said no. So, the next night, Caden dragged me to Wingaersheek Beach to do the séance with Ms. Brontë. Then the next day, he interrupted my date with Isaac, swearing it was life or death. Granted, in a way it was, because had I not magically buffed out the scratch in his car's sleek black paint, he would've killed the guy who'd let a shopping cart roll into it.

But realizing that Caden hadn't been bluffing about "every single day," I made the promise. I was pretty sure he knew about the S-shaped wreath in Isaac's bedroom, though. He seemed to let me have that small victory.

The door to Mystic Endeavors closed with a bang, bringing me back to the present.

"You should have let me send him back to hell," Isaac said. He'd made the offer last month.

"I'd still owe him. Besides, it's better to—"

"—know the demon that lives near us. Yeah, yeah, yeah."

The scent of lavender and sage greeted us. Mystic Endeavors was a quaint shop with just about everything a witch might need. Small bags of herbs lined the wall to our right. There were tables with an array of gems and crystals, shelves of ointments and lotions, books, scrying bowls, and more. Mixed in with the practical items were ruby slippers, golden snitches, and other movie memorabilia. The table in front of us had a rectangular basket full of colorful glass spheres. The sign next to the display read "Witchballs."

I picked up an orange ball and read the rest of the sign.

> Witchballs were very popular in 18th-century England. For well over 300 years, hollow glass spheres have been hung in windows to ward off witches' spells, evil spells, and ill fortune. The evil spirit is attracted to the ball and is mesmerized by its reflective beauty. When the spirit touches the sphere, it is absorbed and trapped in the web-like strands inside the ball.

"It's a good thing you cast using positive emotions." A woman in her forties picked up one of the spheres. "Or you'd have been sucked inside, trapped until someone broke the glass."

I hadn't thought about that when I'd picked it up, but the idea of being sucked into a glass prison wasn't what had me staring back at her. "How'd you know?"

"That you're a witch? I sensed it." She placed her sphere back in the bowl. "Plus Isaac doesn't bring many people to my store." She bent closer, although she didn't lower her voice. "I think he's afraid his mortal friends will discover his secret."

Isaac took the witchball from me and tossed it in the air a few times, catching it with ease. "Put in a few pool tables or a basketball court outside, and I'll bring them by."

She caught the ball mid-toss and returned it to the display. Then she held a hand out to me. "I'm Anastasia."

"Madison."

A slight sting, like static electricity, happened when I shook her hand. I knew it was our powers colliding. She studied me a moment, emerald-green eyes seeming to look right into my soul. I wondered if she'd be able to see that it was tied to Isaac — compliments of a spell we'd cast to keep the Prince of Fae from feeding off my life essence. Isaac and I had planned to reverse it once Reed was back in Sanctus, but having my soul tethered to Isaac's had saved me from a couple of supernatural threats. I couldn't help but think of it as a safety net, and I'd decided to leave things as they were for the time being.

Anastasia let go of my hand and eased a hip against the table. "What brings you kids by today?"

I looked at Isaac. He was the one who knew her, so I figured he should be the one to do the talking.

"We've been going through my grandfather's books and came across binding chains," he said, sticking to the part of the story he and I were comfortable sharing. "The spell used to create one requires some pretty obscure items and some time to make." He twitched a shoulder. "You know me, always looking for a challenge." His gaze met hers when he added, "But I don't fully understand what the talisman is used for or how it works."

Anastasia's brows knit together. "I haven't heard of a binding chain. What does it look like?"

"It's a necklace," I replied.

"Well, it can't be too hard to dig up information on it." She walked behind the counter where the register was and pulled out a thick midnight-blue book. "When I was your age, I found a potion to clear acne." She let out a tiny chuckle. "It actually required eye of newt and took twenty-nine days to make."

"Did it work?" I asked.

A dazzling smile graced her face. "Like a charm. In fact, it's one of my number-one sellers."

She opened the book and flipped through its pages. I bent closer. At first glance, the book looked like an encyclopedia. Upon closer inspection, though, I realized it was a book of charms, talismans, and other items bewitched with magic.

Anastasia ran her finger down a page. "Binding amulets, binding beads, binding dolls—" She looked at Isaac. "Are you sure it's a chain?"

"Positive."

"It's not in here, but you're welcome to look through the books I have in stock. *Modern Day Amulets* might have something." She indicated with a nod to the bookshelves on the other side of the store. "And I'll do some digging to see what I can find."

"Thanks." Isaac headed over to the bookshelf.

I went to follow, but Anastasia caught my wrist. "The answer to the question that plagues your mind is yes, and Isaac has a right to know."

"What question?"

"I don't see it," Isaac said as he scanned the different titles.

"It has a mauve cover." She went to help him, leaving me to stare at her retreating back.

Several things kept me up at night. Reed invaded my dreams on a regular basis. At least with him in Sanctus, I no longer felt as if I couldn't survive without him. But sending Reed back to his home hadn't undone the effects of eating faerie food, and I was pretty sure that if he found a way back to our realm, I'd be on my knees, begging him for a bacca drop. Then there was Caden and his comment about me enjoying our excursions. I was afraid he might be right. While I didn't look forward to his interruptions, I didn't hate our trips. And I couldn't forget about Shane. Isaac did have a right to know that my best friend had accidentally brought someone back to life.

Shane had to be what Anastasia referred to. I wondered if she knew Kaylee and I were in over our heads. Maybe she knew that one day Shane would lose all sense of what it meant to be human and would kill people. I'd have told Isaac about Shane right then and there, but it was important to Kaylee that we fix this on our own. So, I decided to give us one more week. If Shane was still with us come next Friday, then I'd ask Isaac for help even if I had to break Kaylee's trust to do it.

Happy that I'd set a personal deadline for the zombie crisis, I joined Isaac and Anastasia by the books. Unfortunately, none of the ones she'd stocked mentioned binding chains. Anastasia told Isaac she'd let him know if she found anything, however. We thanked her for her time and headed over to The Grill to meet up with our friends.

Chapter 7

Hidden Message

The Grill was packed when we got there. I recognized several people sitting at the soda bar. Caden was bent over one of the pool tables as he lined up his shot. By the way the muscles in Isaac's jaw twitched, I knew he saw Caden too.

"Let's see if Josh and Kaylee are here." I laced my fingers through Isaac's and led the way through the tables to the other side of the room.

We found them sitting at a table not far from the jukebox. The waiter had just set their drinks down when we reached them. "What can I get you?"

"Coke for me." Isaac looked at me. "Lemonade?"

I nodded and sat next to Kaylee.

Isaac scowled at the far end of the restaurant as he lowered himself into a chair. "Does he have to show up everywhere we go?"

I followed his gaze to the pool tables. Caden didn't seem to know we were there.

"Technically, we showed up where he is this time." I slung my purse over the back of the chair. "Let's not let him ruin our evening before it starts." To Josh and Kaylee, I said, "Sarah texted. She and Mark are running late."

"That gives us a few minutes to talk about other things." Josh leaned in. "What did Anastasia say about the necklace?"

Isaac shook his head. "Nothing useful, but she's going to do some research and get back to me. Did you find anything?"

"Nah." Josh relaxed, slouching in his chair. "I went through my dad's books, but all the good ones are written in Latin, and that's not a language I'm anxious to learn."

Kaylee listened silently, a faraway expression on her face as she rolled and unrolled her straw wrapper.

I rested a hand on her arm. "Is everything okay?" I wanted to add "with Shane," but we still hadn't told the guys about her houseguest.

"Yeah."

When my gaze fell to her hands, she pushed the scrunched wrapper to the middle of the table.

Josh took her hand. "Babe, you sure? You've been jumpy all afternoon."

"I'm fine, really." She gave him a quick kiss. "It's just…today is supposed to be a witchcraft-free, demon-free day, and that's all we talk about."

Josh pulled her closer and playfully nuzzled her neck. "I thought you liked practicing magic."

She offered him a smile that I think was supposed to be sweet, but it came across a little forced. "I do, but the idea of today is to focus on the good things."

Kaylee's gaze met mine, and the look she gave me screamed, *A little help here.*

"She's right," I said. "Being cheerful is sort of the unspoken rule of the night, and even though we changed the venue, we should stick to it."

"Right." Kaylee sat a little straighter. This time when she smiled, it reached her eyes. "Tonight is all about friends pigging out on junk food, skipping down memory lane, and having a good time."

Josh smirked. "How far back are we going, because I can still remember a certain little girl who dressed up as an angel for Halloween."

Kaylee laughed. "I was six, I was a princess, and you didn't even know me then."

"Yeah, but I had said to myself, 'I'm going to know that girl.'"

I remembered the costume he referred to. Kaylee and I had been in kindergarten. Kaylee wore a pale pink gown, and her mom had put a ring of baby's breath in her hair. I wore a deep purple gown and had small violet flowers in my hair.

"Hi." Sarah said from behind me. She and Mark sat. "Sorry we're late."

With Josh and Isaac distracted, I bent close to Kaylee and whispered. "Is everything okay with Shane?"

"Yeah. He's keeping himself busy."

I was glad to hear that.

We ordered dinner, then talked about our day—minus all the supernatural things that were happening around us. I hadn't realized how badly I needed a quiet dinner with friends. No powers or demons or zombies. Just good food and great company. I was enjoying myself so much that when Mark said he didn't care for the latest zombie film, I didn't press.

"Can I get you anything else?" our waiter asked once the dinner dishes had been cleared.

"Yes," Sarah said quickly. "The brownie turtle tower and six spoons."

Five layers of sinfully sweet goodness—that's how The Grill advertised their very generous square of fresh-baked brownie topped with vanilla ice cream, hot fudge, caramel, and pecans.

"I'm stuffed." I placed a hand over my stomach for emphasis.

"There's always room for dessert," Kaylee and Sarah cooed together.

It was what my mom used to say, so who was I to argue.

Sarah hit her fork against her glass. When she had our attention, she raised her soda. "To Mrs. Riley, an amazing mom and baker."

I clinked my glass against hers. "To Mom."

Our friends followed our lead.

"Man, your mom made the best brownies," Josh said as he sliced a hunk of chocolate and ice cream from the dish in front of us.

"And chocolate chip cookies," Sarah added.

"And don't forget her cinnamon rolls." Kaylee leaned against Josh, her head on his shoulder, and let out a little moan. "She made them from scratch. The pastry literally melted in your mouth."

"Remember when she tried to show us how to make them?" Sarah asked.

I laughed. "Ours made better hockey pucks."

"Madison, what was your favorite?" Josh asked.

"Her tiramisu. She made it every year for my dad's birthday."

Sarah threw a napkin at me. "You only liked the tiramisu because she'd soak the ladyfingers in liquor."

"Oh my God!" Kaylee exclaimed. "Remember how we swore—"

"We were drunk," she, Sarah, and I sang out. We burst into laughter at the memory.

"Mine and Sarah's moms worked," Kaylee told Isaac. "So we used to go home with Madison. Every afternoon, Mrs. Riley would sit down with us at the kitchen table and help us with our homework."

"More like insisted we finish it before we could play," I said.

"Yeah, but she made the time go by quickly," Sarah pointed out. "I secretly loved that about her."

Isaac smiled. "She sounds like she was an amazing woman. I'm sorry I didn't get to meet her."

"Me too," I said.

Sitting in the restaurant remembering the little things Mom used to do warmed and broke my heart at the same time. Before Mom died, she had asked two things of me. "Maddie, I want you to always be true to yourself," she'd said. "And watch out for our guys."

I swore I would. But when she died, I had been so upset with the world that I ignored her dying wishes. I let my grades slip, avoided my friends, and pretended that Chase had never been born. I'd have probably slipped further into my depression and might still be there if it hadn't been for Kaylee and Sarah. I'm sure that if Mom had been alive to see my behavior, she'd have been disappointed in me.

"Excuse me." We looked up to find Caden standing next to our table. "Madison, can I borrow you for a moment?"

"Are you kidding me?" Isaac replied.

I rested my hand over his and squeezed, a soothing reminder for him not to let Caden push his buttons. I looked at Caden. "Tonight's not a good night."

And I have a feeling you know that, I added silently in case Caden felt the need to pick thoughts out of my head.

"It will only take a minute," he insisted.

Isaac glared. "She said no."

Caden fixed him with a cold stare. "I only asked to be polite, but it wasn't a question."

I could feel the air sizzle with power. Isaac stood, knocking over his chair in the process. Josh and Mark followed his lead.

Isaac stepped in front of Caden. "I've had it with your games."

Strands of iridescent blue magic radiated between the fingers of Isaac's right hand. By the way Sarah's eyes bulged and her mouth hung open, I was sure she noticed the light show taking place in Isaac's palm, so I quickly muttered the confusion spell to make her oblivious to what she saw.

The temperature in the restaurant rose a good ten degrees, which was no doubt Caden's doing. And the amount of power emanating from Isaac had me thinking he really might explode. I jumped up, positioning myself to block Isaac's hand from being seen by anyone else at nearby tables.

"Stop it!" I placed my hands on his chest and whispered, "You need to calm down before you expose what you are to the entire restaurant."

"He's taking advantage of the situation," Isaac growled.

"Maybe he is." I lowered my voice even more. "But it's partly my fault for not ironing out the details of our agreement." At the time I had made it, I was too upset to care about anything but saving my brother. "Two minutes, Caden." When Isaac didn't sit back down, I said, "Giving him a couple minutes of my time is worth my brother's life."

"What does she mean—" Mark began, but Josh was already mumbling the confusion spell. The smell of hot apple cider—his powers—filled the air. Mark sat back down and started a conversation with Sarah.

"Please," I begged Isaac. "Sit down with our friends, and I'll be right back."

He looked over my shoulder at Caden. "This is the last time you abuse your control over her."

Josh groaned and cast another spell on Mark and Sarah.

I followed Caden to the soda bar. He sat on one of the red stools. I didn't.

I folded my arms over my chest, pissed that he'd ruin what had been a nice evening. "You said you were going to stop interrupting me when I'm with my friends."

"You're always with your friends or family. Or have you not noticed this."

"Sorry I'm not sulking around my house waiting for you to decide you need me."

He tapped a folded sheet of paper on the bar. "I'm surprised that you're here and not at the cemetery." When I said nothing, he went on.

"I did share with you a spell that allows you to talk to the deceased. I would have thought you'd want to spend tonight with your mom instead of walking down memory lane with the people you see every day."

"I like walking down memory lane with my friends. Besides, I don't cast dark spells."

"It's not a dark spell. Really, Madison, have I ever asked you to tap into your darker side?"

"No."

When I had done the séance to communicate with Ms. Brontë, I had drawn upon positive emotions to fuel my powers. The spell required a white candle, an item that had once belonged to the deceased, and dried wormwood. Chocolate and strawberries had kissed my taste buds as I recited the incantation. The pleasant taste of my magic proved I had used hope and happiness to pull her spirit from the afterlife.

But I'd never thought I'd see my mom again, let alone have the opportunity to talk to her. I wasn't sure what I'd tell her first. Maybe how great Dad had been or how Chase had her eyes. I could ask her if she knew about the powers, or what it was like on the other side.

"Can I really see her again?"

"On a limited once-in-a-while basis, yes," Caden said. "Being yanked through the veil is taxing on the spirit and on you, if you recall."

I'd been so weak after the séance, Caden had to help me back to the car.

"Do you think she can see me? I mean, from the other side."

"Before, when you were talking with your friends, I heard your thoughts. Your mom isn't going to be disappointed in you."

I bit my bottom lip, letting hope override my annoyance with Caden. I'd have run out of the restaurant if I didn't think there was a catch to doing the spell. Isaac missed his grandfather, yet he hadn't used witchcraft to talk to him. There had to be a reason, and I'd learned my lesson about casting spells I didn't fully understand when I had invited a vindictive faerie into my life this past December. Caden was a demon. Demons lied, or at the very least twisted the truth.

In my peripheral vision, I could see Isaac watching me. His right hand was clenched in a fist. With how often Caden showed up claiming he needed my help, I couldn't blame Isaac for being upset.

"Is that why you wanted to see me? To tell me that I should be in the cemetery and not here with my friends?"

"No." Caden handed me the paper he'd been tapping against the bar. "I need you to read this out loud."

I took the paper from him and unfolded it. It was heavy like parchment and more yellow than white. I glanced at the front and the back. "Is this a joke?"

"Not at all." Reaching over the bar, he grabbed a pen from near the register. Then he nodded at the paper. "What does it say?"

"Ah...'under the full moon with Irene Abbadia mare, *ostendo sum vestri specialis.*' What does that even mean?"

"Let me worry about that."

I looked at him. "You dragged me away from my friends for this?"

He plucked the paper from my grasp and held it so I could see. It was blank. "It's spelled to only reveal its message to one like who had written it."

"Someone who possessed the powers." I scooped my hair away from my face. "Wonderful. I can add hell's decipherer to my résumé. May I go now?"

He bent forward. "Are you sure you wouldn't rather see your mom? I'd be happy to say I require your assistance to give you an excuse to ditch Witch Boy."

I pushed him away from me. "His name is Isaac, and I don't want to cut my evening with him short." I turned to leave but stopped. "You need a hobby. Something to keep you busy."

"I have one." His eyes flashed red, revealing his demonic side.

I placed my hand on my hip. "I thought that was your job."

"I wasn't talking about my crossroad duties." He winked. "Plus, I still have my job with your father."

Had he not added that last comment, I would have convinced myself the job with my father was the hobby Caden had meant. No witty rejoinder came to me, so I settled for shaking my head as I walked away.

The rest of the evening went off without any more drama. I made sure to keep my mind and gaze from wandering away from our table. Isaac said nothing about Caden's interruption, and thanks to the confusion spell, Sarah and Mark had barely noticed the intrusion.

After dessert, we headed our separate ways. Isaac and I stopped by Annisquam Harbor Lighthouse. He parked so that we could watch the moon glisten over the dark water.

I gave him a kiss. "I had fun tonight."

"Me too." He slipped a hand behind my neck and pulled me closer. His powers reached out to find mine, eliminating my need to concentrate on anything but his lips. When he broke our kiss, his eyes held a glint of mischief. "You should call your dad and tell him you're sleeping at Kaylee's." His mouth skimmed my jaw on its way to my ear. "And come spend the night with me."

We kissed again. He used his powers to slide his seat further back and teleport me on top of him so that I straddled his lap. My hair fell in curtains over one side of his face as I unbuttoned his coat. Mine vanished, reappearing on the passenger seat.

"Show-off," I teased between kisses.

A low chuckle escaped his lips even as his tongue danced with mine. Every nerve in my body became super sensitive, compliments of our powers mingling. When his thumb skimmed my waist just along the top of my jeans, a moan bubbled up my throat.

"Stay with me tonight, and I promise to let you get a little sleep."

My phone buzzed, announcing I had a message.

He sighed. "If it's Caden, I'm going to fry the guy."

I chose not to remind Isaac that fire didn't hurt Caden, being from hell and all. Instead, I reached in my purse and grabbed my phone. It was Kaylee:

OMG! Shane is evil.

Chapter 8

Trouble

When I texted back, *Details!* Kaylee simply responded that I had to see it to believe it. As much as I hated to cut another evening with Isaac short, I had to know what was going on with Shane.

"Is she okay?" Isaac asked.

I'd almost forgotten I was sitting on his lap. "Ah…yeah."

What had Shane done? The worst-case scenarios sprinted through my thoughts: he'd found a way past the barrier spell and attacked her parents or his parents or some unsuspecting person on the street. Had he killed them? Had he been seen? When I noticed Isaac staring at me, I added, "Girl stuff. Would you mind dropping me off at her house?"

A mix of disappointment and concern etched into his features. "Sure."

I climbed back into the passenger seat, slipped on my jacket, and buckled up. He backed out of the parking space.

"Madison…" His grip tightened on the steering wheel. I thought he was going to say he'd had it with me and all the interruptions. Instead, he asked, "Kaylee's had a lot of girl stuff lately. Is she okay?"

"Yeah." At least I hoped she was. "It's Kaylee, the most all-right person I know."

He stopped at a red light and looked at me.

"You know whatever you tell me stays between us, right?" He took my hand in his. "You've been preoccupied lately, and Josh told me tonight that he's worried about her. If she's in trouble..."

I opened my mouth, the truth ready to spill from my lips, but I just couldn't betray Kaylee's trust.

"She's good." *I think.* "I'm good." *Or I would be if you'd start driving.*

His eyes narrowed. "Why do I get the feeling you'd say that even if it wasn't true?"

Because if it meant keeping you from worrying, I would.

But in this case—at least as far as I knew—it *was* true. "Isaac, I appreciate your concern, but I told Kaylee I wouldn't say anything. In another week, things will be back to normal. You'll see. Right now, though—"

"You need to get to her house." Without another word, he drove, pushing the speed limit to make up for lost time.

He pulled to a stop in front of her house. "Call me if you need anything."

"I will."

I sprinted up the front steps. The door creaked open before my knuckles made contact with the dark red wood. Fingers wrapped around my wrist and tugged me inside. My scream caught in my throat as I stumbled. Afraid Shane was about to attack, I quickly righted myself and sent a stream of power outward.

"Whoa!" Kaylee threw up a shield, blocking my strike from hitting her.

"What the heck, Kaylee! You scared the crap out of me." I glanced around. We were alone. Nothing in the foyer or living room was out of place. "Where's Shane?"

"Upstairs." She slammed the door closed and raised her voice. "And he'd better stay there if he doesn't want to be set on fire!"

"So, he did find a way past the barrier spell." Or maybe the spell had worn off.

"Not exactly." Kaylee scrunched up her button nose. "Earlier today, I might have brought down the spell so that he could get some fresh air."

"You what?" I wasn't sure if I should arm myself with an energy ball or prepare to see the worst.

"He's been fine, and he looks almost normal." She was right. Shane looked like a kid who could use getting outside in the sun, but he no longer looked like the walking dead. "And, at the time, I didn't think we should treat him like a prisoner."

The whole idea of putting a spell on her brother's room had been to make sure no one saw Shane, but what was done was done. We'd deal with the aftermath, as soon as I figured out what that was. "Where are your mom and dad?"

"At the movies, thank goodness."

That meant Shane hadn't tried to eat them, and we had a little time before they'd be home. Speaking of not being eaten, Kaylee seemed fine. Her hair looked as if she had run her hands through it a few dozen times, but she'd had time to change into sweats and a tank top since I'd last seen her, and Shane wasn't tied to a chair. That allowed me to deduce that he hadn't gone on a killing spree.

I dropped my purse just inside the living room doorway and looked at her. "Well, are you going to tell me what Shane did, or do I have to guess?"

"He's gotten too comfortable in my house, for one." She walked to the kitchen. I followed. "And then there's this."

I missed what "this" was. She reached into the freezer and grabbed a pint of chocolate and peanut butter ice cream, closed the freezer door, and plucked two spoons from a drawer.

"Kaylee! You sent an S.O.S. What did Shane do?" I couldn't help being annoyed, and I missed being in Isaac's arms. Not that I wanted someone to be hurt, but I did want there to be a reason I'd cut my evening short.

"That." She pointed to a glass vase on the counter. It was stuffed with yellow roses and pink carnations.

"Those are from Shane?" Honestly, if Kaylee weren't so upset, I would have laughed at how silly it was to be this disturbed over flowers. Instead, I bent over the arrangement. The roses smelled amazing. She leaned against the counter and stuck her spoon into the frozen treat.

"This is what you text me about." I took a spoon from her and scooped out a large chunk of chocolate goodness. "They're pretty."

"Josh saw them." She kept eating.

I wasn't seeing the big deal. "He probably thought your dad got them for your mom."

She handed me a small rectangular card. *Thanks, Kaylee. You always were great to me,* had been handwritten in blue ink.

"Josh read this?" I asked.

Not that Josh was the jealous type, but everyone knew he and Kaylee were a couple. They'd been dating for two years and, well, fit together perfectly. But let's face it, everyone had a breaking point. And Josh's would no doubt be a large, expensive floral arrangement sent to his girl. "What did you tell him?"

"She said they were from you," Shane replied from the doorway. He gave a nod toward the pint of ice cream in Kaylee's hand. "Hey, is that rocky road?"

Kaylee's reply came in the form of an energy ball whipped at his head. Shane ducked. The energy ball hit the doorframe and left a burn mark. She held another glowing ball at the ready.

"Kaylee, you need to calm down!" I raised my hand and called her weapon to me. Once in my grasp, it disappeared as I vanquished it. I then fixed the wall with a wave of my hand.

She pinned Shane with a glare that could wither a plant. "I told you not to step foot out of Chris's room."

"I heard Madison's voice." Shane snatched the spoon from me and the ice cream from Kaylee. "My dad loves chocolate and peanut butter."

He lowered himself into a chair.

"He's eating us out of house and home," she griped. "My parents think it's me. As if I suddenly have the appetite of a teenage boy. They've even joked about it in front of Josh."

"Did you really tell Josh I got you flowers?" Something I would never do. If Kaylee needed cheering up, I'd buy her Jelly Bellies or a *grande* mocha. I'd hand-deliver them along with a pint of ice cream and two spoons—one for me and one for her—like she and I always did when the other was upset. Like we were doing now, minus the jelly beans but plus a zombie.

Kaylee massaged her temples as if warding off a headache. "I was caught off-guard. Shane's lucky Josh didn't see him."

"I was downstairs when they got here. I hid in the dining room," Shane explained through a mouthful of ice cream.

The doorbell rang.

Kaylee went to answer it, but not before saying, "Josh knows something's up."

I looked at the bouquet. If I were Josh, I'd be suspicious too.

"They are pretty," I said to Shane.

"Don't encourage him," Kaylee called over her shoulder.

"Where'd you get the money for them?" No way was he buried with a pocketful of cash.

"Her brother's dresser drawer. I only took fifty. I wanted to thank Kaylee for bringing me back."

It hadn't been intentional, but we all knew that. And as soon as we found a counterspell, we would have to send him back. Although, the more time I spent with him, the more I questioned if that was the right thing to do.

Kaylee re-joined us. "I tried to tell him to go away, but he wouldn't listen."

I didn't have to wait long to find out whom she was talking about. "You're tracking me down at my best friend's house now? Seriously, Caden, you need a hobby that doesn't involve me."

"This can't wait." Caden eyed Shane. "Madison, I thought you were opposed to raising the dead."

"You can tell he's dead?" Kaylee sat in the chair opposite Shane.

Caden nodded. "He doesn't have an aura."

An aura was a person's life force.

"I am," I said in reply to his earlier statement. "He's Kaylee's doing."

"He's a little young for you, isn't he?" he asked.

"I didn't bring him back on purpose!" She folded her arms over her chest. "And Zombie Boy and I are not dating." There was emphasis on the last two words.

"He's not a zombie." Caden's body tensed, and the rest of his comments went unsaid. Instead, his fingers curled into fists at his side, and his eyes closed as if he were struggling with an unseen force. When he opened them, his irises burned liquid red. "Madison, we have to go."

His sudden change told me now was not the time to give him a hard time. I looked at Kaylee. "Will you be okay?"

Kaylee didn't seem able to tear her eyes away from Caden's. "Will *you?*"

"Of course she'll be fine." Caden's body shuddered. "Madison, take my hand."

I didn't. "I can walk to the car just fine."

"There's no time to drive."

I've traveled by magic a few times now. Most were by Isaac's doing, as I hadn't mastered that type of magic yet. Being teleported from one place to another by the powers was like walking in a dream. You became weightless as if you were nothing more than a thought for the brief second it took for your body to vanish from one place and reappear in another. Then there was the time the Prince of Fae used his magic to transport us to my house. I had sworn my insides were being pierced by thousands of ice shards. While under his spell, I couldn't breathe. And once at our destination, I'd felt as if my insides were trying to come up my throat. Death would have been more merciful than his magic.

Traveling at the hand of a demon was somewhere in the middle of those experiences. Caden's eyes were fierce, and his hand felt as if he had a high fever. He snaked an arm around my back and pulled me against his chest. "Bend your knees when we land."

"What?"

But my word was sucked into a vacuum of black and red. The air became drenched with the stench of smoke and brimstone. No wonder there were times Caden smelled as if he'd just come from a bonfire.

We landed with a jolt that knocked the wind out of me. Had Caden not been holding me, I would have fallen. Crisp country air filled my lungs as a thought occurred to me: I shouldn't have been comfortable standing this close to a demon. He said nothing as if knowing I needed a moment to steady myself. When I was sure my feet were firmly planted on the ground, I took a step away from him and surveyed the small copse of tall trees around us.

"Where are we?" But as soon as I asked, I saw the old red barn and knew we were near his crossroad.

"We have a problem that I thought would be better addressed by you." He indicated with a nod for me to turn around.

My gaze followed the narrow road to the dark green Jeep parked in the grass. Isaac stood in the center of the crossroad, feet shoulder-width apart.

"Judging by the etching in the dirt around him and the items at his feet, he's planning on sending me to Hades," Caden explained in a tone much too calm, considering why we were there.

A black bowl rested over the spot where I'd once buried the things needed to summon a crossroad demon. Five blood-red candles circled the bowl. If there was a witch who could exile a demon, it was Isaac. The added power he'd been given by his grandfather along with a grimoire full of unusual spells made Isaac a person who wasn't to be messed with.

I wrapped my arms around myself to fight off the night air, glad that I still had my coat on. "You should have thought about the repercussions of messing with a natural witch sooner. Really, Caden, you had to know Isaac would eventually get tired of it and send your ass back to hell."

The corner of Caden's mouth tugged upward into a wily smirk. "You're assuming I'm worried that Witch Boy's little spell might work?"

"I've yet to see a spell of his fail."

"I'd burn him alive before I stepped foot near that crossroad. Any experienced demon would do the same. The only reason he's still breathing is because I don't want to hurt someone you care about."

"Caden…" I wanted to say, *You can't feel that way about me. And even if I didn't have a boyfriend, you are a demon and I am human. You've lived for centuries and I'm not even old enough to vote.* But his compassion was the only reason Isaac wasn't a charred pile of ash and bone.

"Had you not intrigued me, I never would have made a deal with you," Caden said, not hiding the fact that he'd been eavesdropping on my thoughts.

"I'll go talk to him." I stuffed my hands in my jacket pockets and strolled forward.

"Madison."

I stopped and glanced over my shoulder.

"Me giving you a chance to reason with him is a onetime offer. If he tries to pull something like this again, I will respond with the full force granted me."

I nodded and walked forward. It didn't take Isaac long to notice me.

"Hey," I said.

My surprise at finding him at the crossroad was nothing to the shocked expression on his face. "Madison? What are you doing here?"

My gaze traveled over the pentagram drawn in the dirt and the shallow black bowl near his feet. Some type of herb had been sprinkled over fine black power. "I should ask you that question."

The flames of the candles spiked as Isaac cursed under his breath. "Caden saw me and ran."

I was sure Caden hadn't run. More like spent a minute or two debating if he should roast Isaac in hellfire or get me.

Isaac's face flushed. "What does he do, scope out his next victim before he lets them know he's here?"

"Can you blame him?"

Isaac couldn't have been the first person who'd tried to trick a crossroad demon. I stepped closer. The bowl and candles were the only things between us.

"Where is he?" Isaac's voice was level, but I knew from the smell of steel in the air that he was angry.

"Caden thought you and I should talk."

"Of course he did." He paced a couple of steps away, rubbed a hand over his mouth, and looked at me again. "Don't you see what he's doing?"

"He's refraining from killing the guy I'm pretty sure I love."

"He wants you to think he's a good guy, but he's not."

I wet my lips. I didn't want to argue. "I know what Caden is."

"Do you?" He didn't give me time to reply. "You've stopped questioning his intentions. You run off with him day and night. You're standing up for him now."

"Not because I want to spend time with him." I dragged a hand through my hair. "I made a binding agreement with him. I promised no questions asked. Promised, Isaac. I *have* to go with him when he calls. And I'm not here for him. I'm here because I don't want you to get hurt."

"I'm ready for him."

Maybe Isaac was. Maybe he'd cast a spell that would keep Caden from being able to draw power from hell. Maybe he'd found a spell to protect him from a demon's magic. But Caden wasn't stupid. He wouldn't get close enough for Isaac's powers to touch him. And even if Isaac managed to get the upper hand, it wouldn't solve anything.

"Isaac, if you vanquish Caden, another demon will take his place."

"Your contract is with Caden. Another demon shouldn't have any hold over you."

I could be free. On the surface, that possibility sounded great. No more cutting my evenings short. No more late-night trips to do a demon's bidding. No more worrying about binding chains and what they could do. Problem was, we still weren't sure that would be the case. Somehow I knew that sending Caden away wasn't a permanent solution.

"Caden will eventually claw his way out of the pit, and he will come for you."

"I'll be ready."

So will he. "I'd prefer not to have to worry that a pissed-off demon might show up on your doorstep." Caden would probably burn Isaac's house down with him inside, no warning. I closed the distance between Isaac and me and rested my hand on his arm. "Isaac, give this up. For me."

He rubbed the back of his head. "Caden's not going to show up here, is he?"

"Would you walk into a trap?"

Isaac waved his hand over the things at his feet, and they vanished.

I wrapped my arms around his waist. "I want you to promise me that you won't try this again. I made the deal with Caden, and I'll keep it. You make that promise to me, and I promise I'll tell Caden he and I are going to set some ground rules."

"He'll never agree to that."

"I'll ask nicely." If I had to add a few years to my current contract, I would.

"You get him to agree, and I'll make that promise."

"Okay." I'd accept that for now. "Think I could get a lift home?"

Chapter 9

Dreaming of a Prince

It was past eleven o'clock when Isaac dropped me off at my house. I called Kaylee as soon as I walked in the door. I caught her up on my evening and then asked how things were going over there.

"You should have seen him, Madison. Following me around like a lost puppy. It reminded me that his return is just as difficult for him as it is for me. And, really, the flowers are beautiful, so I thanked him, and we hung out awhile."

I chuckled at the image of Shane trailing behind Kaylee and her trying not to notice. "Where is he now?"

"Knocked out asleep in Chris's room. Did Caden tell you what he is?"

With everything that had gone on with Isaac, I'd forgotten to ask Caden about Shane. "No. Sorry."

"Remember when the only thing we had to worry about was homework and if the guys we liked would ask us to a dance?"

I stretched out on my bed, looking at a glow-in-the-dark ladybug Mom had put on my ceiling when I was eight. "And the only witches we knew went to Hogwarts."

"Yeah." Her voice drifted away as if she was checking the display on her phone while she talked. "Josh is calling. I'll catch up with you in the morning."

"Okay. Good night."

Sleep came to me almost immediately, and with it came the dreams of Solstice Balls and a very handsome Prince of Fae. Reed's back was to me. His snowy white hair brushed the collar of his dark green tux as he looked out over a frozen river. Around us, the forest was filled with faeries in long dresses and fancy suits. The celebration was held under a deep purple sky. A sad melody serenaded the guests gliding gracefully over the glade in a synchronized waltz. My breath caught when the prince turned. He was more beautiful than I dared remembered.

"You came." He held a pale hand out for me to take. "Come and I'll get you some wine."

I placed my fingers in his. We walked along the edge of the field where the others danced. The sweet scent of bacca wine laced the crisp air, awakening my senses. We stopped in front of a large mushroom. Its flat cap was the refreshment table.

Reed picked up two rose-colored flutes and handed one to me. I sipped mine. The fruity liquid coated my tongue and warmed my insides. One sip led to another until my glass was empty and Reed was handing me another.

"Tell me," he inquired. His snow-white gaze fixed on my eyes. "What made you change your mind about being here?"

I opened my mouth to answer, but movement to my left caught my attention. Isaac stood there, hand held out much like Reed had done a moment ago. "It's time to go."

I reached for him, but our fingers didn't connect. Then Isaac was gone, and I was in Reed's arms, twirling around the dance floor with the others. Faster and faster until my head felt light and my heartbeat became heavy. I broke free of Reed's grip, turned to flee, and found myself in the arms of another faerie. He was thinner than Reed but just as tall.

"Sorry." I stepped around him and into yet another faerie. Again and again until I was back in Reed's arms.

"Stay with me, my flower."

Over the ballad, I heard my name.

Reed placed his fingers under my chin, tilting my head up. "Madison."

I jolted awake and found myself standing in the middle of my room with my sheet wrapped loosely around my body. A dark figure loomed over me. I raised my hand and whipped an energy ball at its head.

Instead of ducking, it caught my weapon. "It's just me."

I glanced at the light, pushing out power and turning it on. Caden stood next to my bed, holding my weapon.

I pulled the sheet higher over my tank top. "How'd you get in here?"

"Same way we got to the crossroad earlier this evening." He glanced at the energy ball. "You want to do something with this, or shall I?"

"I should make it explode in your face." But instead, I waved my hand in front of me and canceled the spell.

"Do you always dance in your sleep?"

"I must have been sleepwalking." Something I had never done before, but I had other things to worry about. "What are you doing here?"

"Our link went supersonic. I thought you were in danger."

Every person who made a deal with Caden was linked to him. It was how he kept track of his clients. Most of the time, he let them live whatever was left of their lives in peace. That was because most of his clients had traded their souls for whatever it was they wanted. I was one of the few exceptions.

I rubbed my eye. "I was dreaming."

"I noticed." Caden lowered himself onto the edge of the bed. "I thought the cravings for bacca wine died when Reed returned home."

It was no use denying that I was dreaming about Reed. Not with Caden's ability to see inside my head. "They did. But sometimes he sneaks into my dreams." I groaned. "That sounds so much worse when I say it out loud."

"You haven't told your friends?"

I shook my head. "I'm fine. I just need a drink."

I tossed the sheet — my makeshift dress, I realized — on the bed.

Caden smiled. "Cute pajamas."

I was wearing lavender cotton shorts with a matching top. Nothing sexy. My bare feet padded over the carpet. "I'm good now, thanks. You can go."

He didn't. "I can take away the effects of the faerie food you consumed last December, if you ask."

For a price. "I can handle a dream or two, so the next time our connection goes supersonic in the middle of the night, feel free to ignore it."

I left him in my room and headed to the kitchen to get a glass of pineapple-orange juice. It was the closest thing in our house to Reed's faerie wine. I'd just poured myself a glass when I heard Caden behind me.

"I'll do it at a discount. Ten years."

"No."

"You're being stubborn."

"I'm being smart. I don't need to owe you more time than I already do. Now get out of here before my dad sees you." I put the juice back in the fridge and realized this was my chance to question him. "Before you go—"

But when I looked back up, Caden was gone.

Saturday morning, Dad had to replace the water heater at a house on the other side of town. That left me to watch Chase. I tried calling Caden, but he didn't answer his phone.

"It's Madison. For the third time." As if he didn't know that from my other messages. "Call me when you get this."

I decided to use the time I was trapped at home to do laundry. I'd folded the whites and was waiting for the jeans to finish drying but still no call from Caden. Isaac called, though.

"What time will your dad be back?"

"By noon, but I need to stop by Kaylee's. You know, I sort of ditched her yesterday." And I wanted to make sure Shane hadn't done anything new to have her wanting to set him on fire again. There seemed to be a lot of that going on—people I knew wanting to set someone on fire.

"How about I pick you up at four?" Isaac asked.

"Perfect!"

We hung up. I walked in the family room to check on Chase and found him bouncing on the couch.

"You're supposed to be putting away your Matchbox cars while you watch cartoons." I picked up the remote control and turned the TV off.

"That was the best part."

The television clicked back on. It had to be Chase's doing, but he must have thought I'd only changed my mind, because he went back to staring at his show as if nothing unusual had happened. I hit the off button again.

"Hey!" he exclaimed.

When I heard the faint sound of the TV powering back up, I quickly canceled Chase's unintentional spell and acted as naturally as I could. "Hey, nothing. Promise me you'll clean up your mess before you turn the TV back on."

"I promise." His words were loaded with sarcasm, but when he went to move closer to the TV as if to turn it on himself, he stumbled over his own feet. "Fine."

He might not have known what stopped him from disobeying my wish, but I did.

I smiled, wishing all my problems were so easily solved.

Kaylee was way too happy to pick me up and bring me to her house. Her parents were out for the afternoon. Shane sat on the edge of the coffee table in the family room playing Xbox. We hadn't even been there two minutes when Kaylee grabbed her keys.

"Your turn to zombie-sit," she announced.

"Whoa!" I popped up from my seat on the couch. "Where are you going?"

"To spend some quality time with Josh before he dumps me." She grabbed her coat and made a beeline for the foyer.

I got there just as she opened the front door. "He's not going to dump you."

"Yeah, well, I've been cooped up keeping an eye on Shane while you've been having fun. It's my turn to get out." She raced to her car.

"You're the one who brought him back to life!"

She didn't hear me, though.

I blew out a breath, sending my bangs flying. "Great, I go from brother-sitting to zombie-sitting." I looked at the back of Shane's head. "Or whatever you are."

I took a seat on the loveseat and watched the living dead on TV rip a pedestrian apart.

"Out of all the games Chris owns, this is the one you chose to play?"

Shane pounded on the green A. "It's my favorite."

How ironic.

"Have you figured out how you're going to get me back home and in school?"

"Not yet." Even though Shane's behavior since his return had been that of the caring boy I'd known when he was human, Kaylee and I had still been focused on sending him back to the grave. But if Caden was right—if there was no danger of Shane turning into a decaying, flesh-eating zombie—then maybe we needed to start looking for ways to warp time in such a way that he'd be able to stay.

"I saw my mom yesterday. She didn't see me, though." Shane paused the game. "Her smile's changed."

"She lost her son less than a year ago." I bent forward and took the game remote from him. "When I lost my mom, I thought I'd never truly be happy again, but eventually it got easier, and I was."

His big gray eyes met mine. "Do you think she's forgotten me?"

"No. She could live to be a hundred, and she wouldn't forget you."

Shane's longing to see his mom hit home with me. It made me realize Kaylee and I had to help him return to his old life, but to do that, we needed to know what he was. I dug my phone out of my purse and sent a quick text to Caden.

Sorry I was rude last night.

After all, he had invaded my privacy to see if I was okay; I could cut him some slack. I then sent *I need to see you* followed by *Please.* All I could do now was hope he'd forgive me and stop by.

Shane switched remotes with me so that he could be player one. We'd just killed a nest of rotting living-dead avatars when the doorbell rang.

I set my remote on the coffee table. "Stay here."

Relief filled me when I caught a glimpse of Caden's familiar green pea coat through the sidelight.

I opened the door and stepped aside. "Thanks for coming."

Caden winked and sauntered by me. "How could I resist a girl who begs to see me?"

"Don't make me sorry I asked you here." Which might just happen if he continued on with that type of teasing. I shut the door before Kaylee's nosy neighbor could see a guy entering her house. Thank goodness her parents liked Josh, because Mrs. Cramer never missed an opportunity to run over and tell them that Kaylee let Josh in the house when they weren't home. "I left you three messages."

Caden leaned against the wall near the door. "I was out of my calling area." He didn't reek of brimstone, so I highly doubted that. "Did you change your mind about my offer? I don't often give discounts."

I'd almost forgotten that Caden had offered to heal me of the lingering effects of faerie food, but if I was going to make another deal with him, it wouldn't be for that. His brow rose questioningly, and I halted my thoughts.

"Is hell running a special?" I asked. Maybe I could get a two-for-one deal.

He laughed. "Sorry, I don't do BOGO deals." His expression grew serious. "Derek hasn't bothered you again, has he?"

"No." And as far as I knew, he hadn't bothered my friends either.

"Good." He clapped his hands together once. "So, did you need something, or were you simply missing my company?"

I stopped myself from saying *You wish.* "Two things. First, you said Shane wasn't a zombie."

Caden nodded.

"Then what is he?"

The television in the other room went silent. Shane obviously wanted to know the answer to that question as much as I did.

"He's a ghoul." Caden's eyes narrowed. "You really didn't know that?"

"No." And I had no idea how that differed from a zombie.

I was about to ask, but Shane beat me to it. "What does being a ghoul mean?" He stood in the doorway to the family room, the remote still in his hand.

"Unlike zombies, ghouls remember who they were." Caden twirled his keys around his finger, catching them in his palm as he spoke. "They're capable of feeling and learning, which makes it possible for them to blend into society."

That described Shane and explained why he was so…Shane.

He nodded. "Madison and Kaylee are working on getting me home."

I forced a smile. "That's the plan." *Now, anyway.*

Caden's gaze fell on me, one eyebrow raised.

I pretended not to notice his quizzical expression and asked, "How long will the spell last?"

"Forever."

It wasn't the answer I'd expected. Forever was a very long time to be fifteen.

"It's forever or off with his head," Caden said, having clearly read my mind. He pushed off the wall.

Shane took a large step away from us, hands raised in fists—though I think he forgot he was still clutching the game remote in one of them. "Try and we will have a problem!"

"No one's chopping off your head." My stomach lurched at the mere thought. Shane might be undead, but he was still the same guy I'd grown up with. "What I don't understand is how Kaylee managed to bring him back." I groaned. "Sorry, that sounded cold."

"It's okay." Shane relaxed his stance and rested a shoulder against the doorframe.

"It's just that Kaylee and I weren't practicing magic." I told Caden how we'd gone to visit my mom's grave and how Kaylee had been telling me about the spells she'd learned. "We've discussed spells before. Unless we're trying to cast, nothing happens."

Caden rubbed his mouth, thoughtfully. "Is Kaylee a natural witch?"

"No. Josh and Isaac shared a little of their powers with her." My eyes narrowed. "What does that have to do with anything?"

"Everything, considering they shared the powers with someone who has necromancer blood running through her veins."

"I know what that is," Shane interjected. "There's one in my game—Glenda. She's a sorcerer that raises the dead."

"Most only raise their spirits." Caden looked at me. "But the powers would amplify Kaylee's necromancer abilities, and she went to a cemetery and decided to recite a few spells."

He said it as if Kaylee knew she was a…whatever Caden had just called her. I lowered myself onto the bottom step of the stairs and processed this information. "I think Kaylee would know if her ancestors could talk to spirits."

"Really?" Caden challenged. "Some people would think a person would know if they possessed the powers, but more than half of those who do go their whole life without knowing they're special." He had me there. If it hadn't been for Emma Scott and Paige Osborn, I may have never discovered my powers, let alone embraced them and be practicing magic. "After I met Shane," Caden continued, "I did a little research. Traced Kaylee's family tree. From what I could find, no one in her bloodline has practiced in centuries."

I wondered if Josh and Isaac knew about necromancers. Yet even if they did, I highly doubted they knew Kaylee was a descendant of one.

Caden checked the time on his watch. "You said you had two things for me."

"Ah, yeah." I looked at Shane. "It's sort of private."

"Say no more." Shane went into the family room. He was fighting zombie avatars before he sat.

I motioned for Caden to follow me into the kitchen. I hadn't given much thought to how I would approach this next subject. When I told Isaac I'd talk to Caden, I'd been confident it would be easy. The worst thing that could happen was Caden refusing.

He pulled out a chair, turned it sideways before sitting, and watched me with a bored look on his face. After a few more seconds, he said, "Just spit it out, Madison."

"Right." I sat next to him. "Look. The deal we made was that when you need my assistance with an issue that requires magical intervention, I help you. It wasn't that I'd be your gardener or car repair service, and it certainly didn't include me dropping everything to rush off with you so that I can snatch a little devil's shoestring from the homes of clients that have years left on their contracts."

He smirked, a playful glint in his chocolate-brown eyes. "Go on."

"You and I need ground rules." I squared my shoulders. No way was I going to back down now. "No coming to get me when I'm with my friends. That includes Isaac."

He leaned back. "So, you'd like me to get you when you're in school or watching Chase instead."

"No!" I couldn't afford to miss class, and it wasn't like I could leave my brother alone while I ran off to do hell knew what. "I want you to plan ahead."

"You mean schedule appointments with you."

"Yes."

He seemed to consider this a moment. "There might be a time when that's not possible."

"That's fine, for exceptions." I paused. "Do we need to go over what qualifies as an exception?"

"No. I think I can figure that out. But, Madison, you do realize that would be a change to our existing contract and would require payment in the form of years?"

I figured as much, but I needed Caden to agree or Isaac would keep trying to send him back to hell. As powerful a witch as Isaac was, I feared his magic wasn't a true match for Caden's.

I raised my chin. "How many?"

"Five."

That seemed steep, considering we were talking about changing a line or two in my existing contract.

"It's as low as I'm willing to go," Caden said.

You need Caden's cooperation to get Isaac's, I reminded myself.

"Fine." I combed my fingers through my hair, feeling better about Caden's and my arrangement. "And no more flirting."

At this, he smiled. "I'm all right with you coming on to me. No need to change that."

My cheeks warmed, and I knew a blush had crept into them. "I have not come on to you!"

"Believe what you'd like." He stood. "Shall we kiss on it?"

I groaned. He was like talking to a spoiled child used to getting his way. "Caden, this is exactly what I mean. I'm dating Isaac."

Who was smart and funny and who'd been more tolerant of my problems than most boyfriends would be.

Caden's irises bled to red, but he didn't look angry. Standing with his feet shoulder-width apart and his hands folded in front of him, he looked businesslike. "We need to amend our existing contract."

My left arm started to burn like it had the other day in the graveyard. Red glowing letters formed, spelling out *Beck-and-Call, who will come when told.*

"We're not kissing." Ignoring the pain, I held out my hand. "We can shake on it."

His mouth pulled upward into a smirk I was beginning to hate. "Afraid you'll enjoy yourself? That you might start having dreams about me, perhaps?"

"Jerk." I ground my teeth against the ever-present sting in my arm and kept my hand raised to say it was a handshake or nothing.

His gaze never left mine. "Our deal was sealed with a kiss. The only way to make the changes you desire is through another kiss. Hell's rules, I'm afraid." He didn't look the least bit remorseful. "I've been more than giving with you, but this is not something that can be negotiated."

I bit my bottom lip and scrutinized him. His teasing smile had been replaced by a stern expression. I could see fire flicker in the back of his eyes, the look that he got whenever he conducted his crossroads business.

"Fine." I stood. "A quick kiss."

His lips were as soft as I remembered, and his arm around my waist was as unyielding as it had been that cold day in December when I'd made the deal. He was solid too. All muscle. My heart raced as my hand slid to his hip. My nails dug into the fabric of his jeans as the sting on my arm grew to be unbearable. It was as if the old part of my contract was being scraped away with a dull knife. I whimpered, sure I'd pass out before it was over. Caden pulled me closer, deepening our kiss. As he did, the pain lessened from excruciating to throbbing. It was the difference between having a rusty old blade rammed through your forearm over and over again and being grazed by a scalpel. Realizing Caden's kiss was like an anesthesia, I squeezed my eyes shut and kissed him back, focusing on the feel of his mouth and not the letters being etched into my skin.

He had a way of moving his tongue just so, skimming mine almost as if in challenge, that sent my pulse racing. Under the scent of brimstone and sulfur that was his demonic side, I could smell the deep woodsy aroma of his cologne. It suited him.

After I'm not sure how long, Caden ended our kiss. His eyes faded back to brown as his fingers tucked my hair behind my ear. "Happy?"

"Yes. Thank you." I couldn't look him in the eye. I was embarrassed I'd kissed him back, mad at myself for liking the feel of his lips on mine, and slightly breathless. Unfortunately, the last sensation wasn't because I'd been fighting not to scream.

I put much-needed space between us, hoping Caden couldn't hear the accelerated beat of my heart. I also worked hard not to think about Isaac, even though I had amended the contract for him. No way would Isaac have wanted that if he'd known it meant kissing Caden.

Caden looked at the clock on the stove. "I have to go."

I walked him to the door.

"Shall I pick you up at eight?" he asked.

"Why?"

"Because it's the first night of the full moon, and I'd prefer not to have to wait another month to retrieve the next piece of my necklace."

"*Under the full moon with Irene Abbadia mare.*" That's what the message had said, and it stood to reason that if it took a person who possessed the powers to read it, then it would take a person who possessed the powers to retrieve the next link. That didn't necessarily mean Caden needed to be there. If I could get to the next piece before him, then I could stop him. All I needed to know was where we'd be going.

I quickly changed my thoughts to Isaac. "I have plans."

"With Witch Boy?"

"Yes, and I'm not canceling them. Pick me up at eleven." I paused. "Is it far?" I asked, fishing for more information. I replayed our last trip together in my mind to keep him from knowing my true intentions.

He laughed. "Distance isn't really a problem for me."

"Yeah, but it is for me. I wasn't too fond of being zapped to the crossroad yesterday." I placed a hand over my stomach. "I felt queasy most of the morning."

"No, you didn't." He frowned. "But if it will keep you from worrying about it, we'll be taking my car. We might even have time for a midnight stroll."

I couldn't stop the image of the moonlight hitting Caden's eyes from flittering through my thoughts, and I cursed inwardly. "No strolling. We get your trinket, and you bring me home."

Caden smiled devilishly. "I like seeing you in the moonlight too. Did you know it brings out a pink glow in your cheeks?"

"Stay out of my head!"

"See you at eleven, Madison." Caden opened the door.

He was halfway down the walk when I said, more to myself than him, "Damn, I should have made him add a clause to the contract that stated he'd refrain from reading my mind."

Caden stopped next to his car. "Want me to come back inside? We can discuss another amendment…"

And kiss you again? "No, thanks."

"Face it, Madison, you like bad boys." He got in his car.

I closed the door, glad to be alone with my thoughts. I did not like bad boys. I liked good guys with a dangerous side, like Isaac. Sweet and protective most of the time, but when push came to shove, he could handle himself against the evil in the world. And just because my heartbeat had increased when Caden and I kissed didn't mean that I *liked* him. Altering the contract had hurt. His kiss took that pain away, or at the very least, masked it. I rubbed my arm and chastised Caden for being what he was.

If it was because he was smug, a demon, or a temptation I didn't need was a question I couldn't answer.

"Can we order a pizza?" Shane called from the other room. "I'm starved."

I'd almost forgotten he was there. I called in our order, then texted Kaylee to find out how long she expected me to keep Shane company. I went back in the family room and waited for her reply. She didn't take long.

Parents won't be back until 3. Another hour? A second message came through. *Tell him to go upstairs when you leave.*

Aren't you coming home?!

In Peabody.

"Great," I muttered to myself and typed another response. *Aren't you curious to know "what" Shane is?*

YES! Tell me.

Sure. When you get here.

Tease. Still not hurrying home. Talk later.

Considering that *what* Shane was didn't change the fact that he was here and ready to blend back into society, I couldn't blame Kaylee for not rushing home. I picked up my game remote. I might as well kill a few zombie avatars while I waited.

Chapter 10

Abbadia Mare

I filled Isaac in on my visit with Caden as we drove to Isaac's house. I tiptoed around how I'd managed to get Caden to agree to my conditions. Some details were best left a secret. In turn, Isaac promised he'd stop trying to send Caden back to hell. He did add a stipulation that went along the lines of *as long as Caden abides by this new agreement.* Since my contract had been amended, I knew Caden would, and therefore I could stop worrying about Isaac getting himself killed by hellfire. I then told Isaac about my appointment with Caden later that night, and Isaac was all for getting to the next piece of the chain before him.

"Tell me what the message said again," Isaac said.

We leaned over the kitchen counter and his tablet.

"Under the full moon with Irene Abbadia mare. Then *ostendo sum vest special*, or something like that."

His fingers tapped the keypad. "The last part has to be a spell."

A few seconds later, he slid the tablet closer to me. I had part of the saying wrong, but the search engine still managed to translate the Latin incantation: "reveal your secrets."

"Maybe I'm remembering the name wrong," I suggested.

We'd already searched the white pages for an "Irene Abbadia" and then anyone with the last name of Abbadia living in the area. We came up empty.

"It's Latin." Mr. Addington opened the fridge and grabbed a soda. I hadn't seen him come into the kitchen. "*Abbadia mare* refers to 'Abbey by the Sea.'"

Mr. Addington was a tall man with brown hair like Isaac. Only, he wore his hair shorter and combed to one side. He unscrewed the top of his drink and took a sip. "Isaac was young when we heard it, but I bet he remembers the pipe organ."

"The one at Hammond Castle?" Isaac asked.

His dad nodded. "John Hammond christened the castle *Abbadia mare* because the great hall resembled a medieval church. Remember?"

Isaac shook his head.

"Who's Irene?" I asked.

"Hammond's wife." Mr. Addington pointed his soda at us. "The place is amazing. You two should take the tour."

Isaac and I exchanged glances. That's exactly what we planned on doing.

There was tons of information on the Internet about Hammond Castle. One site called Hammond's wife a recluse, stating she would often lock herself in her room when Hammond threw a party.

We sped down Western Avenue. Isaac and I had less than four hours to search the premise and get me home. I hoped Hammond Castle was really just a large house and not a sprawling fortress or the task ahead of us would be daunting.

I scrolled further down the article I'd been reading. "We have to get to the chain before Caden does."

"I know." Isaac reached over the stick shift and covered my hand with his. "Madison, I want to apologize about yesterday. I shouldn't have gone behind your back to try to get rid of Caden."

It meant a lot to me that he would admit that. I twisted in my seat so I could see him better. "No, you shouldn't have, but I think I understand why you did it."

Caden purposely pushed Isaac's buttons, and he didn't hide the fact that he was doing it.

"I hate the way he looks at you," Isaac confessed.

"He only does it to piss you off." I turned my hand over and laced my fingers through his. "Isaac, you can't let Caden know it bothers you, or he'll keep doing it."

He stopped at a red light. "That's why I want to send his ass back to hell."

"I know." There were times I wanted him to. "But what if the demon who takes over Caden's crossroad is hungry for power and seeks out souls? Or if my contract is with that crossroad's demon in general and not necessarily with Caden. Right now I'm doing small things." And I trusted Caden to keep it that way.

Isaac ran his free hand over his hair, messing it up more than it was. "I know. That's why I made the promise I did."

A few minutes later, we pulled up to Hammond Castle and parked in the guest parking lot. I gaped at the building in front of us. "It's huge."

"It's a castle."

Complete with towers and drawbridge—I didn't expect that.

An arctic wind nipped at my face and went straight through my jeans when we got out of the Jeep. Isaac raised his arm. With his palm facing the Jeep, he slowly moved his hand from left to right. As he did, the Jeep vanished, starting with the front bumper. It was as if the vehicle had been drawn on an Etch-a-Sketch and was being wiped from existence with the swipe of a lever.

"It's still there," Isaac said. "The spell will last until we touch it."

I nodded and stuffed my hands into my jacket pockets. The castle was enormous, with narrow windows housed in large archways along the curtain wall. Gargoyles stood guard over the grounds from various perches high and low. The only thing that was missing was an actual moat.

Our shoes padded softly over the lowered drawbridge. Vanilla and spearmint wafted through the air as Isaac used his powers to open the massive dark wood doors in front of us. We quickly ducked inside. With a wave of our hands, the doors swung shut. I closed my eyes, allowing my powers to fully surface, and then pushed them outward in the form of a dozen glowing orbs the size of grapefruits. They hovered around us, illuminating the entry hall.

"Where do we start?" I asked.

"The tour took us this way." Isaac gave a nod to the stone staircase.

We followed it upward and through a large archway that led to an elaborate office. I could just make out a hazy full moon through the tall narrow windows behind a centuries-old couch. Isaac opened a couple of drawers in the five-drawer hutch to our left, glanced inside, and closed them again.

I stood in the center of a red and gold area rug and turned in a slow circle. "It will take us an hour just to search this room."

"Maybe not." Isaac raised his hand, palm out. As his lips moved silently, a mix of vanilla and spearmint filled the room. The air in front of him shimmered as his spell took form. I'd seen Isaac use this spell once before to find his car keys. It was like watching a thin sheet of water travel over, under, and through everything in his room. When it had reached his keys, the transparent sheet turned into a hand and pulled his key ring from under a pile of clean clothes. This time, however, the spell circled the entire room and faded without finding its target.

"Nothing." His arm dropped to his side. "There are probably wards protecting it. My spell might not work even if it's hidden in here."

I thought about what Caden had said about my powers being stronger than I gave myself credit for. Caden had shown me what the chain looked like. That meant I knew what I wanted. Maybe I didn't have to be able to see it to summon it. I held my hand up. "Binding chain."

We waited a beat.

"Nice try," Isaac said when my hand remained empty. He recited the second half of the message Caden had shown me. Nothing mystical happened. "You try."

I did and had the same disappointing results.

We went room by room, repeating these steps. When we reached the great hall, Isaac let out a low whistle. "I'd forgotten how big this place was."

With a thought, I sent two orbs soaring beyond a glass case containing a suit of armor toward the pipe organ. The orbs then backtracked and hovered in front of a dark throne. As my gaze traveled upward, so did the orbs. Two stone balconies overlooked the great hall. We were in another impossibly big room with way too many places to hide a small piece of jewelry. We recited the spells we knew with no more luck than we'd had in the other rooms.

Isaac rubbed his temple in what I took as frustration. A muffled creak followed by an eerie squeal broke the silence and startled me. I closed my eyes in an effort to pinpoint the direction of the noise. The sound of metal knocking on glass had me doing a one-eighty so that I faced the armored suit. The soldier inside the display motioned with its finger for me to come closer.

I swallowed my fear and did as it asked, ready to throw up a magical shield if it broke free. I stopped a foot away. It beckoned me to come even closer. When my nose was a mere inch from the glass, it let out a ghostly *boo!*

I screamed. Isaac chuckled, and I realized he had animated the suit of armor.

"That is so not funny!" Although I laughed along with him.

"I'm sorry." He reined in his laughter. "But we've been at it for an hour and needed something to break up the monotony of the task."

He was lucky I hadn't wet my pants. Being in a deserted castle was creepy enough without the décor jumping out at me.

"Maybe we should ask it if it's seen the necklace," Isaac said.

I couldn't tell if he was serious or joking. When he didn't actually start a conversation with the suit of armor, I guessed it was the latter. "Let's check out the rest of the place."

We continued our search, going from incredible room to incredible room, repeating the same process. In one of the guest rooms, I got back at him for his prank by using my magic to open a hidden door I'd discovered. I cracked up laughing when he spun around ready for a fight. A few rooms later, we came to a locked wooden door. I used my magic to open it and stepped into a cavernous room fit for a queen. The air was stale, and a layer of dust covered everything from the window dressings to the hardwood floors.

I crossed the room and peered out the small window into a courtyard. "This has to be Irene's room."

Hope surged in me as my gaze met Isaac's. He gave a nod, indicating for me to say the spell.

"*Ostendo sum vestri specialis.*"

A faint scent of rose water saturated the otherwise musty air as the room became charged with power that danced over our skin. A high-pitched *tap-tap-tap* turned into a whisper of a melody. Isaac and I scanned the area around us. Our gazes settled on the baseboard to our left and the raspberry hue seeping through a narrow gap between the wall and the floor. We rushed closer.

Isaac ran his hand along the striped floral wallpaper. "Feels like there's a gap."

I felt it too. "Another hidden door?"

"I think so."

We pushed, expecting to release a hidden latch and the door to swing open, but it didn't. Isaac then passed his hand over the seam, pushing out his powers as he did a simple unlocking spell. Instead of the door opening, the glow faded.

"It's in there. I know it is." I held a hand in front of me. "Binding chain." Nothing happened. I drew in a slow, deep breath. Caden had been convinced my summoning spell had failed because I lacked faith in myself, and Isaac felt the spell only worked when it was something I really wanted.

Well, I really wanted to get that chain before Caden did. "Binding chain!"

My hand remained empty. I kicked the wall with the toe of my boot. The damn door still didn't open. "Maybe it takes a witch to find it and a demon to retrieve it."

"I don't think so. It wasn't forged by hell." Isaac continued to examine the wall. "Caden's been feeding you spells since you made that deal."

He'd said it as an afterthought like one might say, *You've always liked blue.*

"Yeah." I leaned against the wardrobe, feeling defeated. "So?"

"Where does he get the spells?" Isaac rested a hand on the wall and met my gaze.

I hadn't given that any thought. When Caden wanted something done, he wanted it now. He didn't want to hear excuses any more than he expected me to know every spell ever performed. He brought the tools needed to get the job done. Sometimes it was a spade to dig with, and other times it was a slip of paper with the magic words needed to make the impossible possible. Now that I was thinking about it, he obviously had more than a few tricks up his sleeves. "He gets them from a witch."

"And if Caden knows a witch, why involve you?" Isaac wet his lips. "Think about it. Caden would know that you'd tell your coven about the necklace. He has to know we'd figure out what it does. Why risk us interfering with his plan?"

I shrugged. "He doesn't consider us a threat. He likes to piss you off. He likes my company more than this other witch's. Take your pick."

A knowing look flittered across Isaac's face—the expression of a person who had done a little scheming of his own. For a moment I thought that under different circumstances Isaac and Caden would make a good team. "What if it's none of the above? What if he hasn't been dreaming up things for you to do?"

I fidgeted with my rings, trying to follow Isaac's train of thought. "You think an important piece of his master plan will require me to grow grass?"

"I think he's preparing you for what's to come." Isaac bounced his knuckles against his mouth as he thought. "Caden researched your family tree, right?" When I nodded, he went on. "I'll bet my Jeep he needs *your* help to find this piece of the chain. That would explain why he's waited until now to retrieve it."

"Blood of the witch who created the talisman?"

Isaac nodded.

If Caden could discover Kaylee was a descendant of necromancers, why couldn't he find out that I was the great-great-great-granddaughter of one of the witches responsible for making the binding chain? "I suppose I should be grateful that this isn't dark magic, or I'd have to be drained of all my blood or something equally as sinister to make the thing work."

Isaac turned away from me, but not before I saw the muscles in his jaw twitch.

"Oh my God." My knees almost gave out. "You think before this is over, I will have to be sacrificed?"

He rubbed the back of his head. I grabbed his arm and turned him to face me.

"Isaac?"

His troubled gaze met mine. "I was going to tell you." He closed his eyes a moment. "But then you told me about this piece of the chain. If we can find it…"

"Go on," I nudged when he went silent.

"Anastasia spoke to the spirits and was able to find a source that has seen a chain like this. The four pieces have to be linked by blood, but that's not the worst of it." His hands swept through his hair. "The spirit said that to bind someone with the chain, you have to bind another to the place of the first. It's vague, but Anastasia believes that in order to become master of one person, you have to offer someone else in his place."

I shook my head, confused. "What does that even mean?"

"It means that in order for Caden to bring Death here to our world, he has to offer up a soul to send to wherever Death now resides."

"Oh." I was sorry I asked.

I rubbed my arms to fight the chill that settled in my bones, more than uneasy over the power of this chain and why I had to be any part of Caden's search for it. I thought about the spells I'd done for him so far. There wasn't any devil's shoestring in the castle, at least none that I'd seen, and Isaac and I had searched more than half of the place. Caden didn't need me to remove that plant just so he could enter this building. He'd also been pushing me to learn the summoning spell, but I'd been trying that one on and off since Isaac and I had entered the castle. Either it didn't work on the chain or I still needed to be able to see what I was looking for.

I glanced around the room. My gaze reached a tarnished candelabrum on the dressing table. My thoughts went to Ms. Brontë. "Give me one of those candles."

As Isaac went to grab one, I dug in my purse, looking for something sharp. "Remember the ghost I told you about? The one Caden had me do the séance with?"

"The famous author." The corner of Isaac's mouth tugged upward into the sly smirk of a fox. "You're going to bring the late Mrs. Hammond's spirit here."

"'Under the full moon with Irene.' I do believe she needs to be present." My fingers curled around a thin strip of metal. "Yes! A nail file should work just fine." I tucked one side of my hair behind my ear. "Let's hope I remember the spell and that Irene is in a chatty mood, because according to Caden, ghosts don't have to cross the veil."

Isaac and I sat cross-legged on the floor.

"I'll need wormwood." My eyes narrowed. "Can you get that?"

A moment later, he held the dried plant in his hand. "Mom keeps some in the kitchen."

It took me a few minutes to engrave her name into the wax. Using magic would have been faster, but I had to think *Irene Hammond* with each letter I carved. Isaac rubbed his hand on his thighs, his eyes darting to the hidden door. We were close to our goal. We both could feel it.

I blew tiny wax shavings from the candle, made sure I hadn't missed a letter, and said, "Done."

We cast our circle, and with our hands linked, I called upon the spirit who once called this room her home. The air grew cooler.

A glimmer of light had us looking at the dressing table. The ghost of a woman dragged her slender fingers over the antique mirror and brush. I imagined if she had been solid and in color, her long dress would have been as black as a crow's feathers. She wore her hair in a bob and, even though she was a specter, her cheeks had a warm gray glow to them.

Isaac and I scrambled to our feet.

"Mrs. Hammond?" he asked.

She flickered in and out of view. One moment she'd been admiring her dust-covered possessions, and the next she was looking at us, brow furrowed.

Isaac cleared his throat. "Ah, Mrs. Hammond, we were hoping you could help us locate a length of chain. It's silver and about this long." He held his hands approximately five inches apart and then let them fall to his side. "It's part of a longer necklace."

"There's no chain like that here." She did the flicker thing again, this time reappearing next to the four-poster bed.

Isaac's incredulous expression mirrored mine. *She's lying,* it said, and I agreed. We had to get Mrs. Hammond to trust us. It stood to reason that if Caden had buried the other piece near Godspeed's grave, he'd been the one to hide this section as well.

Here's hoping I'm right. "Caden asked us to retrieve it for him. He told us it would be in a secret room located in your bedroom." I pointed to the wall where the door remained annoyingly closed.

"Caden?" she echoed as she floated to the window. "He and John were such friends." A whisper of a smile tugged at her lips. "You say he sent you?"

Isaac nudged me with his elbow, prodding me to keep going. "Yes. Um…he mentioned a spell, but it only reveals the chain's location. *Ostendo sum vestri specialis.*"

The dark pink hue illuminated the floor brighter than it had been before.

Irene stood — floated, really — motionless. Several heartbeats later, she said, "I was beginning to think my John had fibbed when he said Caden would one day return for it." She glanced around the room. "Why didn't he come himself?"

"He's been busy," Isaac said. "He asked that we give you his regards."

She blinked out of site and reappeared next to the door. Her lips moved soundlessly. A faint click occurred a moment before the door creaked open. "Touch only what is yours."

She inclined her head as she drifted backward, straight through the wall on the opposite side of the room.

The hidden door led to a walk-in closet. The glow came from the top-most drawer in a floor-to-ceiling cabinet. There had to be thirty or forty different compartments, each with a unique knob.

Isaac used his powers to slide the drawer out, then it sailed through the air and into my hands. I reached into it for a sheer white draw-string bag.

"Open it," Isaac said.

Eager for a closer look, I loosened the ties and let the chain fall into my hand. This piece was made of rose-colored gold, and it was surprisingly heavy for how small it was.

I bit my bottom lip. Now that I had a piece of the necklace in my hand, a tinge of guilt scratched at my conscience. Caden had trusted me with the information he'd shared; he'd be angry if he found out I had betrayed that trust.

Before I could dwell on that thought, Isaac wrapped his arms around my waist from behind and pulled me against his chest. "You did it."

"We did it." I held the chain up higher, admiring how the light of my orbs glistened off the shiny metal. "We make a good team."

Isaac's fingertips brushed my neck as he moved my hair to the side. His touch was warm. Comforting. It squashed my lingering guilt.

He kissed behind my ear. "You know, we have an entire castle to ourselves and an hour before you're due home."

I craned my neck to look at him over my shoulder. "What about Irene?"

"It's a big castle, and she has a lot to see before the spell wears off." Isaac spun me around and trailed a line of kisses along my jaw. "Let's make the most of being here."

His mouth found mine. With the chain gripped tight in my right hand and my powers tucked deep inside me, I rose to my tiptoes, loving the feel of his lips on mine. Vanilla and spearmint encompassed us a moment before his powers brushed mine. Isaac's hands slid down my sides, over my hips, and cupped my butt. A squeal bubbled up my throat as he lifted me off my feet.

"Isaac, maybe we shouldn't."

His smile grew wider. "Oh, I think we should."

I giggled and held on tighter as he carried me out of the hidden room and back into Irene's bedroom. The orbs that had followed us inside zoomed around us. With a jerk of my head, the door in the wall swung closed.

"Not the bed," I said when Isaac headed straight to it. "We'll disturb the dust, and I still have to come here with Caden."

Isaac came to a stop, and his powers withdrew from within me. "You had to say his name."

He relaxed his hold on me, allowing me to slide down the front of him until my feet touched the ground.

I took a step back, the mood killed by my slip of the tongue. "We talked about this. Caden has to think that he misunderstood the clue or that someone else found this—" I held up the chain "—before he did. I really don't care which he believes as long as he doesn't know we have it."

"That doesn't mean I want to hear his name when we're making out."

"Right."

Caden wasn't around and he'd still managed to mess up my evening with Isaac. The sudden withdrawal of Isaac's powers left me empty, but I didn't want to tell him. The feeling would pass.

Instead, I just dropped the chain back into the sheer bag and tucked it safely inside my purse. We left Irene's bedroom, scattering dust over the floor to cover our shoe prints before we locked the door behind us.

Chapter 11

Flirting with the Devil

Isaac and I arrived back at my house with ten minutes to spare.

He parked in the driveway and took my hand in his. "I've been practicing teleporting individuals long distances, and I no longer need to see the person or animal I'm calling to me."

It wasn't easy magic. It took a great deal of concentration and control to teleport the living even when they were right in front of you. Most people who possessed the powers didn't dare try it, because messing up a spell like that meant crippling someone for life. Isaac had once confessed that the only reason he'd attempted it was because of his added powers.

I had tried to zap a houseplant from the family room to the kitchen. The short trip turned a healthy fern into a wilted mess that looked as if it hadn't been watered in weeks.

"Who have you been practicing on?" I asked.

"Neighbor's cats. Don't look so worried; I didn't kill any of them."

"Glad to hear it."

He ran a finger under my hemp bracelet. "Promise you'll call if you need anything."

I trusted Isaac. I really did, but I wasn't so sure about being the first human he beckoned with magic. "I'll call you," I assured him, careful not to use the word *promise*.

"Remember not to think about our trip tonight."

Like I needed reminding of that. "I won't."

He leaned over the center console and kissed me. It was a slow, sweet kiss that left my heart racing and my knees weak. "Text me when you get home."

"Kiss me like that again, and I might just have to tell Caden to reschedule." Not that he'd let me.

Isaac's lips met mine again—a too-short, tender taste. "Be careful."

After one last kiss, I was out of the car and heading up the walk. I had a few minutes to hide the binding chain and splash cold water on my face before I had to pretend I didn't know where Caden and I were going or that our trip would be in vain.

Dad lounged in his favorite chair in the family room, watching late-night television.

I stopped in the doorway. "Hi."

He turned to face me. "You're home early." He looked at his bare wrist. "Curfew isn't for a few more minutes."

"Ha-ha."

He laughed. "Did you have a nice evening?"

"Yeah. Isaac and I went for a drive along the coast."

"It's a good night for that."

"It was. You staying up late?" I needed him to go to bed so that I'd be able to sneak back out.

"Nah." But he didn't get up.

Here's hoping that means you're going to sleep after this show. "I'm going to bed. See you in the morning."

He nodded, then I waved and went upstairs. After a quick stop in the bathroom, I walked into my bedroom to find Caden sitting at my desk, flipping through one of my yearbooks.

A glance over my shoulder let me know that Dad wasn't behind me. "What are you doing here?"

"We have an appointment."

I closed the door. "I know that, but Chase or my dad might have seen you."

"I stayed out of sight." He closed the yearbook. "You'll be happy to know they respect your privacy and don't come in your room when you're not home."

I already knew that. Had my dad or Chase been in the habit of coming into my room when I wasn't home, they would have seen the frozen bouquet of daisies and lilies given to me this past December by the Prince of Fae.

"I wish I could say the same thing about you," I quipped.

Caden ignored my comment and stood. He wore faded blue jeans with holes strategically placed over one thigh and his knee, a tight-fitting gunmetal gray T-shirt, and black boots. His dark hair fell over his eyes like always. To keep myself from thinking that he looked hot, I started to sing to myself. By the sly way the corner of his mouth quirked upward into a smirk, though, I knew I hadn't started singing soon enough.

"Leave your jacket on." Caden grabbed his from the back of the desk chair.

I paused, purse dangling from one hand and the other still gripping my zipper. "We can't leave until my dad goes to sleep."

"We aren't going out the front door. Take my hand."

When I didn't, he frowned, wrapped an arm around my waist, and pulled me against him. He didn't give me time to protest. The crimson void and smell of brimstone consumed my words before they reached my lips. A jarring moment later, we stood next to his car a block north of my house. Frigid air nipped at my cheeks. I closed my eyes, waiting for the stench of smoke and the shock of our landing to pass. When I felt steady, I slapped Caden's arm. "Warn me the next time you're going to do that!"

He let me go. "Why? Are you going to hold your breath or something?"

Maybe. "At least I'll be prepared." I zipped my jacket and put on gloves. I couldn't decide if I wanted to throw up or if I needed some water to wash the taste of the smoke out of my throat.

"There is a way to negate the after-effects of travel." His eyes flashed red.

I rubbed my arms in an effort to stay warm. "Let me guess, it requires us kissing."

He shrugged. "We might have to add *clairvoyant* to your list of gifts."

"And I guess *smart-ass* to yours."

We got in the car. To help me keep my thoughts off Isaac and our trip to Hammond Castle, I immediately struck up a conversation.

"So, what does it mean to be…what was it you called Kaylee?"

"A necromancer." He started the car and pulled away from the curb.

"Necromancer," I echoed, letting the word become embedded in my memory. "Shane said that was the same thing as a sorcerer. How's that different from a witch?"

"A witch can't yank a person's soul out of the afterlife, and a necromancer shouldn't be able to perform magic."

"I brought the ghost of your friend back." I forced myself not to think, *and Irene Hammond.*

"You lowered the veil and allowed me to talk to her spirit. Kaylee literally pulled Shane's soul from his final resting place and shoved it back into his body. I'm surprised she could do it without knowing what she was and without focusing on him."

"We'd been discussing how he died. In a way, she was focusing on him."

Caden's eyebrows rose, and he shrugged as if to say, *I suppose that would do.* "Who dug him up?"

"No one." I double-tapped the button to turn on my heated seat. "His casket just sort of rose." Now that I thought about it, Kaylee and I weren't going to be able to leave it sticking out of the ground much longer. We'd have to find a way to rebury it. "Kaylee's going to freak when I tell her that she can communicate with the dead." That Jeremy and the other ghosts being drawn to her hadn't been a one-time accident.

"It's a rare gift." Caden gave me a sideways glance. "Necromancers used to be held in high esteem. They were respected by kings and coveted by emperors."

"Why?"

"For one thing, ghost and ghouls feel a sense of loyalty to them. They'll protect a necromancer with their very existence, which made being in a room with one often the safest place to be when war raged."

"Undead bodyguards." Smart.

"It's hard to kill what's already dead." He took a right at the light and continued driving. "And imagine what one could learn about their enemies from the recently deceased."

"Souls were shoved back into their bodies to be questioned?" That seemed disrespectful, if you asked me.

"Only those who received orders from higher up. They were offered a second chance at life in exchange for information that would help defeat the enemy."

"You mean they became ghouls." When he nodded, I asked, "What if they refused? What would happen to them then?"

"That depended on the person whom the necromancer served. Some lost their heads. Others were buried alive."

"That's awful!"

"That's war. And don't look at me as if I did this personally. I may have known a king or two, but I was never a consultant. My job was and will always be a crossroad demon."

It wasn't until Caden blew through a red light that I realized we were the only ones on the road.

"What are you going to do with Shane?" he asked.

That was the million-dollar question. I fidgeted with my rings. "I don't know. We'll figure something out." We always did.

We were quiet after that. When my thoughts wandered back to why I was driving down a coastal road with Caden, I sang "Party in the USA" over and over in my head. It was the only thing keeping me from thinking about the binding chain still tucked inside my purse. Caden didn't take the direct route to our destination. Not that I should have known that, but it did make me wonder what he was doing.

After fifteen minutes of seemingly aimless cruising and me silently singing the same song over and over in my head, I said, "I thought we weren't going far."

"We aren't, but it's a nice night for a drive." He smiled. "Isn't that what you told your dad?"

"Yes." The sky was a midnight-blue palette dotted with stars and smudges of dark clouds. The moon sparkled off the water and small traces of snow that stubbornly clung to the frozen ground. It was a gorgeous night. "But we aren't on a date, and it's late. I need sleep."

His smile vanished. "You're loads of fun."

I wasn't there to be fun.

"What's with the song you keep singing?"

"It's stuck in my head." I shrugged and went back to singing.

"Or maybe you don't want me reading your thoughts."

I didn't see any harm in him knowing that much. It wasn't like I hadn't already told him I hated that he could invade my mind. I tapped my finger to my nose and then pointed to him.

Shortly thereafter, we were driving up the roadway leading to the massive castle. Caden parked in the same place that Isaac had. Only, when we got out of his car, he didn't head toward the drawbridge. I hesitated, dying to ask him where he was going, but I couldn't do that without letting on that I'd figured out the clue.

Instead, I whined. "Please tell me your trinket isn't hidden in the gardens."

He just kept walking.

"But it's freezing."

"Stay close to me, and you won't feel the cold." When I didn't join him on the cobblestone path, he added, "Or warm the air yourself. I don't care." He strolled along the path, leaving me gaping at his back.

My gaze bounced between Caden and the wooden front doors. Maybe there was more than one piece of the necklace here. I left my purse in the car and slammed the passenger door shut. I then breathed in deep, drawing in energy from the nearby trees and shrubs and pushed out a small amount of power. The air around me became bearable. Unfortunately, I wasn't in a bubble, and the little pocket of warmth I'd created didn't follow me like my orbs had earlier. To keep my teeth from chattering, I had to settle for catching up to Caden.

He lowered himself onto a cast iron bench that overlooked the grounds and patted the seat next to him. Reluctantly, I sat. To my surprise, the metal was warm, and I guessed that was his doing. We had a clear view of several yards of manicured lawn, a low half-wall made of stone, and a calm Atlantic Ocean.

He leaned forward, elbows on his thighs, and stared into the distance. "I bet you could draw a lot of power from this place."

"Nature fuels a witch's magic." I cast the spell to increase the temperature around us. "But you know that."

The ocean reflected the night sky, giving the impression that the full moon bobbed merrily in the water, but that wasn't what had my attention. "You haven't lit a cigarette."

"You don't like the smoke."

"That never stopped you before."

He didn't reply, and I didn't know what to make of his overly considerate behavior.

I pivoted in my seat. "So, is a piece of your necklace hidden outside?"

I'd almost thought the words to the spell he'd shared with me—the ones that had helped Isaac and me find the rose-colored chain. To stop myself from spilling my secret, I quickly rushed through the lyrics of "Party in the USA" again.

Caden ignored my questions. He took his cell phone from his pocket and flipped though the screens. "I used to come here when John Hammond was having the place built. He was a believer in the occult. Did you know that?"

I shook my head. "Did he make a deal with you to be able to afford this place?"

"Nah. The man had vision. Probably helped that he had great mentors. We'd met at a party, and when he found out I'd spent time in Germany, he invited me over. We became friends."

"Did he know what you are?"

"No."

I was beginning to realize that Caden must have always given off the persona of a fine, upstanding member of the community.

Scott Stapp sang out softly from his phone. Caden set it on the bench between us.

"I love this song."

"I know." When I looked at him questioningly, he said, "You think that every time it comes on the radio. I thought hearing it now would get you to stop singing the other one."

I scrunched my nose. "It was getting annoying."

"There's the smile that's been missing this evening." Caden bumped me with his shoulder.

The grounds at Hammond Castle were amazing, all twisting paths through meticulously kept gardens, magnificent statues, and welcoming patios. We were at the edge of that, staring into a horizon filled with opportunity.

I wanted to know if Caden had made deals with anyone famous. Had Emily Brontë been the only person he'd talked out of one? Why had he done it? Demons were supposed to be on hell's side, buying up souls by the dozens. Not befriending humans.

"Aren't you in a hurry to get your trinket?" I asked, needing to be away from Caden and his soft music.

"No."

"Why not?"

"Because I'm enjoying your company, as erratic as it is tonight."

"Caden…" I tucked my hair behind my ears. "You have to stop acting as if we have anything more than a business arrangement."

He placed a hand over his heart. "And here I thought we were friends."

We were, but because of our deal. Not like Josh and I, who'd been lifelong buddies.

A new song began. The singer enticed an unseen lover to stay the night.

The music seemed to get louder in the stillness of the garden. Being outside with Caden under the moonlit sky with such a passionate song serenading us was too much. I could see myself letting my guard down and simply enjoying his company.

I couldn't let that happen. He was hell's spawn.

The male vocals sang of tangled tongues and lips. It was all I could do not to look at Caden's mouth.

I snatched the phone off the bench, stood, and whipped it toward the ocean. It landed in the grass by the rocky wall.

Caden jumped up. "Hey! I just got that."

I pulled my hair away from my face and held it at the back of my head. *He's messing with your head. Just have him look for the damn necklace.*

He pointed in front of him. "Get my phone. I'm not asking."

I held out my palm. "Cell phone."

It vanished from near the wall and reappeared in my hand. I hit a button to wake the dark screen and stopped the music. "Can we get down to business?"

He took his phone back and examined it. "Go ahead. Summon the length of chain hidden here."

I rubbed my temple and sighed in exasperation. "Caden, I have to see what I'm aiming for."

"Or maybe you just need to know what it looks like," he challenged.

"Great." I'd play along. "Do you have a picture?"

"No." Apparently happy that his phone still worked, he slid it into his pocket. "But you were here earlier tonight and already found it, didn't you?"

"I wasn't —" The rest of my words caught in my throat. I grabbed my neck and drew in a ragged breath.

Caden crossed his arms over his chest. "Want to try that again?"

"I don't know —" I gagged and fell to my knees. My powers choked me, making it impossible to breathe.

Caden crouched down in front of me, his expression stern. "Shall I remind you that you *promised* not to lie in response to a direct question?"

Bastard.

It was part of our contract sealed not only with a kiss but with a promise too, so no matter how hard I focused, I couldn't force my powers to relent. I'd pass out soon if I didn't tell the truth. As soon as I admitted that to myself, I was able to gulp down a lungful of air.

I glared at him through strands of dark bangs. "How'd you know?"

"I was standing next to you in Kaylee's kitchen when you decided you didn't need me to retrieve it. I wanted to see if I could trust you. Now I know I can't."

"I'm trying to protect people."

"So am I."

I ignored the hand he offered and got up without his help.

"I'll take my trinket, as you like to call it."

"It's in the car." I turned to go there, but Caden grabbed my wrist.

"Use your magic to get it."

"But I can't see it."

"Try."

I looked at his hand, but he didn't release me. Sighing again, I said, "Chain." I then held my free hand up to show him it was empty. "I have to be able to *see* what I'm summoning."

"You need practice." He kept his hold on me. "I have all night."

"You're serious, aren't you?"

"Dead."

"Why do you need it?" I searched his eyes for either a hint of malevolence to signal his evil plan wasn't going well or an inkling of arrogance to gloat that his diabolical endeavor was right on schedule. What I saw was a mix of exhaustion and frustration. "You have the fires of hell at your disposal, why do you need Death too?"

I hadn't meant to let him know I had figured out whom he planned to bind, but it was too late to take my words back.

"I never said I wanted anything to do with the horseman."

"But you said you wanted to tame Death."

"The angel, Sammael. Not the horseman. You'd have to be crazy to attempt that. My turn to ask a question. Why do you work so hard to hate me? I've done nothing to deserve that."

I was about to say that it didn't take work, but my powers pinched the inside of my stomach as a warning not to lie again. "Fine. You want the truth, it's because you're a demon, Caden — one of hell's children. You hurt people."

He wet his lips as he seemed to consider this a moment. "Fair enough. Try the spell again."

I shifted my weight to my left to put a small amount of distance between us and did the spell. It still failed.

"Do you like spending time with me?"

My gaze snapped to his. "What?"

"It's a direct question." I went to turn away from him, but he grabbed my other arm to keep me from moving. "Answer it."

A montage of replies streamed through my thoughts. *No!* My powers clawed at my stomach. *Yes.* Stopped the torture. *As business associates.* My lungs tightened. *Okay, friends.* The burning subsided. *But that's it.* A pang shot through my side. *Damn it!*

"You're not the worst being I've met." *There,* I thought smugly. *A truth we can both live with.*

He had to have heard my internal argument too, but he didn't comment on it. Instead, he released my right hand. "Try the spell."

It failed, again. "Why is it so important to you that I like you?"

"Because you're not the worst company I've kept." He studied me a moment. "Earlier today, did you enjoy our kiss?"

I would have barked out a solid *NO*, but my powers squeezed my stomach with enough force to make me wince. Instead, I yanked my arm free from Caden's grasp. "Binding chain!"

The sheer white bag appeared in my hand.

Caden took the bag from me and checked its contents. "Are you afraid to answer the question because I won't like the answer or because you won't like it?"

"Go to hell."

"If you still want to go inside, we could start a fire. Warm up."

I hugged myself and shook my head.

"Because I'm a demon or because you're with Witch Boy?"

I bit my lip. "Both."

"Are you ready to hear what I think?"

I'd forgotten he had asked me that once before. Whatever he thought, it wasn't going to be good. Sure, he'd come across as charming. Maybe being charismatic and likable was all part of his repertoire to get humans to trust him and make the deals that cost them their souls.

"I don't need to hear your theories, Caden. Take me home." I stormed off.

All I had to do was touch my hemp bracelet and think Isaac's name, and he'd teleport me to his house. The risk of being the first human he teleported a long distance seemed small in comparison to being alone with Caden under a pensive night sky.

"You'd really chance being maimed to get away from me?" Caden said from right behind me.

I whipped around and glared at his wary face. "Stay out of my head!"

"Stop acting like a spoiled child who isn't getting her way, and maybe I will!"

"I am not acting like a child."

"In all the time I've been in charge of the crossroad, I've never met anyone as infuriating as you." He yanked the collar of his jacket around his neck as if the night's chill bothered him and walked past me. "I should let you dig your own grave."

"Isaac wouldn't have told me he could do the spell unless he was sure," I shot back.

"You assume everything is about Isaac." Caden disappeared around the corner of the castle.

It took me a few minutes to get my feet to move. Tonight was supposed to be my victory. Instead, Caden had dragged things out of me that I hadn't wanted to admit to myself or to him. I expected him to be gone when I reached the parking lot. He wasn't. His car was running, though. A stream of thick white exhaust blew into the night like the breath of an angry dragon.

Caden's focus remained on his dashboard when I got in. I'd barely gotten my seatbelt on when he shifted into drive. He didn't stop at red lights, let alone say another word to me. "Party in the USA" played in a constant loop in my head to keep my thoughts from running wild. The fact that I'd gotten in Caden's car instead of calling Isaac meant that I trusted a demon to get me home safely over my boyfriend.

I had cursed myself seven ways to Sunday when I couldn't get myself to call Isaac. It wasn't that I didn't think he believed he could do the spell, and half the power of any spell came from a witch's confidence that he or she could perform it. But what if Isaac was wrong? What if there was a difference between a cat's structural makeup and a human's that he didn't take into account? What if I arrived with my nose on my chin or missing an arm? I liked my body parts right where they were.

Caden parked down the block from my house. He surprised me by getting out of the car when I did.

"You're not walking home alone at this time of night."

I hitched my purse higher on my shoulder. "I can protect myself."

"Not from everything."

"Fine." It was only a block, but if he wanted to walk with me, I'd let him.

The headlights on his car flashed when he locked the doors. He joined me on the sidewalk, only instead of strolling next to me, he wrapped an arm around my back and pulled me against him. His fingers tangled in my hair as his mouth crushed mine. I tried to push him away, but he just held me tighter, forcing my lips apart with his tongue.

His lips were warm and his kiss hungry. The cold vanished, and in its place came cinnamon-scented air. Still, he held me close, his lips moving over mine until I was breathless. Then the hand on the back of my head slid to my neck as the fire in his kiss waned. I pushed him away from me.

"You had no right," I said with less fury than I'd wanted. I barely registered my lavender bedspread.

"You want so badly to hate me. Now you have a reason to."

He dematerialized, leaving me trying incredibly hard to despise his very existence.

Chapter 12

'Fessing Up

"A ghoul?" Kaylee eyed Shane suspiciously like it was his fault he was sitting on the foot of her bed and not buried six feet under. "And I raised him because I'm the long-lost relative of a necromancer?"

"I wouldn't call you long-lost." I leaned against her dresser as she tried to accept what she was.

She paced from the closet to the closed door and back. "I'm not chopping off his head!"

"Neither am I." I'd had a frustrating sleepless night trying to come to grips with the idea that Shane was here to stay.

She continued to pace. The cranberry-scented candle next to me lit and extinguished with each pass she made across the room. She didn't seem to notice she was doing it. "Well, he can't live in Chris's room forever!"

"I know."

Shane remained silent, his gaze volleying between Kaylee and me as he listened to our exchange.

"We have to tell Josh and Isaac," I said for the third time. Seeing as neither of us was willing to run a blade clean through Shane's neck and we didn't know what to do with him, we had no other option.

"No." She chewed on the nail of her thumb. "There has to be another way."

The flame of the candle flared skyward. I pushed my power out and blocked its path to the ceiling. "Kaylee, we need their help."

It took a while to convince her, but she finally agreed to tell the guys about Shane. I sent them a text, asking them to meet us at Isaac's house.

Kaylee took forever to get ready. I knew she was stalling. I'd seen her dress and do her makeup in less than ten minutes when she wanted to. Of course, normally she didn't keep secrets from Josh—at least nothing big like this. Plus, she'd lied to him about the flowers. We agreed not to mention that when we saw him.

Shane was excited to be getting out of the house. He referred to our excursion as a field trip. I supposed if I'd spent as much time as he had in someone else's bedroom, I'd consider going over to Isaac's a field trip too.

We piled in Kaylee's MINI Cooper. She drove the speed limit, stopped for gas, grabbed lattes from the drive-through at the coffee house, and ran into the grocery store for a box of donuts.

"I'll drive." I snatched her keys from her hands and got in the driver's side of her car before she could argue. There was still a car wash and drug store between us and Isaac's house, and I was sure she'd find an excuse to stop at both if she remained in charge. "Josh will understand." It might take him a moment—or three—to get past being mad that she'd lied to him, but he'd help us.

She bounced her head against the back of her seat. "I promised him I'd be careful if I practiced magic without him."

"And you are." I backed out of the parking space. "Trust me; the powers would stop you if you weren't."

Shane scooted forward so that his body was wedged between the front seats. "I don't see what the big deal is. I haven't hurt anyone, and I'm not a zombie."

I glanced at Kaylee. "He's right."

She groaned. "You can smile because you're not the one that messed up."

The way she was behaving, you'd think our boyfriends were tyrants.

"I'm sure Josh has made mistakes. And we know Isaac has." I eased the car to a stop in the turn lane leading to Isaac's subdivision. "And let's not forget about the vindictive faerie I brought into our lives. Did Isaac or Josh ridicule me?"

She shook her head.

"No. They rolled up their witchy sleeves"—figuratively speaking—"and helped me get rid of him. They aren't going to do any less for you."

"We are trying to find a way for me to stay, right?" Shane asked.

I met his gaze in the rearview mirror. "That's why we need the guys. If there's a way to make it so that you can go home, they'll know it."

Traffic cleared, and I drove.

Josh answered the door. His black hair was ruffled, giving the impression he'd been tugging at it. He pulled Kaylee into an embrace, almost spilling her mocha in the process. "You okay?"

"Yeah." Her eyes met mine even as her head rested against Josh's chest.

Shane and I glanced away. It felt wrong to watch their private moment.

That's about the time Josh noticed Shane. His eyes narrowed. "I know you."

"Yep. He's why we're here." I didn't wait for Josh to reply. Instead, I grabbed Shane's hand and breezed by Josh and Kaylee with Shane in tow. We descended the stone steps to Isaac's room. He was sitting on his bed, a book and a sheet of loose-leaf paper on his lap.

I let go of Shane and went to sit next to Isaac. "Isaac, this is Shane. Shane, Isaac. He moved to Gloucester last fall." A few months after Shane's funeral.

Shane nodded his hello and then held up the bag with our spoils from the store. "Want a donut?"

"I'm good." Isaac looked at me, his forehead creased in obvious confusion.

"Josh and Kaylee should be down any minute." I wondered if Josh had figured out how he knew Shane yet.

Shane leaned against the dresser, munching on a glazed donut while Isaac eyed him but didn't ask the questions I knew had to be on the tip of his tongue. I was sure he was waiting for Josh and Kaylee to come downstairs. I took that time to fill Isaac in on the important details of Caden's and my trip to Hammond Castle, leaving out Caden's interrogation about my feelings toward him and that he had kissed me. There were some things you just didn't tell your boyfriend.

116

Josh and Kaylee joined us in time to hear me say that Caden had the second piece of the binding chain.

"Caden's still not saying why he wants to bind Death?" Isaac asked.

"He's not after the horseman." I told Isaac about Sammael, the Angel of Death. "To be honest, I'm not sure that's much better."

I crossed my legs like a pretzel and looked at the book Isaac held. It was his calculus text, and the sheet of paper was covered with numbers and symbols. I made a mental note to do my homework when I got home.

"You're that dead kid." Josh's eyes were wide. "The one who died last year."

That got Isaac's attention. I felt the teensiest bit of guilt for welcoming the change in subject. Kaylee, on the other hand, looked as if she wished we'd continue discussing our demon issues.

Shane peered at Josh from beneath the brim of his baseball hat. "We had Foods together."

"Yeah. You were sick." Josh lowered himself into the sphere chair. "Leukemia?"

Shane nodded. "It's good to see you."

Stunned silence filled the room. Kaylee and Shane leaned against Isaac's dresser, looking like two cats caught with mice in their mouths.

Josh rubbed his face and then studied Kaylee. "You're not pregnant?"

"What?" Kaylee's hand went to her stomach, which I thought was a very pregnant thing to do.

Isaac bent close and whispered. "Is she?"

"No! Why would you think that?" But I knew the answer as soon as the words were out of my mouth. I'd kept saying Kaylee had female issues. And then there were the very out-of-character flowers Josh thought I'd given Kaylee, along with her weird behavior. "That's why you asked if she was in trouble?" Had Kaylee and I not been playing house with a ghoul, I probably would have caught his word choice before now.

"What else were we supposed to think?" Isaac asked.

"I don't know. She had cramps?"

"I would have wanted you to keep it," Josh said, halting any further conversation between Isaac and me. "I would have found a way for us to still be able to go to college and travel like we planned. We would have done it as a threesome."

"We would have?" Kaylee muttered.

"It's all he's talked about," Isaac said.

Kaylee crossed the room. Josh scooted back, making room for her to sit on his lap. "You really thought I was pregnant, and you would have been okay with it."

He gave her a squeeze. "You're my girl. I would have been whatever you needed me to be."

"He was totally freaking out," Isaac whispered so that only I could hear.

I smiled. I'd bet my savings — the entire one thousand, fifty-two dollars I'd saved for a car — that Josh and Kaylee would end up married with three kids before the age of forty. I'd go double or nothing that they'd make great parents. But marriage and children weren't something they talked about. Kaylee, Sarah, and I had discussed it once, during our yearly sleepover. We agreed that we were going to live life to the fullest in our teens and early twenties. Then we'd worry about settling down.

"If a witch and a necromancer have kids, which gene overrides the other?" All eyes turned to Shane. He shrugged. "Brown eyes trump blue, at least that's what my dad says. He has light blue eyes. Mom has brown." Shane's were brown. "Maybe the kid would be both. I bet Caden would know if the bloodlines have ever been mixed."

Isaac set his calculus book on the bed behind him. "What's he talking about?"

Once Kaylee and I picked our jaws up off our laps, we took turns filling him and Josh in on Shane's miraculous resurrection. Shane played with the Rubik's Cube he found on Isaac's dresser as he waited patiently for us to get to the part about helping him.

Isaac had gone rigid next to me. "You went to Caden before me?"

"Of course not!" I rubbed my palms on my thighs and looked at Kaylee. If I'd had my way, Isaac would have known about Shane when we'd still thought he was a zombie. "I was at Kaylee's yesterday morning. Caden saw Shane when he stopped by."

"Don't be mad at Madison," Kaylee quickly interjected. "I made her promise not to say anything."

A wave of relief that Kaylee had said it flooded me. I didn't want Isaac to be mad at me, but I also hadn't wanted to point fingers and say this was all Kaylee's fault. "We were going to reverse the spell."

"But we couldn't figure out how," Kaylee said at the same time Shane blurted, "Thank goodness they didn't know what they were doing."

Josh looked at Kaylee. "Back up. Shane's staying at your house?"

"He's been hiding in Chris's room," she confessed.

"Sleeping, eating, building models, staring at the walls bored out of my mind," Shane added.

"He's why you've been acting so crazy when I'm at your house." Josh inhaled deeply, the vein near his left temple pulsating. "I knew something like this would happen. I knew it was too soon for you to be practicing magic on your own."

Kaylee jumped up and came to sit by me, arms folded over her chest. She shot me an I-knew-this-would-happen look.

"This is why she didn't want to tell you," I said. "She wasn't *practicing*. She came with me to the cemetery to visit my mom. And like we've all done, she was talking about the spells she'd learned. She didn't know she had necromancer blood running through her veins. None of us did."

Josh rubbed his eyes. I knew the feeling—shock, speechlessness, amazement that ghouls existed. He opened and closed his mouth a couple of times before finally saying, "You shouldn't have kept it a secret."

Shane set the Rubik's Cube down. "Can we fast-forward to the part of this meeting where we get me back home?"

Josh pinned Shane with a disbelieving glare. "You've been dead… what, a year now?"

"Eleven months," Shane replied.

"You should be…" Isaac paused as if lost for words.

"Gross-looking," I offered, glad to see his shoulders had relaxed and that he no longer looked upset with me. "And smelly."

"Yeah." Isaac held out a hand, which I took. The gentle squeeze was all the apology I needed for him assuming I'd ask Caden for help before him. Isaac looked at Josh. "That's one heck of a spell. Where'd you get it?"

"My mom casts it all the time to make the house plants and the flowers outside healthy again. It's not supposed to work on anything with a heart. Believe me, when Leo my pet gecko died, I tried it and half a dozen other spells. Nothing brought him back."

Isaac's gaze fell on Shane. "That's the thing. He's not human. Kaylee didn't bring him back, she made him something else. Something unnatural. She broke the natural order of things."

"But he's not dangerous, and he's here," I said.

"And I won't become dangerous!" A red flush crept up Shane's neck as black spider veins spread away from his eyes like lightning. For the second time since his return, he looked unstable. His next words came out in a menacing growl. "You said they'd help!"

The aroma of hot apple cider filled the air a split second before a greenish-black fog appeared at Shane's feet. Quick as water over the side of a mountain, the dark mist consumed him. He became immobile, face frozen in anger, and fingers curled into fists at his side.

"What did you do to him?" I asked.

"He's petrified." Josh held his hand out toward the pissed-off ghoul not ten feet from us. "But it's only temporary. That doesn't worry you?"

Even in his rage, I didn't think Shane would hurt us. And that wasn't because we were witches. "He's just as confused and scared about being here as we are."

"We have to help him," Kaylee said, her eye riveted to the fog in front of us.

Josh pressed the balls of his hands to his eyes. "We need time to discuss this, and he needs time to calm down."

I wondered if it was possible for Shane to calm down while he was frozen like that.

When Kaylee gave Josh a wide-eyed what-the-heck glare, Josh said, "If he wakes with his head still attached, I think he'll figure out we didn't kill him."

I got the distinct feeling there was a silent *yet* at the end of that sentence.

"He won't age," Isaac said. "Even if there was a way to erase the memory of his death from every single person who knew him, they'll notice that he isn't getting older." Isaac looked at me. "Fifteen forever is not a way to go through eternity."

"Not to mention there's no telling if he'll change for the worse over time." Josh closed his eyes and shook his head. "Isaac and I aren't just your boyfriends. We're part of your coven. You should have told us what happened the day Shane showed up on your doorstep."

"We should have," I agreed. "But if we had, wouldn't we still be in this predicament? Wouldn't we still try to help him?"

"Maybe." Josh stood.

"Caden said—" Kaylee began.

"You told us what Caden said." Josh paced. "But did he happen to mention why necromancers and witches don't make it a habit of turning the deceased into members of the living dead?"

Kaylee shook her head.

"Immortality comes with a price, Kaylee." There was forced calm in his words. The battle over doing what he thought was right and wanting to do what Kaylee was asking was clear in his eyes.

"Josh's right," Isaac said quietly. "The civilized thing to do would be to return him to his grave."

"Kill him?" I said. "How is that humane?"

"You can't kill what's already dead," Josh said.

Kaylee shook her head and pointed to herself and me. "We've spent time with him. He wants to go finish school, to hang out with his friends, to have a future. He's no different than us."

"Except for the not-human part." Isaac pinched the bridge of his nose. "If you'd have told us—"

"We've been through that," I said. "How do we help him now?"

Isaac scooted off the bed and knelt in front of a stack of books on the floor near the closet. "We find a more permanent spell and rebury him."

Josh picked Kaylee's and my purses up off the floor where we had dropped them. "Let Isaac and me take care of it."

Kaylee whipped a pillow at his head. "Joshua Corey, we are not letting you bury him alive!"

If Shane were a monster, I'd back the guys, but he wasn't. Ghoul or not, Shane had feelings. "If you aren't going to help us—"

Isaac's velvet brown gaze met mine. "This is that important to you?"

"Yes."

He wet his lips as he scrubbed his hands over his face. A long moment later, he said, "I guess we could keep an eye on him if he were close by."

"We will," I promised.

Isaac turned his attention to Josh, who had gone back to pressing his fingers to his eyes. "Josh?"

Josh dragged his hands to his temples, making his eyes slits. "Fine."

Kaylee smiled. "He'll be like an adopted brother, part of the family." She paused. "Only living at his house."

Isaac grabbed a book from the pile and handed it to Josh. He then held his hand up, his palm facing Shane, and moved it from right to left. The green-black fog evaporated.

"And don't think I'm going to let you chop off my head!" Shane exclaimed as if no time had passed.

"Wouldn't think of it." Isaac tossed him a book. "Start reading. Look for anything that we can use to explain away your death and absence for the past eleven months."

Chapter 13

Brother Issues

As soon as Shane realized Isaac and Josh were his allies, the black veins in his face faded. We spent a good part of Sunday searching for a spell that would allow him to go home.

Every hour devoted to helping Shane was an hour we could have been looking for information on the binding chain. Isaac brought up a very good point about that: Caden might already have all four pieces of the necklace. As Caden liked to put it, I was on a need-to-know basis, and I was sure he felt I didn't need to know his every move.

Well, he didn't need to know mine either, and I planned on putting an end to his plan to control Sammael.

At one point, my friends and I had taken a break from Project Ghoul and attempted to summon the chain. One by one, Isaac, Josh, Kaylee, and I gave it a try.

"Knowing Caden, he probably has the thing stashed in hell under a block of brimstone," I remarked when we failed. Caden was smart. No way would he leave it in a place where magic could reach it.

After that, we remained diligent in our efforts to help Shane. We kept revisiting the idea of casting the bewilderment spell. It wouldn't be too difficult to use it on Shane's parents and his siblings. We could make them believe Shane had never left. And if our coven—four strong—took the divide-and-conquer approach, we would be able to cast the spell on the administrative staff at the high school. That still left the problem of how we'd alter the memories of Shane's friends and their parents and the friends of their friends, the doctors, the store owners that knew him by name, and so on. The sheer number of people who were aware Shane had died was the reason Kaylee and I hadn't cast the spell a week ago.

We discussed alternative living arrangements, but we couldn't expect a fifteen-year-old to move to another state and start a new life on his own. Josh thought of Kevin, our friend who had moved to Minnesota last summer. If we could come up with a story on why Shane was alone and needed a place to stay, we were sure Mr. and Mrs. Hobbs would open their home to him. Kevin knew about the powers, so we could tell him the truth. He'd keep an eye on Shane and help him adjust. Problem with that plan was that Shane hated it. I'd love to have called him a baby, but I knew I would have felt the same way as he did if I were in his shoes.

"There's something we're missing," I finally said. "We need a break. To get out of the house."

Kaylee flopped across the bed. "And food that doesn't come in a bag marked 'no saturated fats.'"

Shane perked up visibly at the mention of something to eat. "Can we go to The Grill?"

He received four simultaneous noes to that question.

Josh dropped the book he'd been skimming on top of the pile near the closet. "I know a great little diner in Ipswich. There's less of a chance we'll run into someone you know."

I got home as Dad and Chase were cleaning up after their din-ner—fish sticks and French fries, one of Chase's favorite meals. Dad's too, because it was easy. Plus Dad felt anything that could be dipped in ketchup was man food and therefore gourmet.

"Hey, sport." I ruffled Chase's hair. "Hi, Dad."

Dad put the ketchup in the fridge. "Where've you been all day?"

"With Kaylee and the guys." I opened the garbage for Chase to drop in their plates. "How was your day?"

"We went bowling," Chase announced.

"Sounds like fun. How'd you do?" I plucked a grape from the bowl on the counter and popped it into my mouth.

He puffed out his bird-chest. "I got a two-ten."

"You did!" I said it enthusiastically but guessed he was exaggerating—unless they played on the lane with bumpers, but usually Chase refused to bowl on what he called the kiddie lanes.

Dad bent closer and whispered, "The machine was acting up, giving him more pins than it should have. Don't tell your brother."

I suspected that the machine worked just fine and it was Chase's powers bubbling over that gave him his record score. It could have been worse. Chase could have used his powers to knock the pins over. Still, I had to do something before Chase realized what he was doing.

Dad's phone rang. He checked the display. "It's a potential client. Can you finish here?"

"Sure." It wasn't like there was much to clean up. Plus, it would give me a chance to talk to Chase.

Dad slid his phone open as he walked out of the room.

I decided to take Mr. and Mrs. Addington's approach on the matter and crouched in front of Chase. "I need to tell you a secret, but you have to promise not to tell anyone. Can you do that?"

His hazel gaze stared back at me. "Not even Dad?"

"This has to be our secret, for now." I glanced at the hallway. Chase and I were still alone. "You have to say, 'I promise to keep this a secret.'"

Chase loved it when he and I knew something no one else did. All our secrets were harmless things that made him feel special. Like staying up past his bedtime or hiding the picture frame he'd accidentally broken so Dad wouldn't find out he'd played ball in the house.

He huddled closer. "I promise to keep it a secret."

I lowered my voice. "You know that show you like so much. The one with Merlin?"

"And Arthur?"

I nodded. "Well, you and I are like Merlin. We're wizards." I used the word he was most familiar with and tried to keep my explanation of the powers as simple as possible.

His eyes grew wide. "I knew it!"

I lowered my voice even more to show I'd just shared a humongous secret with him. "I shouldn't be telling you this, but you're my brother, and I know I can trust you. But we can't let anyone find out, or we could be in danger."

"Like mutants?"

His reference was to the X-Men. "Something like that." I furrowed my brow. "No practicing magic when I'm not around and absolutely no magic in front of other people. Promise?"

"Promise!" He drew a cross over his chest.

I definitely liked that word when it came out of Chase's mouth.

"Great." I stood and stuck the cookie sheet in the dishwasher. "You go wash your hands. I'll be upstairs doing homework." I scrunched my nose and stuck my tongue out.

Chase giggled.

"You're lucky you're in first grade. All the fun of learning, one-tenth the homework."

I studied for the history test I had the next day and was more than halfway through the chapter Mr. Chapin had assigned in English when my eyelids grew heavy.

I dreamed of Reed. I'd had the dream before—the one at the Winter Solstice Celebration. His snow-white eyes drank in every inch of me, from the winter-white flowers that adorned my hair to the white satin pumps poking out from beneath the pure white dress I wore. He was dressed in a white tux, his pallid hair shimmering under the twinkle lights strung between the trees. Mesmerized by his beauty, I couldn't take my eyes off him. The sweet smell of *bacca vinus* laced his breath. Then the dream turned into a nightmare. The enchanted forest melted to gray. Reed vanished. I was alone in a gown fit for a princess, craving the wine I could smell but couldn't see.

I woke with a start to the sound of my phone vibrating across my nightstand and my left hand wrapped around my wrist and the hemp bracelet I never took off. I had four missed text messages: two from Kaylee, one from Isaac, and one from Josh.

What dance? And then *Madison, are you dreaming?* from Kaylee.

Reply in three minutes or I'm driving over, from Isaac.

And finally, *No more rum cake for you,* from Josh.

As if the rum cake we'd split for desert had enough alcohol in it to get us drunk.

This was the first time I had invoked our link when I slept. They had to think I'd lost it. I touched my hemp bracelet and thought, *Sorry, bad dream.* To be sure my message made it to them, I sent a group text too.

I fell back against my pillow and stared at the ceiling, hating my eyelids each time they drooped over my eyeballs. There had to be a way to get a dream-free night of sleep.

"There is. All you need to do is ask," a tired voice said from the darkness.

My heart nearly jumped out of my chest. With a flick of my gaze to the lamp on my nightstand, I turned on the light. Caden stood near the window with his shoulder against the wall.

"Admit it, you're afraid to fall back to sleep."

"Am not!" I was, and since he could read my mind, he knew I was lying. "Jeesh, Caden! You need to stop showing up uninvited."

"I'd love to, but your signal went supersonic again."

"Try ignoring it next time." I scooped my bangs out of my eyes. "I don't need your help."

"You don't *want* it. There's a difference." He shoved off the wall. "Get dressed."

I glanced at the time on my phone. "It's three in the morning."

"And you can't sleep. I need to run an errand. I was halfway there, actually." He paused. "Come with me."

I rubbed sleep from my eye. "Caden, it's the middle of the night."

"What if I told you the destination is in London?"

"England?"

He nodded.

"The answer would be hell no."

"Even if we'd be picking up another piece of the binding chain?"

Okay, that piqued my interest. I pursed my lips. He was right; I didn't want to fall back to sleep. Not if it meant I'd be dreaming about Reed and his stupid faerie wine. Plus, I'd never been to London. And I did wonder what the next links in the necklace looked like. Who knew, maybe Caden would say or do something that would tell me if this was the last piece.

In Caden style, he answered my unspoken questions. "It's not, and if you come with me, it's on your promise of no games. I'm not in the mood."

"I really hate that you can pick thoughts out of my head."

I flipped the covers off, padded barefoot over the carpet to my closet, and grabbed the first thing I could find: a pair of skinny jeans and a hooded brown sweater. Caden grabbed my pillow and sank down onto my bed.

"Caden, it's bad enough you can read my mind. You are not watching me change."

One dark brow rose. "You don't have anything I haven't seen before."

He was a centuries-old demon, so that was most likely true. "But you haven't seen *my* parts."

"Whatever." He turned his back to me. By the way his shoulders shook, I knew he was laughing at me.

I dressed quickly and then stuffed my feet into my black combat boots. "Okay."

Caden faced me. "No games."

"No games, I promise." I pulled my hair out from under my sweater. "Shall we go?"

"You'll need a jacket."

With a thought, I had mine floating up the stairs and into my room. I put it on.

I didn't bother to ask if we were driving, nor did I object when he put his arms around my waist and pulled me closer.

Caden stood straighter. "London's much further than I've taken you before. I can make the journey…agree with you. I'll leave the choice up to you."

It took me a second to realize what he was referring to. I bent my knees. "I can handle the trip without kissing you." And now that I was fully awake and thought about it, "Besides, I'm still mad at you from before."

"I can see that." He had to lean back and tilt his head to the side to see me properly.

Later, when Caden couldn't read my thoughts, I would admit this to myself—I had a funny way of showing my anger. It was the dream's fault. It messed with my head. Made me want to skip sleep altogether. Not to mention, it was hard to be pissed when I was afraid to be alone.

Caden sighed. "Don't say I didn't offer."

I closed my eyes and nodded.

The heat and smoke hit at once and seemed to squeeze me from all sides. I could feel Caden's breath in my hair. When I inhaled and no air filled my lungs, I forced myself to remain calm. I'd be fine. The blackness continued on. Caden's grip tightened around my waist. My head grew light.

I'm fine.

Caden wouldn't let me die.

I wanted to ask if we were there yet, but couldn't.

Then my feet hit solid ground, and I gasped for air.

Caden kept his hold on me, keeping me upright. "Breathe through your mouth."

"I'm—" I sucked in a mouthful of damp, chilly air and coughed out smoke. "Trying."

I heard Caden say, "Screw this." I would have asked what, but I was too busy trying not to pass out. Then Caden's mouth was on mine. His hand held my head still, and I didn't have the strength to fight him. The stench of brimstone turned to the scent of crisp air, and the smoke in my lungs evaporated. My nails dug into his coat as I breathed in through my nose and savored the relief of my first clean inhalation of London's winter morning. The strength came back to my knees next. Traveling halfway around the world was much worse than a trip to the local crossroads. This time when I went to break our kiss, Caden let me.

His hands rested loosely on my hips. "Can you stand?"

I nodded. He released me.

"Why wasn't there any air?" I drew in another long, deep breath.

"We were in the void—between the veils, if you will."

"Right. Of course we were." I tucked my hair behind my ears. I'd never been able to hold my breath long. When I was five years old, I'd failed swim class because I couldn't breathe right. But since then, small lung capacity had never been a problem, until now.

I glanced up the two-lane road. The sun made its climb through the cloudy sky. I tried to remember if London was five or six hours ahead of Eastern Standard Time. That would make it eight or nine in the morning. We stood on the porch of a tan and white row house. Identical homes stretched up and down the length of the block in this neatly manicured neighborhood.

"Where are we, exactly?"

"Chelsea, London." Caden walked up to the door and knocked.

I waited next to him. It felt weird, like friends visiting a relative. To break the uncomfortable silence, I said, "What, you only barge into my bedroom uninvited?"

He gave me a sidelong glance. "If you want your privacy, then ask me to rid your system of the faerie food you ate."

"I've been doing fine. Besides, it was just a dream." That had me waking my friends. "Another month"—or six—"and all of Reed's magic will be out of my system."

"You know that's not true."

I refused to believe it wasn't.

The door swung open. A slender black woman in her sixties answered. She had ultra-short blond hair and sharp whiskey-brown eyes. She planted a hand on her hip when she saw Caden. "You're late."

"I know," he replied. "I got tied up."

Her disapproving gaze slid from Caden to me. "And you brought company?"

"She's the reason I'm late." After a brief stare-down between the two of them, he asked, "Are you going to invite us in?"

"You're lucky my work is flexible." The woman stepped aside, and we entered the small foyer. Her home was a mix of cheerful colors and antique furniture.

Caden shut the door behind us, blocking the chilled morning air. "Roxie, this is Madison. Madison, Roxie."

"It's nice to meet you," I said.

"American?" When I nodded, Roxie looked at Caden. "You're traveling with your clients now?"

Caden replied, "You know me better than that. Do you have my box?"

"It's where you left it." She pointed with her thumb to the stairs on our left.

"Thanks." Caden took the steps two at a time.

I rocked from toe to heel, not sure if I should follow or not. With Caden gone, Roxie's expression softened.

She eased a shoulder against the banister. "I'd offer you a cup of tea, but Caden never stays long enough to drink it. Not anymore, anyway."

Caden peeked his head out of the room at the top of the stairs and said, "You were the one who had plans the last few times I was here."

"*Pft.*" There was weight to Roxie's response, and I got the distinct impression she would have made time had he asked her to.

"Are you and Caden…or did you…?" I asked.

"Date?"

I nodded and reminded myself that Caden wasn't in his late teens. He was old. Like, really, really old. He'd have been around when she was younger and would probably enjoy the company of this mature woman too. And Roxie was pretty. She looked sophisticated in a pair of camel-color wool pants and a cream sweater.

"No." She smiled. "But, before I moved to London, we were close friends. I even got him to take me dancing."

"The Electric Slide is not dancing," Caden called down to us.

She dropped her voice to a whisper. "I got him to do the Hustle too."

I could almost see her wearing bell-bottoms and a wrist full of bangle bracelets.

"Caden liked disco?" I giggled as a picture of him in tight pants and a flashy shirt flitted through my mind.

"No!" He hollered from upstairs. "Not just no — *hell* no!"

Roxie chuckled. "He was more of a burnout back then. How long have you been seeing him?"

"Oh, we're not a couple." Because her grin reminded me of the Cheshire cat in *Alice in Wonderland*, I added, "Really, we're just friends."

"That's not the vibe I got when I first saw the two of you together." Her mouth twisted to the side as she shrugged. "I'm usually very intuitive."

"We've been spending a lot of time together." Caden and I were familiar with each other's moods and temperaments, and it probably showed. Not wanting to expand on my reply, though, I asked, "How'd you and Caden meet?"

"I was probably a few years older than yourself and living in the States at the time. The bloke I was dating took me on a romantic drive through the countryside. We'd only gone out a couple times. He seemed nice, so when he eased the car off the road, I thought he was having car problems. Then he made his move, and his advances didn't stop when I said no."

I let out a gasp. Even though Caden may have kissed me without my permission, in all the times we'd been alone, never once had he been anything less than a gentleman. And as much as I hated to admit it, I was more upset with myself for liking the feel of his lips on mine than I was that he'd kissed me. I quickly stopped thinking and hoped Caden wasn't still hacking into my thoughts.

Roxie continued. "Next thing I knew, my date was being dragged out of the car by a chap with red eyes."

"What did you do next?"

"Sent the jolt of magic I was about to inflict on my date's nether regions at Caden." She shook her head. "Caden barely registered my attack. He was too busy dragging my date to the boot of the car. Then Caden drove me home before dealing with the arse." She paused. "I never did ask exactly how he did that. Caden only said he'd read his mind, and the punishment fit the crimes past, present, and future. We've been friends ever since."

"He's a good guy," I found myself saying.

She nodded. "He is, and he protects what's his. That includes his friends. You're lucky to be counted as one of them."

"I'm sure he has hundreds of people scattered across the globe that fit into that category."

"Caden has a lot of acquaintances, but few he considers an ally, and if you're here, you're one of them." She looked over her shoulder right as Caden reappeared at the top of the stairs.

Roxie smiled. "I trust you found what you came here for."

He held up an engraved wooden globe the size of a plum. "Thanks for keeping it safe."

She grinned playfully. "If I hadn't, you would have forgotten all about me."

"Roxie, you know that isn't true." He kissed her cheek. "The next time I visit, I promise to stay longer. Today, however, Madison and I are crunched for time."

"I shall hold you to that."

Roxie and I exchanged a round of "Nice to meet you," and Caden and I left through the front door, which surprised me, seeing as he could have just zapped us back to Gloucester while we were standing in the privacy of Roxie's foyer. What surprised me even more was the black taxi parked out front.

"When did you call for a cab?"

Caden open the rear door. "When I was upstairs."

I hesitated. Was that before or after my very private confession to myself while Roxie recounted the past?

"It was the first thing I'd done once upstairs."

That didn't answer my unspoken question, and no way was I going to ask if he'd been tuned into my thoughts while retrieving the link to the chain. "Caden, I have to be back before my dad wakes."

"You will be." He gave a nod at the cab.

Caden told the driver our destination through the open window, and we slid in.

"Why aren't we going home?" Now that I was awake, I wasn't sure if traveling halfway around the world with Caden had been a wise choice.

Caden stuffed the wooden ball into his pocket. "Are you afraid you might enjoy yourself or that, if you do, you'll have to admit you like hanging out with me?"

"That's creepy, replying to someone's thoughts." I stressed the last word, though his question still didn't tell me if my musings at Roxie's had been overheard too.

"It's early, to answer your question." Caden gave me a pointed look. "You know, it wouldn't hurt you to let your guard down. Live a little. Have fun."

"Caden —"

"Friends are allowed to grab a cup of coffee. I did hear you say we were friends."

I couldn't help my smile. "You did?"

He nudged my knee with his. "I bet you've had coffee with Josh and didn't question it."

"Josh is like my brother."

An easy smile graced his face. "I'm glad to hear you don't think of me that way."

I sang "Party in the USA" to avoid reading too much into that comment.

The neighborhood we drove through reminded me very much of Harry Potter and Privet Drive. When we reached the shops, I felt we'd entered Diagon Alley. We eventually stopped in front of a little café called the Troubadour. Getting out of the cab, I took in the A-frame sign listing the day's specials, the potted plants along the inside ledge of the windows, and the brightly colored wood door while Caden paid the driver.

"I feel as if we've stepped back in time," I commented. Old-fashioned coffee pots marched to a cheerful melody across shelves that stretched over the front windows, and a large variety of old musical instruments hung from the ceiling.

"I thought you'd like it."

We settled at a table in the front of the café and ordered our drinks.

"Do you visit London often?" I asked. The world seemed smaller in his presence.

"Not so much these days." Caden leaned back.

"Why not? I mean, if I could travel the world by twitching my nose, I would."

Caden's warm brown gaze met mine. "I've been a little busy lately. You know, two jobs and a coven to keep up with."

"My coven isn't your concern, and you could stop playing handyman's apprentice."

He let out a hearty chortle. "At least one member of your coven wants me dead, and if I quit my job with your dad, he'll go back to working long hours, which means you'll be back to taking care of the house and brother-sitting. You remember how that turned out this past December, don't you?"

Like I could forget about the spell I cast, hoping to get a little help with chores. Even if my dreams weren't a reminder of the dangers I'd brought into my life, my contract with Caden was.

We talked about the office he was helping my father remodel, and then about school. Somewhere in the middle of my whining about homework, our waitress brought our drinks. Caden had just asked me why I didn't get the CliffsNotes version of the book I was reading for English when we were interrupted by a voice next to us.

"On holiday?" We looked up to find Derek standing next to our table. "If you're here, who's tending to your duties back home?"

Caden's features became an expressionless mask as he took a sip of his double espresso. "Go away."

Derek turned a chair around, straddled it, and rested his arms on the back. "So, what brings the two of you to London of all places?"

Caden's dark eyes met mine. "Ignore him. He'll get bored and leave."

I tipped my cup to the side, letting the froth skim dangerously close to the lip.

Obviously undeterred, Derek said, "Visiting Buckingham Palace or maybe Big Ben? I hear Hyde Park is quite nice."

"How's your latte?" Caden asked me.

"It's good." *Let's just get out of here.*

Derek's gaze flicked to me, and I knew he'd heard my thought. *Ass.*

Caden chuckled. I started singing to myself.

Derek thanked the barista when she brought his drink. "Or maybe you stopped by to visit another old friend of yours."

Caden's leg brushed mine as he calmly finished his espresso. I fought not to look worried for Roxie's safety. Caden set his cup down and turned his attention to Derek.

"I was feeling nostalgic." Caden then looked at me. "We lost possession of our souls in England, not too long after Derek rammed a dagger into our father's chest."

My gaze whipped to Derek. "You killed your father?"

"He would have done worse to Caden if I hadn't, and my brother knows it." He said it matter-of-factly as if there was no other option. "One day Caden will thank me."

I couldn't help it; I stopped singing. It didn't really matter. I was too in shock to have an intelligent thought. Caden's reply barely registered inside my stunned brain.

"Maybe I deserved to die."

"Like hell you did!" Derek retorted.

"You're damned because you killed your father." My mind was stuck in a loop. *He murdered his father. His own blood. The man who gave him life.*

"No. I'm damned because my brother's an idiot."

"Derek, she doesn't want to hear the sordid details of our estranged past."

I did want to know more, but I couldn't get my thoughts to move past *murder* and *father.*

Derek shrugged. "You're fond of this one." He studied me as he drank his coffee. "I can see why. Young. Pretty. Chock-full of talent. I'd want to play with her too." He paused. "Maybe I will."

Caden stood so abruptly his chair slammed into the table behind him.

"You're too easy." Derek let out a guffaw. "He always has been."

"Madison." Caden held his hand out, and I took it.

"Caden's well on his way to losing his crossroad." Derek caught my gaze. "But don't worry. I'll be there to take care of his affairs when he does."

Caden's eyes burned red. He leaned close to his brother. "Don't bet on it."

He then ushered me to the exit.

"See you next time, Madison," Derek called. "There will be a next time."

Chapter 14

Taming a Demon's Fury

The heat of Caden's palm bled through the cotton insulation of my jacket as if he'd stuck his hand in hot coals moments before touching me. He didn't slow his pace, nor did he release me until we were a few blocks away from the café.

"Caden, your eyes are red," I whispered when we stopped in the doorway of a quaint bookstore. Steam came off his body. I gathered energy from the air around us and created a gentle breeze in hopes of lowering his temperature at the same time as hiding his unearthly fever. "You need to calm down."

Caden bowed his head, closed his eyes, and took several deep breaths. "He's just trying to get under my skin. He's always trying to get under my skin."

"He's good at it." I ducked down to see his eyes beneath the curtain of dark hair. They no longer burned with the fires of hell. "The only time you lose your cool is when he shows up. Want to talk about it?"

"Sure." He let his head fall back against the brick behind him. "We can have a heart-to-heart as soon as you admit your dreams are connected to Reed's magic."

Admitting that would have been the same as admitting I needed help. I wasn't ready to do that. So, instead of replying, I asked, "Why do you believe you deserved to die?"

"If your dreams are nothing to worry about, why haven't you mentioned them to your coven?"

"Forget I asked." I stormed out of the doorway, made it to the next store, and stopped.

Caden was infuriating. I'd only been trying to understand him. To figure out what he'd done to become a crossroad demon. Maybe help him through his issues with his brother.

No, you were sticking your nose where it doesn't belong.

Caden's past was his business, just as the dreams were mine. I'd get them under control without it costing me additional years in Caden's service, just like he'd deal with Derek.

I bit back my frustration and sauntered to where I'd left Caden. He hadn't moved, and I supposed I should be grateful because I was in another country and did need a ride home. I decided to keep my questioning to things that were happening in the present.

"What did Derek mean by 'there will be a next time'?"

"My boss thinks I need a babysitter, and Derek seems to have noticed we like to hang out."

There was more to it than that. I could tell by the way Caden wouldn't look at me and how Derek had stared at me. I got the distinct feeling that I was Derek's award should he do his job well. No way would I allow that to happen. Nor would I let another witch be hurt.

I pulled my hair away from my face. "Aren't you worried about Roxie? If Derek's following us, he's going to know we stopped by her house."

"Roxie's home is protected by wards, and one of them hides supernatural signatures. That's why we arrived on her front porch and not on the sidewalk." He pulled a pack of cigarettes out of his pocket, tapped one out, and put it between his lips. The tip glowed orange before he put the pack away. "She's a solitary witch. Very few people know what she is. Her wards keep it that way."

I switched which direction the breeze blew, sending his smoke away from us. "If you already know a witch who's willing to help you, why do you need me?"

"I don't." He took a long drag of his cigarette. "You needed me."

Funny how the supernatural world worked. Witches were bound to their promise. The Fae couldn't enter our realm without being invited. And a crossroad demon couldn't help someone without making a deal. No exceptions. Nature—or Hades, in Caden's case—governed the rules we abided by.

He took one last drag on his cigarette before flicking it into the street.

I frowned and used my powers to snuff it out, then transported it to a nearby trash can.

"Let's get you home. Shall we?"

"Caden." I grabbed his hand. "Please, talk to me."

"Do you know why you dream of Reed?"

I let go of his hand and grabbed my elbows to keep from fidgeting. "Because I'm overtired and, like many girls, I dream of princes and fairy tales. Because there never seems to be an end to the supernatural threats in my life, and with Reed gone, he seems like the most harmless. Because there's still a minute trace of Fae magic in my bloodstream. The reason doesn't matter. The worst of my withdrawal symptoms are gone."

Caden's gaze bore down on me. "You dream of Reed because it's when you sleep that you're the most vulnerable. It's the only time he can still get in your head. You wondered if you could summon him in your sleep. The answer is yes. If you want to keep from doing just that, then get rid of the dried rose you keep taped to your dresser mirror and remove every last acorn from your property, because if you don't, one night you might just find yourself standing over a bowl of water with these ingredients floating inside and the Prince of Fae at your side. If that happens, neither Isaac nor I will be able to save you." He turned and punched the brick wall behind him.

I flinched, even though he hadn't struck me. The anger rolling off him was almost tangible. I placed a hand on his shoulder, but before I could say anything, he asked, "Is a few more years in my debt worth risking your life here with your family and friends?"

"Caden, I…They're just dreams." I didn't want to believe they could be more than that. "Not even three months has passed since I made the deal with you and I've already added five years to my…"

"Sentence, that's what you were going to say." He looked genuinely hurt.

"Caden, I'd rather be your friend than your Beck-and-Call Witch."

He considered me a moment. It would have been nice to get inside his head for a change. I half wished the bookstore were open.

I'd browse the shelves just to have something to focus on other than Caden's pensive expression. Finally, he glanced at his watch. "Your father will be up soon. Do you want help traveling or are you going to pass out on me?"

"I know what to expect this time. I can make it on my own."

I took a deep breath as his arms encircled me. The red and black void came immediately. To keep my mind off the lack of air, I counted. I made it to thirty-three before instinct took over and I tried to take a breath. I remember gagging and Caden's crimson eyes. Then nothing.

I woke to the sound of waves lapping over sand and Caden's mouth on mine. Since blue sky showed over his shoulder, I guessed we weren't in Hades.

He lifted his head. "I was only joking about passing out."

My brain felt as if it were floating in gelatin, but other than that I was okay. I propped myself up on my elbows and surveyed our surroundings. The sun glistened off the ocean directly behind Caden, and to my right, green mountains rose to meet the sky. "Where are we?"

"Azores. You did worse this time. Didn't even make it halfway."

"Great." I went to stand, swayed, and decided I'd sit on the shore a little longer.

He fell back on his butt and rested his arms on his bent knees. "You must not have fully recovered from the trip to London. We need to either find the airport or you accept my help."

My phone chimed, announcing I had a message. It was from Isaac, letting me know he'd be late picking me up. A glance at the time told me Dad and Chase would be downstairs eating breakfast already. The fact that I didn't have a text from Dad meant he hadn't noticed me gone, yet.

"You could tell your dad you left early." Caden let a handful of sand slowly escape his grasp like grains in an hourglass. "With luck, there will be a flight that gets us into Boston before evening."

"And Isaac? What do you suggest I tell him? That I couldn't sleep, so you and I snuck off in the middle of the night and went to London?" I slipped my pinkie ring off and on my finger. "I'll be single and on the outs with half my coven before our flight takes off."

Kaylee might understand, but I was pretty sure Josh would say *What did you expect?* and side with Isaac due to an unspoken guy code.

"I'm afraid there are no other options."

"Perfect." There I was, magic coursing through my veins and powerless to avoid an argument with my boyfriend without lying to him. Plus, I had a test in history that I'd actually studied for. When my teacher discovered that I ditched — and she would — she'd never let me make it up. The school would call my dad, and I'd still end up in trouble with him.

I stood and brushed sand off my butt. "We use your hoodoo to get us home now."

"As you wish."

He got up and waited for me to move in front of him.

"Why do I feel as if I'm cheating on Isaac?"

"We can still catch a flight." He indicated with a nod to our left. "Sounds like the road's that way."

"Caden, zap us home before I change my mind."

His hand came to rest on the side of my face as his other arm pulled me closer. I watched his irises bleed to red as his scent became smoky. His thumb followed my jawbone and sent shivers through my body. I may have had a very good reason for kissing him, but standing that close to him and it being my choice to do it was definitely cheating on Isaac. Before I could hate myself more than I already did, I closed the distance between us.

His lips were firm and moved tenderly over mine. I braced myself for the overwhelming heat to consume me. When that didn't happen, I peeked and saw we were still standing on the coastline.

As if in reply to an unspoken question, Caden's tongue brushed my lips, and I knew the gentle nibbles weren't enough to get me from Azores back to the continental United States. My hands found his hips as I gave in to our kiss. His fingers tangled in my hair a moment before I felt his hold on me tighten and the ground beneath me vanish.

It would have been easier on my conscience if he were a bad kisser — if he opened his mouth too wide or used an excessive amount of tongue. But he didn't. So, I concentrated on not allowing my hands to wander, and I didn't let the little moan of pleasure that stewed inside me pass my lips. In no time, the familiar smell of my bedroom found me. Caden cupped my face.

"You know what your problem is?" His lips brushed mine for one last taste.

I was too busy trying to catch my breath to answer, and this time it wasn't because of the lack of oxygen. Caden had a way of messing with my head and, unlike Reed, he didn't use magic to do it. I closed my eyes and pretended I needed a moment.

His thumb caressed my cheek. "You've convinced yourself that your first love can be your only. That's such an innocent belief." Caden's mouth skimmed mine again. "Just imagine what the world could hold for you if you let yourself be wrong."

"Caden, this was a onetime thing to get us home."

But the warmth of his hands no longer held my face. I opened my eyes to find myself alone.

The banging on my door nearly had me leaping out of my skin.

"Madison! You're late!" Dad hollered through the door. "Again."

"I'm up! Jeesh."

I checked the time. If Isaac hadn't been running late, he'd be parked out front waiting for me. I was beginning to think fate was on my side.

My hair and clothes reeked of brimstone and smoke. I draped my jacket over my lamp, opened the bedroom window, and created a warm breeze to circle it, hoping it'd be enough to air it out. Next, I took a speed-shower, changed clothes, and brushed my teeth. The quick *beep-beep* of Isaac's Jeep announced he was out front.

With a wave of my hand, my window closed. Just in case my jacket still smelled like Caden, I grabbed my thickest button-up sweater and jogged down the stairs.

"See you tonight," I called to Dad and Chase as I raced out the door.

I climbed in the Jeep and gave Isaac a kiss good morning.

He pulled a strand of my wet hair through his fingers. "And here I thought you'd use the extra time to your advantage."

"Overslept."

He shifted into gear. "No more nightmares, then?"

"No."

Guilt at being dishonest with him settled in the pit of my stomach. I opened my mouth to tell him that Caden had shown up. I didn't have to say I volunteered to go with him. I could let Isaac assume I'd completed another task as part of my contract. Isaac wouldn't be mad that I'd gone. He'd understand even if he didn't like the idea of me spending more time with Caden. But when the words passed my lips, they came out as "Sorry I woke you," instead.

My next attempt to come clean went pretty much the same. I gave up after that. My instincts evidently knew better than my conscience.

"I've been giving the situation with Shane some thought," Isaac said. "It might be enough to cast the confusion spell on his parents—go with the story about a secret medical study that his parents couldn't talk about until now. And there are elixirs we could brew to make Shane age. We might need to tweak the formula some, but he's undead. It's not like we'll kill him if we get it wrong the first couple of times."

Kaylee and I had already nixed the idea of a medical breakthrough, because someone somewhere would dig into a story like that, and odds were it would come back to bite us. But still, I couldn't help but stare at Isaac. While I'd been enjoying a latte in a cozy café in London, he'd been devising a plan to solve my best friend's ghoul issues.

I sank lower in my seat, feeling about three inches tall.

Kaylee placed a carton of milk on both of our lunch trays. "Let me get this straight. You dreamed you were dancing the night away in Sanctus with Reed, you actually ran off to London with Caden, and then you caught a ride to school from Isaac. All before seven o'clock in the morning."

"When you put it that way, I sound like a tramp." I swiped my school ID through the reader to pay for my lunch.

She did the same and followed me to a table in the back of the lunchroom.

"Caden really thinks Reed's influencing your dreams?" She took a bite of her pizza.

"Yeah."

She swallowed what was in her mouth. "Maybe you should let him help you."

"What? No!" I squirted ketchup over my fries. "I've already committed to twenty-five years of service."

"Doing simple spells." Kaylee shook her head. "Madison, we don't want a repeat of last December. And if we thought Reed was pissed before, imagine what he'd do if he came back—who he'd hurt to get to you."

He'd start with Chase and my dad, then work his way through my friends. Reed had told me that much when he was here. That was why I had risked everything to get him to return to Sanctus.

"It's not just the years." I pushed my tray away from me, not really hungry. "Any deal I make has to be sealed."

Kaylee froze mid-bite. Slowly, mechanically, she set her pizza down. "You'd have to…"

"Yes."

We had agreed to never mention that I'd kissed Caden to seal my original deal. Good to our word, we hadn't. Until now.

She leaned in, palms on the table on either side of her tray. "Did you…when he amended the contract?"

I nodded.

She did this thing where her nose sort of crinkled and her mouth tilted up on one side in a thoughtful way. "Is he still a good kisser? I mean, he has been around for a *long* time."

"Kaylee!" I threw a stack of napkins at her.

She plucked one off her shoulder. "You did it for Isaac. It doesn't count."

According to Kaylee, kissing a demon as part of a business transaction was not the same thing as cheating on your boyfriend. I loved how her mind worked.

Her candy-brown eyes looked at me through her lashes. "So, is he?"

"Kaylee, focus."

"Right. So, you 'sealed the deal'"—she made air quotes—"two times."

I must have winced or made a face, because she pushed both our trays to the side and rested her forearms on the table between us.

"You kissed him more than that, didn't you!"

I sucked in a breath. This was my best friend. She knew all my secrets and never told anyone, not even Josh. So, I told her about the side effects of traveling with him, how I'd passed out halfway between here and London, and how I'd managed to make the last leg of the journey home.

She was silent until I finished. "No wonder you didn't tell Isaac about last night."

"He can't know. Promise me you won't breathe a word of this to anyone."

"I promise." She rested a hand on mine. "Madison, your arrangement with Caden is complicated, and a bit unorthodox, but your reason for being in it is selfless. And it could be worse. It could have cost you your soul." She paused. "So what if you have to kiss a supernatural hottie once in a while. Your soul is intact. You'll live a long life."

"I don't hate it," I admitted. "Kissing him."

"Well, duh! He's had centuries to perfect his technique."

I waited until she looked at me to roll my eyes and then changed the subject. "Speaking of hotties, I heard there's one subbing in Mrs. Crawford's class." I believe the words Sarah had used when I'd seen her in the halls between classes were *smokin' hot* as she fanned herself with her hand.

"You don't know?"

I shook my head and took a drink of milk. I didn't have chemistry this year.

Kaylee bent closer. "It's Derek."

I choked on the milk.

Kaylee handed me a napkin and continued in a low voice. "Talk about making a hard class even harder. To keep myself from thinking *Omigod, a demon's teaching class,* I spent the entire period copying everything he wrote on the board. I even read the textbook word for word. My brain hurts from concentrating on the molecular structure of sucrose."

I shook my head, still processing the fact that a demon was posing as a teacher. "Caden wasn't kidding when he said Derek would find a way into the lives of my friends."

Kaylee snatched a fry off my plate and pointed it at me. "Well, he picked the perfect class. Josh and Isaac have him next period. I already gave them a heads up." The fry went in her mouth.

"Did Derek say anything to you?"

"Just 'If it isn't Miss USA.' Get it? The last time I saw him I had been singing 'God Bless America.' That's why I focused on the lesson today." Her shoulder rose and fell. "Other than that, he conducted class as if subbing was his life's profession, but I could tell by the way his focus would land on someone that he was reading their minds."

I set my milk carton on the tray and stood. We headed to the tray return.

"Derek has a deep, almost seductive voice," she said. "Can you imagine what was going through the minds of the girls?"

"Ew!"

She bumped my shoulder with hers. "You only say that because you know what he is."

True. "Hopefully, one day in the heads of teenagers will be enough for him."

More importantly, I hoped Derek didn't decide to make Gloucester his home.

We set our trays on the return belt as the bell rang.

"I'll call you later." She hurried in the direction of her next class.

I dug my phone out of my purse and typed a message to Caden as I headed up the south staircase. My finger hovered over the send button as an image of him barely able to control his temper flashed through my mind. Even if Caden knew his brother was here, there was nothing he could do. If he stormed into school and demanded that his brother leave, Derek would laugh in his face or, worse, start a fight. Derek might even suspect I had something to hide. Certain that it was better not to make a big deal out of Derek's presence, I dropped my phone back into my purse. My confidence, however, shattered the moment I reached the top of the staircase.

Derek leaned against the wall. He wore dark dress slacks, a white shirt, and a tie. He was clean-shaven for his role as Respectable High School Teacher.

"Ugh. When Kaylee told me you were teaching class, I hoped I wouldn't see you." I turned right and kept going. Derek fell in step with me. Since it was obvious he wasn't going to leave me alone, I asked, "Aren't you a little far from the science wing?"

"I wanted a word with you."

"I have nothing to say to you."

"Then I'll do the talking, and you can do the listening." He grabbed my arm and pulled me into an empty classroom.

Derek was taller than Caden and more imposing. He was the type of guy you wouldn't want to run into in a dark alley. It occurred to me that I never felt in danger when I was with Caden. Derek, on the other hand, caused the skin on my arm to prickle. I didn't like being alone with him. I liked it even less when he closed the door. My fingers curled around my hemp bracelet, ready to call Isaac and Josh so that I'd have backup.

"Don't. Or I will burn it off your wrist." He indicated with a nod to my hand.

I released my wrist and hugged my books to my chest as if they'd protect me from him. He strolled over to the desk nearest the door and leaned on it.

"Does Caden know you're pretending to be a substitute teacher?"

"Does your father know he has a demon working for him?"

"Leave my father out of this," I growled.

"I didn't think so." Derek had the same dark brown eyes as Caden. I hadn't noticed that before. And they produced the same disapproving glare I'd seen on Caden's face. "You know the problem with my brother?"

I could think of a few things. None of which Derek would have been referring to, so I shook my head.

"He cares about humans."

I considered that a quality more people should possess. "Compassion isn't a crime."

"It is when you're a demon. It gives him a weakness he can't afford to have. I see why he likes you." Derek rose to his feet and came closer. I backed up a step. "And I get why he allows himself the pleasure of friends." He inhaled deeply. "Especially ones as tantalizing as yourself."

I took another step back. "Why are you here?"

"To keep an eye on the prize."

I bit my bottom lip. "Me." Derek didn't blink. "That's not going to happen."

"Says the teen witch who can't even bury a coffin. Where's the binding chain?" He stepped even closer and ran a strand of my hair through his fingers. "You don't have to say its location out loud. Just think it, and I'll be on my way."

"I don't know. But even if I did, I wouldn't tell you."

Derek studied me a moment. "You're telling the truth."

I glanced at the door. "Is that all? Can I go now?"

Derek didn't move. "My brother pissed off a high-ranking demon. If he's not careful, he's going to get himself killed."

For a brief moment, I saw something behind Derek's fierce gaze that made him look younger. It softened the deep creases near his eyes and made his scowl less menacing.

"You're watching out for him. Aren't you?" I asked.

His brow pulled low over his eyes as he snarled, "I stopped protecting Caden the day we landed in hell."

"Did Caden kill you?" Maybe that was why they'd both been damned.

"He didn't tell you the rest of our story?"

My back pressed against the wall. I hadn't realized that I'd been backing up until I had nowhere else to go.

Derek planted his palm on the wall next to my head. "Caden did worse than kill me."

"You murdered your father. I'm sure you deserved what you got."

Derek's face was inches from mine. "Our father drank from sunup to sundown, and his favorite pastime was beating the crap out of Caden. He'd been drunk the night I rammed a knife through his lung. He was still swearing he'd whip my brother until he saw blood when I twisted the blade and shredded his heart."

"You killed him to protect Caden." I held his gaze, thinking I understood Derek's anger. "And now you feel betrayed because you risked everything to help your brother and he didn't do the same for you."

"Not exactly."

"Then what happened?"

"Ask Caden."

Like he'd answer me. "He's still your brother. Don't you think you guys should make up?"

"I'm having too much fun watching him screw up the perfect existence he's managed to create. But don't worry. I'll be there to take care of his affairs when he's gone. If you're lucky, I won't make you do anything that will taint that pretty little soul of yours." Derek pushed off the wall and left.

My heart hammered in my chest, and my legs gave out. Derek thought this was a game, and I was the prize.

Chapter 15

Chicanery

Several days had passed since my encounter with Derek. As expected, Caden closed up whenever I asked him about his past, leaving his and Derek's demise a mystery. Derek continued to teach Mrs. Crawford's class. His lessons were pure torture, according to Kaylee. But Isaac and Josh must have convinced him they were ignorant of the demons around them, because the wrath of hell didn't rain down on us. Our resident ghoul was also behaving himself. And, best of all, I managed to avoid any more interactions with Derek.

Thursday, I met Isaac at the double doors leading to the student parking lot. Our focus was on finding a way to get our hands on a piece of the binding chain to keep the complete talisman out of demonic hands. We drove to my house.

I scanned the messages on my phone while Isaac checked in with Anastasia on his. I had one text from Dad saying he'd pick up dinner on his way home and a group one from Sarah telling Kaylee and me to study the last chapter we'd gone over in history, because Mrs. Parris had hinted there'd be a pop quiz tomorrow.

"Anastasia was able to acquire an old grimoire," Isaac said after he ended his call. "She's not sure how much of it is accurate—something about being written by a madwoman—but it did mention binding chains. The spell in it was incomplete, but there was a drawing."

"There's a drawing in your grimoire too."

"Yeah, but this one included a poppet." He downshifted and made a left onto my street. "Anastasia thinks the miniature doll represents the person you're binding."

"Like a hex doll used in voodoo?"

"Pretty much."

Our coven had made a poppet once. We used it to bind a friend from using the powers to harm others. Ours required some very specific items for it to work.

"Do you think Caden has a strand of Sammael's hair and a feather from his wings? Do angels even have wings?"

"I don't know." Isaac pulled into my driveway. Dad's truck wasn't there, so I knew we were the only ones home. "Has Caden called to set up another appointment?"

"No." It wasn't a lie. Caden never called. He just showed up. Like at two o'clock this morning when he'd woken me from yet another bad dream. This time, I had made it to the kitchen, and I had three acorns gripped tight in my hand; I must have summoned them in my sleep. While I had tried to look at the bright side—I'd summoned something I couldn't see—Caden had scowled and used hell's fires to destroy every acorn on my block, including the ones in my hand. He had tried, yet again, to get me to ask for his help, but I had refused. He left after that, but I don't think he went far. I could smell his smoky scent as I drifted back to sleep.

"Caden's suspiciously absent all of a sudden. Maybe you should call him," Isaac said, pulling me out of my reverie.

And have him thinking I miss him? No way. "We amended my contract, remember? He's not to bother me at school or when I'm with friends, unless it's an emergency."

"I'd feel better if we knew how close he was to becoming Master of the Angel of Death."

I was less worried. Of course, I knew he still needed one more piece of the chain.

"I think we should avoid giving Caden an excuse to find me, take a break from research, and enjoy this." I used my powers to cause his seat to slide further back, leaving me room to climb over the stick shift and onto his lap. I ran my fingers through his silky hair. "And this." I nibbled at his neck. "And this." I bit his bottom lip.

"I could get on board with that plan." Isaac cupped my face in his hands and ran his thumb over my cheek just as Caden had done that morning, but when Isaac's lips met mine, there was no mistaking they were his. Vanilla and spearmint encircled us. Weightlessness took over, and the next thing I knew, we were lying on my bed with me on top.

I needed to feel Isaac's powers touch mine. I broke our kiss and tugged my top over my head.

"Your dad—"

"Won't be home with Chase for another hour."

Isaac grabbed the neck of his T-shirt from the back and yanked it off. His hands caressed my sides on their travels up from my waist to my shoulders. He pulled me back to him. As our tongues did a slow dance, my powers fought to break free. Isaac's arm found its way to my lower back a moment before he flipped us over, switching positions so that he was on top. And then it happened—the flow of his powers searching for mine and finding them.

He trailed a line of kisses over my collarbone. "You sure? I'd hate to get you in trouble."

I ran my fingers over the hard muscles in his abs and unbuttoned his jeans in reply. The scent of his powers grew stronger, and then the shades were pulled and music drifted out of his cell phone. I used my power to light the candle on my dresser. We had one hour, and I didn't want to waste one minute of it.

Isaac and I went downstairs before Dad and Chase got home. We had our schoolbooks spread across the kitchen table, but I couldn't concentrate on homework. At some point during the day—at least I hoped it was during the day and not while Isaac and I had been preoccupied—Caden had stopped by. He'd left the wooden ball we'd retrieved from Roxie's house on my dresser next to the candle. Had I not been busy kissing Isaac, I would have seen it sooner.

With everything that had happened since London, I'd forgotten to ask Caden about it. Isaac watched me use two fingers to pick it up. His brows knitted together. I stared at it as if it were the devil himself.

I considered telling Isaac that I'd seen Caden with it, but that admission would most likely lead to questions I'd have to answer with lies. The number of secrets I kept from him grew with each passing day, and I hated it.

Acting as if I had no idea what the ornate ball was or who put it in my room took a monumental amount of effort.

Isaac sat at the kitchen table, turning it over in his hands. "I've seen markings like these before. They're used to create a protective barrier."

He shook it and something inside rattled against the walls, giving a sound similar to the maracas we had in grade school.

A piece of the chain. It had to be, but why would Caden give it to me?

I held out my hand. "Let me see it."

Caden had said he was retrieving a box, which meant the ball had to open. I ran my fingers over the etchings, trying to find a seam. Its craftsmanship was amazing. It was perfectly round with symbols circling it as if telling a story. I paused to look at the All-Seeing Eye.

"It can't be that simple." I rested the tip of my finger over it and pressed. There was a faint click and the ball cracked open. Grains of sand I recognized as being from the beach at Azores spilled onto the kitchen table along with a folded Post-it.

I didn't appreciate Caden's not-so-subtle reminder that I had chosen to go to London with him nor that I had willingly kissed him.

I couldn't put my finger on the exact moment my life had gotten so complicated. Was it when I'd first asked Isaac not to send Caden back to Hades or the moment Caden had bent the rules and made a deal without claiming my soul? Maybe it went back further than that, to the day I had invited a faerie into my home—or the day my hand had brushed Isaac's and the powers I hadn't even known I had collided with his. I supposed the *when* didn't really matter. I couldn't go back in time and change my future.

"What's the note say?" Isaac asked.

"Um…" I plucked it out of the sand and closed the ball. "It's from Caden. He's picking me up at eight to retrieve the last piece of the puzzle." I turned the note so that Isaac could see it. "His words, not mine."

"He must have gotten a section of the chain without you."

"Yeah. Isaac, I —"

Chase ran into the kitchen, a fast-food bag clutched in his hands and his shoes and backpack still on. "We picked up fried chicken!"

I had been about to come clean and tell Isaac everything, but maybe Chase bursting into the room was Fate's way of saying not to, and who was I to argue with a deity?

"Great!" I said with forced enthusiasm. I grabbed the take-out bag from him. "Go take off your shoes and wash up."

"'Kay!" Chase turned on his heels and jogged out of the kitchen.

"Hi, princess," Dad said.

I groaned at the mention of his nickname for me; he knew I hated when he called me that in front of my friends. "Dad, you promised."

He held his hands up. "Sorry."

Isaac smirked and diverted his eyes. He'd already told me he thought my nickname was cute.

Dad looked at Isaac. "There's plenty. You're welcome to stay."

"We could finish" — that is, *do* — "our homework afterward," I said.

Isaac smiled. "I'd love to. Thanks, Mr. Riley."

Isaac and I cleared our schoolwork off the table. Chase returned, rubbing his hands on the front of his shirt.

"There's a towel in the bathroom for a reason, Chase." I handed him a stack of paper plates and pointed to the table.

When he saw there were four, he looked at Isaac. "You're staying!"

"Is that okay?" Isaac asked and winked at me. I giggled. Isaac always let Chase believe he had the final decision.

"Yeah!" Chase spun on his heels and faced me. "I call dibs on sitting next to Isaac."

My fists went to my hips as I pretended to be surprised. Besides, it was fun to give Chase a hard time. "He's my boyfriend."

"Dibs are dibs." Chase put his cup next to the place Isaac always sat when he stayed for dinner. "You can sit next to Dad."

Dad raised his eyebrows and gave me his don't-tease-your-brother look. It was very similar to his I-don't-want-to-hear-it look, which wasn't far from his I-said-that's-enough look. The only difference in the three was how far he cocked his head to the side.

"You're no fun," I whispered as I squeezed by him and took my seat. Isaac sat across from me.

Dad gave Chase a drumstick and then took a piece of chicken for himself. "I was at Mr. O'Conner's today."

Mr. O'Conner was a widower who lived on the other side of town.

"Any luck convincing him it'd be cheaper to have you put in a new garbage disposal than to pay for all the service calls?" I asked. Mr. O'Conner's disposal had stopped working five times in the last month.

"As a matter of fact, yes. If it breaks again." Dad chuckled. "He's a stubborn one. Kept insisting he had a conversation with Shane Lentz."

I choked on the food in my mouth.

Dad patted my back. "You okay?"

I gulped half my lemonade in an effort to push the half-chewed chicken to my stomach. "Yeah. Thanks. When did he see Shane?"

"Um, last year. But he claims it was just the other day." Dad looked at Isaac and added. "Shane lost his battle with leukemia. Nice kid."

Isaac nodded and calmly ate a potato wedge. I was ready to call Kaylee and ask her if Shane had wandered off. I didn't, though. Instead, I took a bite of chicken.

"I told him it couldn't have been Shane." Dad took a swig of his soda. "Mr. O'Conner was adamant that it was him, though. Apparently, Shane used to live down the block from him."

"Does he know Shane died?" I asked.

"He went to the kid's wake."

Isaac grinned lightheartedly. "My grandfather used to get confused too." Which was a total lie. His grandfather's mind wasn't what had given out on him. "We always found it best not to argue with him."

"So, Chase, how was school?" I asked in an effort to move on to a new subject.

It worked. We spent the rest of dinner talking about school and work. When Chase stuffed the last potato wedge into his mouth, we started to clean up.

Chase went to grab the ketchup, but I snatched it off the table before his greasy little fingers touched it. "You go wash your hands."

Isaac rested his hands on Chase's shoulders. "I'll help."

I mouthed *thank you*. Dad watched them leave the kitchen and then dug a silver ring out of his pocket. He held it out to me. "Caden asked me to give this to you."

My gaze dropped to my pinkie. I hadn't realized I'd lost it.

"It must have slipped off my finger." I tried to remember if I'd been fidgeting with my rings when Caden had woken me this morning.

Ignoring Dad's look of disapproval, I took it from him.

"And Caden wanted me to make sure you got his message."

"Um. Yeah." And Caden was going to hear an earful from me, because he could have given me my ring back tonight instead of using my dad as his personal messenger. I slipped my ring on and reached for a glass container from the cabinet, hoping Dad would let it go. I had no such luck.

He grabbed my arm and glanced at the doorway. We were still alone. "Does Isaac know you're hanging out with Caden?"

"It's not like that, Dad." I removed my arm from his grasp and put the leftover chicken in the container one piece at a time. "And, yes, Isaac knows I helped Caden out."

"Today?"

I paused with the lid a few inches from the top of the container.

"Caden said you dropped it this morning." Dad lowered his voice even more. "Didn't Isaac drive you to *and* from school?"

"I saw Caden for like a minute before class."

"When your ring jumped off your finger?" Dad scrubbed his face.

I put the chicken in the fridge. When I turned, Dad stood in front of me. He rubbed his forehead in the way he does when he's trying very hard to be both a dad and a mom. I could tell the dad side—the one that wanted me to stay his little girl forever—was winning out by the tone of his sigh.

"Madison, Caden's too old for you."

Several centuries too old. "Agreed. Are we done with this conversation?"

"No." He made sure we were still alone. "You like Isaac, right?"

"Yes, Dad." I tried to step around him, but he put a hand on my shoulder to stop me.

"Isaac's a good guy. Keep up whatever it is you're doing with Caden, and you're going to lose him."

I stood a little taller and tucked my hair behind my ear. "I'm not doing anything with Caden."

"That twitch in your left eye and the way you keep playing with that ring you happened to drop during your one-minute meeting with Caden says differently."

That statement would be his mom side kicking in. He was just short of saying *young lady* like Mom used to do whenever she'd known I was hiding something.

My arms dropped to my side, and I mentally told my eye to knock it off. "Look, Dad, I appreciate your concern, but there is nothing going on with me and Caden."

This time when I went to walk around him, he let me.

Chapter 16
Sleight of Hand

I desperately wanted to talk to Kaylee in private, so when Dad and Chase retreated to the family room to watch TV, I told Isaac I needed to use the bathroom and check in with Kaylee while out of my dad's earshot. Isaac started on his homework as I headed upstairs. With a flick of my powers, I turned on the water to keep anyone from overhearing me.

In a hushed whisper, I gave Kaylee a one-minute rundown on Caden and his message. "I'm going to kill him."

"How?" Kaylee's voice drifted out of the speaker on my cell phone with an annoying amount of skepticism.

"I mean it figuratively." I paced four steps to the tub, spun on my heels, and marched back to the close door. "I can't believe he let my dad know we've hung out. My dad! What was Caden thinking? And my dad just confronted me about it now. What if Isaac had heard?"

"Did he?"

"No." I heaved out a sigh and plopped down on the edge of the tub.

Silence followed.

I should have told Isaac about my trip to London the day it had happened. I should have told him about my dreams too. The other night, if I had told Isaac I couldn't sleep, *he* would have been the one to come over and comfort me, not Caden. Because Isaac was always there for me and trusted me. Now, I was drowning in deceit.

Stupid, stupid, stupid. My knuckles bounced off my skull with each word.

"Madison?"

"Yeah?"

"You can't let Caden pick you up at your house. You know that, right? I mean, your dad is easygoing and all, but no way is he going to let you hang out with Isaac all day and run off with Caden tonight."

"Right. Hold on." I quickly sent Caden a text stating I'd meet him at Annisquam Lighthouse at eight. When I put the phone back to my ear, I heard Josh scream out *Oh!* followed by Shane's muffled laughter. Kaylee had already told me that Josh had brought over a twenty-seven-inch television and an old game system to help keep Shane busy. Their voices reminded me that demons weren't the only reason I'd called Kaylee. "Hey, you have to put the barrier spell back up."

I told her about Shane's conversation with Mr. O'Conner.

"Damn it!" I pictured her shooting daggers with her eyes at the back of Shane's head. "He promised he wasn't going to leave the house."

Why she believed him was beyond me. "Kaylee, I can't handle ghoul issues right now." I could barely handle my demon ones. "You need to raise the barrier spell. You need to make it so that he can't leave."

"I'll talk to him."

Not the reply I wanted, but it would have to do. "Are you any closer to convincing him to move to Minneapolis?"

After days of throwing around ideas, we had determined the most logical solution was for Shane to live elsewhere. Kaylee and I had already called Kevin, and he'd said he would help us. He gave us the okay to cast the confusion spell on his parents so that they wouldn't recognize Shane. And we wouldn't have to convince them to take him in. Mr. and Mrs. Hobbs had big hearts; if they found out a classmate and friend needed a home, they'd open their doors. Shane would be able to go to school and finish his education. We'd worry about what to do after high school when the time came.

"He still refuses to move," Kaylee replied.

The bang against the bathroom door had me nearly falling into the tub.

"Daddy said to stop wasting water," Chase yelled.

"Okay!" I got up and turned the faucet off. To Kaylee, I said, "What if we cast the confusion spell on Shane. We can make him excited about the idea of a new life."

"Josh already tried that. It seems a ghoul's mind is harder to manipulate than a human's." There was a pause. "I'll find out who Shane's talked to. Josh can pay them a visit, do a little hocus-pocus, and have them believing they met someone who looked like Shane. Buy us a little more time."

"I should go." I opened the bathroom door.

"Madison, are you going to be okay tonight with Caden? If you want a buffer, I'll come with you. I bet he'd let me tag along."

I appreciated the offer, but there was a very good chance that Caden and I would have to travel through the void to get to where we were going.

"I'll be fine," I reassured both of us.

Kaylee dropped her voice. "Maybe the last piece is in Paris or Beijing."

"I hope not." I took the stairs one at a time, pausing at the bottom.

"Oh. Right! You'd have to make out with him to survive the trip." She didn't hide the chuckle in her voice.

"I'm glad you find this funny."

"Sorry." She let the word drag out a moment. "Call me if you need anything."

"I will."

We hung up.

I just had to get through tonight. Caden and I would get the last section of the binding chain, I'd be able to tell Isaac that Caden had all four pieces, and the guilt of keeping something that important from Isaac would vanish.

What could go wrong?

For the second time since I'd known Isaac, he drove the speed limit, stopped for a count of five at each stop sign, and didn't drive through a single yellow light. His sudden need to obey the law made me late for my appointment with Caden.

Caden's black sports car was the only vehicle in the parking lot when Isaac and I got to the lighthouse. He leaned against the back of his car with one foot on the bumper and a cigarette dangling from his mouth.

Isaac surprised me by parking *and* turning off the Jeep's engine.

"Thanks for the ride." I went to give him a quick kiss good-bye, but instead of meeting me halfway, he got out of the car.

"This should be fun," I said to myself.

Isaac strode ahead of me until he stood a few feet from Caden, feet shoulder-width apart and arms at his side. "Do you want to tell us why your brother is teaching high school chemistry?"

Caden blew smoke out of the side of his mouth. "It's the fastest way to infiltrate Madison's life and meet her friends."

"You knew?" I asked.

"That he was at your school, no, but I'm not surprised." He glared at Isaac. "As long as your coven keeps their thoughts off of me, then Derek will get bored and move on."

"She's on his radar because of you," Isaac spat.

Caden watched Isaac's right hand and the visible white lines of power that pulsed between his fingertips. "She's on hell's radar because of the deal she made of her own free will. The deal she sought out."

"Isaac, this isn't helping." I wrapped a hand around his wrist.

Caden took one last drag of his cigarette and flicked the butt into the middle of the parking lot. He smirked a moment before I waved my hand to magically snuff it out and send it to the trash can. And then I realized: our actions were too in sync. Like those couples where the guy doesn't like olives so he automatically puts his on his girlfriend's plate because she likes the salty fruit. Isaac's shoulders stiffened. He hadn't missed it either.

Caden wet his lips. "I would have picked you up at your house."

I stuffed my hands in my jacket pockets to keep from fidgeting. "Dad and Chase are still up."

"Sneaking you out hasn't been a problem in the past."

Oh, dear God, shut up! I fisted my hands and concentrated on keeping my emotions under control. Isaac wasn't an idiot. If the scent of my powers turned bitter, he'd want to know what Caden was referring to and why it brought out negative emotions like panic and anger in me.

"Isaac and I were already hanging out, so this gave us more time together," I said.

"I'll come with," Isaac added. "Two witches are better than one."

I forced myself not to jerk my head sideways to gawk at him. It wasn't that I wouldn't have liked him to come along—maybe Caden would realize that Isaac and I went well together and back off—but there was no guarantee that the last piece of the chain was within driving distance or that Caden wouldn't mention our trip to London.

Caden's gaze lingered on me, then slid to Isaac. "As much as I appreciate the offer, I only require the services of one witch, and since Madison is bound to me, it will be her. Besides, you want me dead, and I'm not suicidal." He pushed off the back bumper of his car. "I'll see to it that she gets home safely."

I laced my fingers through Isaac's and faced him. "I just want to get this over with." Raising to my tiptoes, I gave him a long, meaningful kiss. Hopefully, my public display of affection would assure him that he had nothing to worry about and convince Caden that he and I would never be more than friends. "I'll call you when I get home."

I walked to the passenger side of Caden's car. "Let's go."

We got in, and Caden started the engine.

"I like a girl who takes charge," he mused. "It's sexy."

I twisted in my seat and fixed him with an exasperated glare. "Let's get something straight. I'm here because I honor the deals I make."

"Because you have to."

"I don't have to be bound to someone to keep my word. You need to stop with the flirty comments and sly little smirks, or I'm going to go back to thinking of us as business acquaintances and not friends."

A stupid smile took over his face. "Noted."

He backed out of his parking space, and I gave Isaac one last reassuring wave.

"And no more using my dad as your personal messenger."

"You have too many rules."

"Caden, I'm serious! Thanks to you, my dad thinks there's something going on between us, and if he…" *If Dad had given me my ring back in front of Isaac…*

Caden snorted. "So what if he told Isaac I had your ring? Isaac knows about me."

"But my dad doesn't." *And Isaac doesn't know everything.* "Besides, you could have just texted me like a normal person. There was no need to sneak into my house when I wasn't home."

"Maybe if you told Isaac everything—"

"You were hoping to mess things up for me. Placing the box in my room, giving my dad my ring. You wanted them to find out we were together last night."

"Now you're being paranoid."

"Am I?" I folded my arms over my stomach and blindly watched the road. There was no way Isaac would stick around if he knew the things I'd done in the name of my contract. And my dad wouldn't want me stringing along two guys. He'd want me to choose, and until I did, he'd find a way to keep me busy, making it hard for me to see either Isaac or Caden.

Caden and I ended up at Hammond Castle, of all places. Seeing the stone structure brought my attention back to the task at hand, and the sooner we got the chain, the sooner I could get away from Caden.

"If the last piece is here, why didn't we get it the other day?" I thought about it a moment. "Is there some mystical rule stating what order they're retrieved?"

"You think too much."

I reached over the center console and rested my hand on his to keep him from turning off the engine. "Caden, it's been a long day. I didn't get much sleep." As he knew. "Would you please answer the question?"

His gaze fell to our hands, but I didn't move mine.

"The order in which I gather the pieces doesn't matter. Normally, the necklace isn't divided." He looked at me. "And the last piece isn't here. We're only leaving from here instead of the lighthouse because I got the impression you didn't want Isaac to find out how you and I get around. Or did I misread your 'shut up'?"

"You drove here for me?"

"We're friends, right? Friends keep each other's secrets."

I slid my hand from his. "You know, your caring about what I want and don't want is at odds with what you are."

Caden shrugged. "Even the devil has a soft spot."

I wasn't sure how I felt, knowing I was Caden's.

"Where are we going?" I asked, needing to change the subject.

"Columbia."

A groan passed my lips when I thought about how far South America was. "Whose idea was it to break the necklace into four pieces and scatter them across the globe?"

"Mine."

I had expected him to say that a witch had done it or maybe a human who had discovered its importance and wanted to keep it out of the wrong hands. "How did you end up with a witch's binding chain anyway?"

"One of my clients gave it to me. He had gotten it from his father."

"And this client gave it to you out of the kindness of his heart or to get out of the deal he made with you?"

"The necklace was in lieu of his soul." Caden frowned. "Do you want to hear this story or not?"

I pretended to zip my lips.

"I knew the necklace was rare. What I didn't know was just how valuable it was. As soon as word got out that I had it, I became every demon's favorite target, so I had Roxie spell another necklace. I put this fake one in a place it would be easily found. Then Roxie reversed the spell that connected the real binding chain's pieces so that we could split them up. She kept one, and two were given to humans I trusted. I buried the last piece near my old friend."

"Vladimir Godspeed. What did the other necklace do?"

"Guarantee nice weather to the wearer."

"Seriously?"

"I needed it to contain positive magic or whoever found it would have known it was a fake, but Roxie wasn't comfortable creating a good luck charm that was destined for demons, so we compromised." He shrugged.

I rubbed my temple. "Caden, why go to the trouble of hiding the chain from other demons only to turn around and give it to your boss?"

"Because, unlike most demons, my boss didn't buy my sleight of hand and, until very recently, he didn't have any leverage to demand I give it to him."

"What changed?"

"You."

"I don't understand."

"And you don't need to."

"But there's no telling how many people will die if you give your boss something that can control the Angel of Death."

"You're going to have to trust me." He turned off the engine and got out.

A disbelieving laugh bubbled up my throat. I had to be available when he called. I had to do as he said. I didn't have to trust him. A chill that had nothing to do with the frigid night slithered down my spine when I exited the car. I pulled my jacket tighter around me.

The words *I won't help you* lay like bricks on my tongue. My powers weren't going to let me refuse, though. I didn't know what angered me more, that my powers would allow me to keep a promise that might cause a lot of people to die or that I'd gotten myself in the middle of another supernatural mess.

There was one thing I did have control over. Sort of.

I raised the hood on my jacket and joined Caden on the draw-bridge. Determined not to kiss him this time, I inhaled deeply, filling my lungs to capacity before slowly releasing my breath. I would hold my breath long enough to get there. I just needed to find my center. Relax.

Caden groaned. "Not this again."

"Columbia's closer than London. I'll be fine." I drew in another breath and repeated the process.

"Do I need to remind you that you blacked out last time?"

"Practice makes perfect." I took a few more slow, deep breaths. He checked his watch as if waiting another minute would kill him. Mentally prepped, I said, "Okay. I'm ready."

Quick as lightning, his arm snaked around my waist, and he yanked my chest against his. My lips parted as a tiny *humph* escaped my mouth. Then he kissed me. His grip on me tightened as the ground slipped from beneath my feet. Caden didn't let go until the salty scent of the ocean was replaced with a spicy herbal fragrance.

I shoved him away from me. "I said I could do it on my own."

"We did it your way last time, and I ended up having to perform mouth-to-mouth resuscitation." He unbuttoned his pea coat and glanced around as if getting his bearings. "Not that I minded my mouth on yours, but I do so like when you kiss back."

I refused to dignify his comment with a reply. Instead, I pushed out a little magic and created a dozen light orbs the size of cantaloupes. We stood at the edge of a wooded area. It looked like your average forest, lush with vegetation, until I turned around.

"No way!" I pushed out more power, increasing the size of my makeshift lanterns and therefore the amount of light they cast over the area, and sent several gliding over a pool of swirling reds and vivid blues. It reminded me of the dye we used to color Easter eggs.

I ducked under a low branch and walked closer to the water. The rest of my orbs followed like obedient dogs. "What is this place?"

"The River of Five Colors."

"It's beautiful." All thoughts of how we got there were forgotten. I held my arms out to the side and twirled on my toes. "Can you feel the energy here?"

Gossamer strands of power sizzled between my fingers, and my skin tingled.

I sent a string of power into the air above us. It exploded like a firecracker. Trickling white sparks drifted to the river like shimmering confetti. "I feel as if I could walk on water."

"You're pulling power from nature."

A tentative tap of my foot on the red water sent ripples speeding toward the center of the river. I closed my eyes and concentrated on making myself light as a feather. The next time I set my foot on the water, it held my weight. I took a few steps away from shore and then turned and looked at Caden in awe. "I feel…"

"Invincible?"

I nodded a moment before I let my head fall back and raised my arms. The power that flowed through me warmed me. Was this how Isaac had felt when he'd first gained his extra power? Did he still feel this way? If I could've bottled the energy in this place, I would have.

Caden smiled. "If you like it here, you'd love Stonehenge. I could take you."

I stopped myself from saying I'd like that, and not just Stone-henge but Niagara Falls and the Grand Canyon also. Strike that. If a demon was my guide, I'd want to visit the Seven Wonders of the World. I'd want to feel the power that pulsed through these mystical places. I'd want to share the experience with my coven. I'd want them to feel as amazing as I did.

I couldn't have both, though. I couldn't travel the world with Caden and share those moments with the people closest to me.

I rejoined him on the shore, feeling more conflicted than I ever had in my life.

"Maybe one day." I tucked my hair behind my ear. "Where's the chain?"

Caden pointed to where the river cascaded over the edge of the earth. "It's at the bottom of the falls."

"Your friend's idea of protecting his piece of the chain was to toss it over the falls?" I walked closer to them and watched the water plummet in pale pink streaks to the basin below.

"He was a bit of a free spirit. Said he gave it to Mother Nature herself. Besides, he knew what I was, and he knew that when I needed it back I'd find a way to get it."

"Me." I leaned forward. The pool below was a mix of yellow and black, adding more colors to the already wondrous river.

Caden stood next to me. "You can use all that newfound energy and call it to you."

Refusal crossed my mind again, but my powers didn't even wait for me to finish the thought. They sent an eye-watering zap to my tongue before I could open my mouth.

I frowned. "I want to go on record as saying that I'm against this. That I think you should leave it at the bottom of the river, bury the other pieces, and forget you've ever seen them. No one should be able to control another person or being. It's not right."

"I'll be sure to mention your objection at the next demon council meeting." When I opened my mouth to ask him if there was such a thing, he quickly added, "There's not. But if it makes you feel better, *I've* noted it." He held his hand in front of him. "The chain, please."

"Fine." With how incredible I felt, I had no doubt I could do the spell. My gaze didn't leave his when I raised my hand and thought, *Caden's stupid trinket.* He crossed his arms over his chest and waited.

A red and orange wave arched over the top of the river and stretched toward me. It shifted into a watery hand, and I plucked a shimmering blue chain from its palm. Then the wave—its watery fingers and all—crashed back into the river.

In this place, I was strong enough to do just about anything, even magically tie Caden to a tree with invisible vines. My magic would hold him long enough for me to re-hide the chain I now held.

"I'd only tell you to give it back, and after you did, I might just leave your ass in the middle of Columbia with no money or cell phone." Caden tapped the side of his head to remind me that no thought was private when he was around.

I handed him the chain and glanced around one last time. It really was pretty here. Had I been dressed for hiking and not for the blustery winter in Massachusetts, I would have suggested we stay awhile.

Caden slipped the chain into the inside pocket of his coat. "It's better to go hiking during the day, but if you're not in a hurry to go home, we could stop at Disney World. It's on our way, and the park's open for another hour or two."

As fun as that sounded…"I don't think that's a good idea."

"You'd hike through the forest with me, but you won't go on a few measly rides if I'm by your side?"

I opened my mouth to reply, but then closed it. Hiking seemed less like a date than a trip to Disney World.

"We'd be two friends hanging out on a Thursday night," he said.

And tomorrow I'd have one more secret haunting my relationship with Isaac. "Caden—"

"I bet you could make it to Orlando without my assistance."

I bit my bottom lip. For that reason alone, I should say yes to Disney World. One hour. A few rides. If I would have been going with anyone else, I'd do it. But I didn't trust him not to be charming and fun to hang out with, and I didn't trust myself not to enjoy our time together a little too much.

I forced a yawn. "Thanks, but I didn't get much sleep last night, and I have school in the morning."

He studied me.

"What?"

"I find it interesting that when given a choice to spend time with me or kiss me, you choose the latter. I'm not sure if I should be insulted or flattered."

I play-punched his shoulder. "Shut up!"

"I'm going to go with flattered." He smirked, causing his dimple to show. "And that you secretly crave being in my arms."

"In your dreams." I had half a mind to try to zap myself home. But as powerful as I felt, I didn't want to take the chance that I'd splice myself in two or misjudge the distance and end up in shark-infested waters. "Wipe that smile off your face."

If there were any other way home, I'd take it. Unfortunately, my options were limited.

I stepped closer to Caden and slid my arm around his waist before I could change my mind. The brown in his eyes bled to red, but I'd seen this side of him too often for it to scare me. The warmth of his hand found my lower back. With his free hand, he tilted my mouth up to his.

Caden really was a good kisser. He started slow, almost teasingly. His fingers slid to the back of my head as his tongue brushed my lips, coaxing me to kiss him back. I gave in. If he wanted a real kiss, I'd give him something to remember. As the fingers of my left hand got tangled in his soft hair, the fingers on my right hand slipped inside his coat pocket. A soft moan escaped his lips when his hand cupped my face. I palmed the chain. I didn't think about what I was doing; I just did it. Our tongues did a slow ballet in our mouths as the ground beneath me vanished.

Don't think, I reminded myself as we entered the void.

Chapter 17

Facing Death

I did it. I had acted without thinking and pulled one over on Caden. The smile plastered across my face when I fell asleep announced just how proud I was of my deceit.

There was no school on Friday — teachers' institute day or something. Isaac and I lay on our backs on his bed. He held the chain above us and examined the ice-blue metal.

"What do you think it's made of?" I had stared at it last night for a long time, admiring its craftsmanship.

"I don't think it's from this earth." Isaac paused, appearing to think it over. "Fae, maybe."

Since each section of the binding chain was a different color — silver, gold, rose, and pale blue — Isaac and I believed they represented the four elements: air, earth, fire, and water. We wondered if the witches who spelled them had been part of a coven, each representing one of the four elements, and if that was important to making the talisman.

"How'd you get it?" Isaac asked.

"Caden let his guard down."

Isaac set the chain on the nightstand next to the bed. "With him able to get in our heads, I wouldn't have thought that possible."

That's because you've never kissed him.

I'd had the chain clutched in a death grip when Caden and I had arrived at my house. When he'd cupped my face with both hands, savoring the taste of our kiss as we stood inches from my bed, I had carefully slid my hand over his chest and around to his back. The guy was buff. I remember thinking that as my fingers traced the curve of his muscles. For a moment, I had been sure our kiss had passed the point of business. I wouldn't have let it go further, though. And Caden must have known that, because his hands never wandered past my arms, my back, my face. But he also must have known that his touch messed with my resolve, because I couldn't help the internal war that brewed inside me. I should have hated the feel of his hands on me. I should have pushed him away the moment my feet had hit carpet. I should have stressed that I was Isaac's girl and there would never be a him and me.

I hadn't, though.

Instead, when our kiss had ended, I'd tucked my hair behind my ear and avoided eye contact.

"Madison, you're one of a kind," Caden had said. He then kissed me one last time. It was the type of kiss that's way too short and leaves you wanting to lean in the moment it's over.

I hadn't done that either, but I think Caden knew I wanted to.

I turned to my side and propped myself up on my elbow. "Because of our deal, I can't lie to Caden. If he asks where I hid the chain, I have to answer. So, you have to hide it."

"I will."

He pulled me on top of him and brushed my hair away from my eyes. "You're as amazing as you are beautiful."

If he knew how I had distracted Caden, he wouldn't say that. "Hide it now, before Caden realizes it's gone."

Chances were Caden already knew, and I didn't have long before he came looking for me.

Isaac spun us around so that I was next to him again. "I'll be right back."

He snatched the chain from the nightstand and jogged up the steps. His footsteps echoed through the room.

I curled up with a pillow. The past week had been long, filled with hours of research and quests to gather sections of the mystical talisman that could destroy mankind. But, thanks to me and my coven, this particular binding chain would never be used to control another living or undead thing.

I had no doubt that Caden would be pissed when he discovered I'd tricked him. Up until last night, he'd always had the upper hand. I smiled, knowing that, for once, I had it.

"Take that, Demon Boy!"

I levitated my phone from the dresser into my waiting hand. Last night I had called Isaac and then Kaylee. Isaac and I had talked for close to an hour, but Kaylee hadn't answered. I figured she'd been playing video games with Shane or had fallen asleep early, so I expected a call from her this morning, but it hadn't come yet.

I had no missed calls and one missed text from Dad.

I replied to Dad, letting him know I'd pick up milk on my way home. I then texted Kaylee: *Good news, call me.*

Isaac rejoined me. "Shall we grab breakfast?"

My stomach replied with a happy growl.

It was a gorgeous day—blue skies accented with big white clouds, mid-forties. I hitched my purse higher on my shoulder and walked to the passenger's side of the Jeep, trying to decide if I wanted French toast or an omelet for breakfast. I was so wrapped up in my thoughts that I didn't notice Caden leaning against the Jeep until I walked around the front of the vehicle.

He blew a trail of smoke out the side of his mouth. "Let's go."

"You don't have an appointment, therefore she doesn't have to leave with you," Isaac said from my right.

Caden glared at him through scarlet eyes. My insides turned to a tangled mass of nerves. Gloating that I had stolen from a demon was much easier when said demon wasn't standing in front of me, looking as if he was a moment away from torching my boyfriend.

"She has something of mine, and I want it back," Caden replied with malice.

"She doesn't have it any longer." Isaac laced his fingers through mine. The feel of my hand in his helped to settle my anxiety. I squeezed, holding on to him as if my life depended on it. For all I knew, it did.

Caden took a long drag of his cigarette. Not liking the gleam in his eyes, I stepped so that I stood between him and Isaac. "I took it. If you're upset, then take your anger out on me."

He flicked his half-smoked cigarette toward the end of the driveway, but I resisted the urge to intercept it. It landed between Josh's feet. He'd just crossed the street, coming from his house. Shane was with him, baseball cap pulled low even though he wore sunglasses. His expression was bleak.

"Is Kaylee with you?" Josh asked once he and Shane were within a few steps of Isaac. If he registered the tension emanating from Caden, Isaac, and me, he didn't comment.

"I thought she'd be with you." Or home with Shane, but that was clearly not the case.

Josh ran a jerky hand through his dark mane. "We were supposed to hang out this morning."

"Maybe she's with her mom." They sometimes ran errands together.

"She was the one who told me Kaylee wasn't home."

He didn't have to tell me why he was worried. Kaylee always told him where she'd be, and if she forgot, she'd answer his calls or texts. She'd answer mine. I dug my phone from my purse—still nothing from her.

"Her car's in the driveway, and I smelled smoke and sulfur when I was sneaking out the back door." Shane took off his cap and twisted it in his hands. "Something's wrong. I can feel it in my bones."

Only one person I knew smelled like smoke.

"What did you do to her?" I shoved Caden. But because he was leaning against the Jeep, he didn't actually move. "If you hurt her!"

The taste of dirty pennies filled my mouth as my powers became overwhelmed with fear and anger. I went to push him again, but Caden grabbed my forearms. In a move quicker than the eye could follow, he had both my wrists in one ironclad grip, and his free hand around my waist. He looked at Josh. "If you hope to see Kaylee again, then meet us in the gardens at Hammond Castle in thirty minutes and bring my chain."

My struggles to break free of his hold ceased the moment we entered the void. Caden's scarlet eyes bore into me like jagged spikes, and I couldn't help but wonder if I'd pushed him too far. Kaylee was the devil-knew-where, and I might be about to join her.

Afraid Caden would let go of me, I leaned into him. I didn't want to be lost in the void. With my small lung capacity, I wouldn't survive in there long.

I expected to end up on the grounds at Hammond Castle, where Caden had told Josh and Isaac to meet us. Instead, I sucked in a lungful of stale air as I took in the patterned duvet on the four-poster bed next to us.

"Let go of me!" I sent a jolt of power into the hand holding my wrists.

Caden tightened his grip. "Do that again, and I'll play rough."

I hated to see what his idea of rough was, so I forced my powers back.

"What do I have to do to get you to stop fighting me?" Caden's words brushed my lips, hot and angry.

My fingers tingled from lack of blood. "Caden, you're hurting me."

He shoved me onto the bed and paced away without saying a word.

I sat, rubbing my wrists, and took in the dusty furniture and heavy wooden door. We were in Irene Hammond's bedroom. "Where's Kaylee?"

"Hell if I know." He said it with cold indifference. Like my best friend was insignificant.

I went to stand, but his frosty glare had me stopping with my butt an inch off the mattress and my fingers digging into the duvet. "Then, why did you bring me here?"

He ignored my question and picked up the ornate silver mirror from the dressing table. "Did you really think I'd leave you in the void?"

Yes. No. I dropped back onto the bed and pulled my bangs away from my face. "Caden, I don't know what to think."

"Because you don't know how I'll react to thievery, or because you've never trusted me?"

I pressed my lips together and studied a knot in the wood floor.

"You should trust me," Caden said.

"No one should control something as powerful as the Angel of Death, especially a demon," I spit back. Didn't he understand that? Did he not care about mankind?

Caden turned the mirror over and over in his hand as he spoke. "Last night, I felt your hand inside my pocket. I knew what you were doing."

My gaze snapped to his. "Why didn't you stop me?"

The corner of his mouth quirked upward. "That kiss was worth losing the chain for a day. Answer my question. You can't lie, so if the words pass your lips, you can be as sure as I am you answered truthfully. Did you think I'd leave you in the void?"

My powers pricked my tongue when I went to say yes. As angry as Caden had a right to be, he wouldn't kill me.

"Not really," I replied. "But if you didn't take Kaylee, then who did?"

"I have my suspicions."

Whatever they were, Caden didn't share them with me. If I were with my coven, we'd scry and find her. I wondered if Isaac and Josh were doing that or if they'd head straight here. I hoped they took a moment to prepare for what was to come. It was the smart thing to do.

I wiped a tear from my cheek. I'd never forgive myself if Kaylee was hurt.

"There is one person I hate more than my brother." Caden used his fingernail to pry a quarter-sized crest from the back of the mirror. "He'll be here tonight. So, let me make this perfectly clear. I expect you to honor our agreement without hesitation. That means you do as I say without the debate and snarky comments. You do that, and I'll do everything in my power to get Kaylee back."

I nodded. I'd have promised just about anything if it meant finding my best friend.

The red in his irises turned to the color of creamy milk chocolate. He indicated with a jerk of his head for me to come closer. I did.

"This is part of Sammael's ring." The silver shined as if it were freshly polished. A fancy six-point star rested inside a circle of symbols I didn't recognize. Caden flipped it over so that we were looking at the back. "This catch will snap into any link on the rose-colored chain."

"Why are you telling me this?"

"Because I happen to agree with you—no demon should have the power to control another supernatural being. So, when the time comes, I want to make sure *you* know how to attach it to the necklace."

"Me?"

"I've known the whereabouts of this crest for over two centuries. If I had any desire to blackmail Sammael myself, I would have done it by now. And I'm certainly not giving Alistair the chance."

I shook my head. "If you don't plan on giving the binding chain to your boss or using it yourself, then why gather the pieces? And why involve the Angel of Death of all things?"

"Because you're the leverage my boss is holding over my head. I give him this chain, or he kills you." Caden gave a sad sort of smile. "I can't allow him to have the chain, and I won't let you pay the price if I don't."

"You could have told me this. I would have helped you."

"Alistair is ruthless and power-hungry, determined to climb the corporate ladder, so to speak. He's also careful, calculating, and not accustomed to losing. I couldn't risk him sending spies who could read your mind." He rubbed a hand over his mouth. "Besides, I don't trust Isaac, and you have an annoying habit of telling him everything."

"He's my boyfriend." And I didn't tell him *everything*, but I wasn't going to correct Caden, because he already knew that and had done a poor job hiding his frown when I'd said *boyfriend*. "What do I have to do?"

He went over the order in which the links had to be connected: silver, gold, rose, and blue. I'd been right; they represented the elements of air, earth, fire, and water. When he finished, he said, "I'm trusting you, Madison. I need to know that you trust me too."

He didn't ask it as a question. I could lie to him and to myself.

I wanted to trust Caden. I wanted to believe he wasn't evil. That he was the caring person I'd grown to know over the last few months. Yes, he was a demon. And, yes, he made deals that cost people their souls. But he was also the demon that had talked a now-famous writer out of trading her soul for recognition. He was the demon who had friends that respected him. He was the demon who had bent the rules to save the kid brother of a girl he hadn't really known.

Thinking back on our time together, Caden had never threatened me. Nor had he asked me to do anything that would stain my soul. He could have, and I would have had to obey. More importantly, I believed he'd help us find Kaylee.

I owed him a chance to prove he was one of the good guys. Didn't I?

His eyebrow slithered upward and got lost under his dark hair, no doubt listening to my thoughts.

"I trust you." I was ninety percent sure I meant it. "Please don't let that be a mistake."

He slipped the crest into the pocket of his jeans. "Promise you won't think about the crest until I tell you to." When I hesitated, he added, "I'm not the only one who can read minds."

"Fine, I promise."

Caden watched out the window for Josh, Isaac, and Shane to arrive. Several minutes passed in silence before he said, "Your friends have trust issues."

I followed his gaze to the gardens below. Isaac stood with his feet shoulder-width apart, head back, and arms out to his side. A thick stream of power traveled over the grass around him, quickly drawing an oversized orange pentagram.

Josh added a series of squiggly lines between the points of the star with a few flourishes of his hand. Shane walked in a large circle around them, placing flat stones at the top and bottom of the symbol.

"What are they doing?" I asked.

"Setting a demon trap."

The orange glow of Isaac's and Josh's magic faded, and I realized the rocks marked the trap's location. Caden's scent turned smoky, and his vow to set Isaac aflame if he tried to send him to hell replayed in my mind.

"Caden, you know they're just doing what they think is necessary to ensure Kaylee's and my safety."

"So am I." His cold glare slid to me. "Stay by my side, and I won't turn them to ash."

He transported us to the gardens, where we arrived several yards from my friends.

"Where's Kaylee," Josh asked.

Shane's eyes narrowed. His hands were fisted at his side, and his stance gave the impression that he was just as dedicated to getting Kaylee back as Josh and I were.

"I'm sure she'll be along in a few minutes." Caden held out his hand. "I'll take my chain."

Isaac pulled it from his pocket and held it out. "Come and get it."

Caden's gaze dropped to the grass around them. "And become your prisoner? Not going to happen. But play nice, and I'll let you test your trap on our guest of honor." Caden wiggled his fingers. "Toss the chain."

"And give you our only leverage?"

Caden didn't take his eyes from the guys. "Madison, summon it."

Isaac gave a small shake of his head. The determined look in his eyes told me he had a plan, but I couldn't risk Kaylee's safety.

I hated going against my coven. Against Isaac. With a heavy heart, I drew in additional power from the gardens and held up my hand. "Chain." It appeared in my palm.

Isaac cursed.

I looked at Josh, knowing he'd back me. "Caden can help us get Kaylee back."

"He has her!" Isaac snapped.

"No, he doesn't."

Caden pulled the other pieces of the necklace from his pocket. "The three of you can fight me, or you can step over here and help Madison build her circle before the others arrive."

Isaac and Josh exchanged a curious look.

"You want us to put up a protective barrier?" Josh asked as if he hadn't heard Caden correctly.

"I will be staying inside it," Caden replied.

Shane was the first to move. Caden waited until Isaac and Josh were within ten feet of us to tell them that was far enough. Shane stood between me and my coven.

Just wanting the evening over with, I raised my arms above my head. "By the power of air."

"By the power of water," Josh said.

"By the power of fire," Isaac declared.

Together we closed our circle. "We shall cast with the powers of three times three."

A translucent orange line raced around us and closed with a faint snap. Nothing could get in as long as the line remained solid.

Caden cupped my left hand in his and placed the chains in my upturned palm. "The outcome of this night depends on you remembering our deal. Do as I say."

"I know."

Caden pulled an army knife from his pocket. Isaac and Josh rushed forward, making it a few steps before a wall of hellfire erupted in front of them.

"We're on the same team," Caden reminded them.

Isaac took a cautious step forward. The flames in front of him grew taller.

"It's okay," I assured him. "The spell only takes a few drops of blood."

Caden had told me this when he'd gone over the steps needed to connect the different sections. Blood was what bound them, but since the necklace had been forged by white magic, it didn't require much.

Nonetheless, my right hand trembled as I held it up.

"Let me mask the sting of the blade," Caden whispered.

He didn't have to tell me how he'd do it. By now, I'd spent enough time with him to know.

"No." When he hesitated, I said, "I'll be fine."

Caden placed his hand under mine. I fought not to yelp as the blade cut a long gash into my palm.

"Do it exactly as I told you," Caden said.

I laid the first two sections of the necklace on my bleeding hand, wincing at the pang that shot through me. I couldn't help it. The metal against the fresh gash was like salt in an open wound. It stung something fierce.

With the last link in the silver chain touching the first in the gold one, I curled my fingers around them.

"Blood to bind, two into one."

A white glow seeped through my fingers. When I opened them, a shimmering red link connected the two chains.

I repeated the process until the necklace was whole. Caden took it and, with his back to the guys and his fire helping to block their view, slipped it over my head. He lifted my hair from beneath it, allowing the cold metal to touch my skin. He then zipped my jacket so the chain was hidden. "Not a word to Isaac or Josh that you have it. And for what it's worth, I'm sorry about this next part."

"What next part? Caden?"

He didn't answer. The fire between us and my coven vanished. Caden motioned for Shane to come closer. "Are you willing to do whatever it takes to find Kaylee?"

"Yes." Shane squared his shoulders.

"Good, then I won't feel as bad about doing this." Caden plunged the knife into Shane's abdomen and twisted.

Chapter 18

Hades' Servants

I screamed. Isaac and Josh rushed forward and caught Shane under his arms, easing him to the ground.

"It's okay," Shane murmured as his eyes rolled into the back of his head.

"Like hell it is!" Josh bit out.

Isaac pressed his hands over the gaping wound. Vanilla and spearmint filled the air as he attempted to heal Shane.

"Calls across the void are tricky. They require the blood of a fatal wound," Caden said in way of explanation. "Shane's a ghoul. The wound won't actually kill him."

"That doesn't make stabbing him all right!" I dropped to my knees. Shane's body convulsed uncontrollably. Ghoul or not, I could tell he was in pain.

Caden held the knife point down, letting Shane's blood drip into his waiting palm. "Would you have preferred I rammed my knife into one of your coven members?"

"I would have preferred you didn't stab anyone!" I squeezed Shane's hand to let him know I was there.

Caden mumbled what I assumed were the Latin words needed to place a long-distance call to Hades. When his lips stilled, he curled the fingers of his left hand over the blood and, with his right hand, tossed the knife. It arched through the air and pierced the center of Isaac's demon trap.

Shane's fingers grew slack, and the little color he had drained from his face.

Josh tore off his own jacket and stuffed it under Shane's head. "Hold on, buddy."

Isaac and Josh's reaction to Shane being stabbed told me they'd grown to like the kid as much as Kaylee and I had. I hated seeing him in pain and prayed it was true that ghouls weren't easily killed. Caden hadn't told me this part of the plan, and I suspected it was because I would have refused to allow it. There had to be more than one way to contact his boss.

A tear slid down my cheek and landed on Shane's jacket, leaving a dark spot. "Don't you dare die! Not after all that talk of how you want to stay."

Shane's hand twitched in mine. I held my breath and waited. Several moments passed. Then Shane's fingers curled loosely around mine. "It's working."

Isaac lifted his blood-coated hand from the wound. Shane had a hole the size of a walnut in his side, but he was no longer bleeding. Isaac rested his hand over the cut. The scent of his powers grew stronger. Shane moaned.

Josh pressed two fingers against Shane's wrist. "His pulse is getting stronger."

"Of course it is." Caden opened his left hand and set the remaining blood on fire. "He can't die of a stab wound, but I'm glad you're helping the process along."

"Stab him again, and I'll ram that knife of yours up your—"

"Isaac! Not helping!" I glowered at Caden. "And you! No more stabbing people."

"Well, this is an interesting scene," Derek called from our right.

He had Kaylee's arm held in an ironclad grip. She tried to jerk free from his grasp. When that didn't work, she slammed the heel of her sneaker into the toe of his fancy black boot.

Josh jumped up, but Isaac was just as quick to block his path.

"Stay within the circle." Isaac shoved Josh away from the orange line that marked the edge of our protected space. "You can't help her if you're dead."

Shane's groan brought my attention back to him. His eyes fluttered open.

"Did we win?" he asked.

"Not yet." The real battle hadn't begun, but Shane would figure that out soon enough. I helped him sit up, glad to see he really was all right.

Shane glanced from his blood-stained jacket to Caden in awe. "I know everyone's been saying I can't die, but I didn't really believe it before now."

When Caden didn't respond with one of his snarky comebacks, I pivoted so that I could see what had his attention. A man who could have passed for a member of the secret service stood to our left. His dark suit was neatly pressed, his expression somber, and his short blond hair parted on the side and combed back. He remained motionless, back straight, and with one hand holding his wrist in front of his body as he surveyed the area. The knife Caden had used was in the ground near his feet. He had to be Caden's boss.

"Your spells won't work." Derek pulled Kaylee closer to him. His red glare pinned me and my friends with a look of pure evil.

I peered back at Josh and Isaac, sure one of them had tried to teleport Kaylee away from Derek and into our circle. Derek positioned himself so that Kaylee stood between him and us. Smart guy, I thought, because Isaac and Josh wouldn't hesitate to strike if it meant getting Kaylee away from him.

To Kaylee, I asked, "Are you okay?"

She stopped squirming. "Yeah."

Caden's boss eyed me up and down. "So, this is the witch in hell's debt."

"In my debt, Alistair," Caden corrected him. He grabbed my arm and yanked me to my feet.

Isaac and Josh stood near the inner edge of the circle—Isaac's gaze locked on me and Josh's on Kaylee. Shane went to stand, swayed, and ended up in a crouch between us.

"How about a trade?" Alistair said. "My witch—" he glanced at Kaylee "—for yours? And I'll be wanting her contract amended to make it official."

"What?" I stammered. That was not the deal. He wanted the chain, which he'd still get.

Caden slid his hand around my back and placed it on my hip—casually, like he was claiming a trophy—and whispered so that only I could hear him, "Stop thinking."

I looked at him. His eyes begged me to trust him. To stifle my runaway thoughts, I sang to myself.

"I'll take the chain too," Alistair added, not hiding his amusement. If it was at my silent singing or my shock at finding out he wanted me *and* the chain, I didn't know.

"Keep singing," Caden warned. He spoke so low I almost didn't hear him. He then pressed something cold and small into the palm of my hand. "You promised not to think about this."

My fingers curled around the object without thought—like my powers controlled my movements.

Louder, Caden said, "It's Madison's choice. If she's willing to make the trade, then so be it."

"No!" Isaac sprinted forward, no longer willing to let the scene play out. Caden let go of me, spun around, and ended up nose to nose with Isaac.

"Madison, make a decision," Caden demanded as he held Isaac back.

Josh raked his hands through his hair. His gaze bounced between Kaylee and me. This wasn't what he wanted. I knew that. He loved Kaylee unconditionally, but he loved me too. We'd grown up together, and I was as much an adopted sibling to him as he was to me.

"I have to do this." My voice came out much quieter than I meant it to. I wanted to sound strong, but that was hard to do when I knew I was about to walk into a tiger's den.

"Madison, we'll find another way," Isaac insisted.

Caden pushed him backward.

I wanted to tell Isaac that it would be okay. That Caden had a plan that I wasn't allowed to think about yet. Instead, I just kept singing to myself, though the song in my head changed to "Don't Fear the Reaper."

"I love you," I said to Isaac. My heart broke when a tear ran down his cheek.

Caden nodded for me to do it. I couldn't stop myself from thinking *I'm trusting you.* The quirk of his lips was enough to get my legs moving.

Derek said something to Kaylee and let her go. They argued a minute. I was pretty sure I heard him growl, "You will," a moment before he shoved her in my direction.

Josh still had his arms over his head and an expression of utter helplessness on his face.

Two more steps and I'd be out of our circle. Fingers clutched mine, and I looked to my side.

"I'll go with you," Shane said. I squeezed, thankful to have someone I knew next to me.

"Madison," Kaylee's voice cracked. "You don't have to do this."

"Yes, I do." And I continued singing.

There was a lot of trust going on, and I still wasn't convinced that it would save us all *and* keep the binding chain out of Alistair's hands.

As soon as Shane and I stepped over the line that created our circle, Josh rushed forward and grabbed Kaylee, pulling her inside the protected space. Caden struggled to hold Isaac back. I could hear Isaac begging me not to do this, but if I turned back now, we'd be trapped in a ten-foot circle with demons waiting for our barrier to collapse. That was if they waited. I'd had one of my circles infiltrated when I had fought the Prince of Fae. I wouldn't risk my friends' safety.

Alistair held out his hand.

"Think of it now," Caden yelled.

And like a veil lifted from my consciousness, I looked at the crest in my hand. Caden's plan came back to me in a rush. I glanced over my shoulder in time to see fire encircle Josh and Isaac, making them Caden's prisoner. He'd done it to keep them from interfering. I liked to think the fiery cage kept them from doing something that would get them killed.

Everything after that moment happened at once.

Alistair sent a line of fire racing toward me. It hit an invisible wall a few feet in front of Shane and me. Derek stared at something behind me. I turned to see Kaylee with her hands raised, palms facing out, and I realized it was her spell that kept Alistair's hellfires from reaching me and Shane. I yanked the binding chain from beneath my jacket and snapped the crest into one of the rose-colored links. Caden appeared by my side and recited the incantation that would summon the Angel of Death.

"I'm sorry," I whispered to Shane. "But I promise it's only temporary."

I repeated what Caden had said, careful to enunciate each Latin word exactly as he had. The ground quivered. Derek winked at me and then vanished, not sticking around for what would come next.

Alistair flickered in and out of view as if he was trying to escape too. His gaze locked on Isaac, who chanted a spell I'd never heard before.

Caden smirked. "I told him he'd get to use his trap."

And it worked perfectly. Alistair wasn't going anywhere.

The sky above us grew dark and stormy as lightning illuminated the shroud of clouds with streaks of blue and purple. Alistair tried more desperately to escape, crashing into the invisible walls of his prison. A particularly bright bolt of lightning struck the ground in front of me, splitting the earth. My foot slipped into the newly formed crevice. My arms flailed as I tried to regain my balance. The gap in front of me seemed to get swallowed by the depths of the earth. Before my mind could register just how deep it was, I was jerked backward.

"Careful," Caden said from behind me.

His arm pinned me to his chest as we stumbled to solid ground.

Another bolt of lightning blasted the earth. Dirt and grass shot upward. In the wake of the strike stood a hooded figure. My coven screamed for me to reenter our circle, but I had to see this through.

Shane was gone. I hoped he'd forgive me for using him to complete the spell—a soul for a soul. But I couldn't send a member of my coven—a living person—to the void.

I swallowed the lump in my throat and rubbed my sweaty hands on my jeans. The Angel of Death lowered his hood. His dark eyes fixated on the chain around my neck, giving me time to take in his gray hair, pallid skin, and gaunt face. He reminded me a little of the frail old man that lived down the block from me. Only, Sammael gave off an eerie energy. It sucked the belief that things would be okay right out of me.

"Madison, you can control him," Caden said.

Sammael's gaze traveled to Caden and back to me. "You dare summon me?"

"We need your help," I managed to say.

"Do you think I care about the trivial problems of a witch or a demon?"

"No." Why should he? Sammael was as old as time. He'd seen species come and go. Why would he care if evil threatened to take over mankind? In his presence, I realized how hopeless the battle I fought was. As long as there were demons, we were all in danger.

"But you have free will," Caden said in answer to my thoughts. "Mankind has free will. That's the power given to them." He turned his attention to Sammael. "And as long as she wears that chain, you'll listen to her."

Caden's voice was much stronger than mine had been. It gave me the courage I needed to finish what we'd started.

I took a deep breath and tried to mimic his confident tone. "An angel should be interested in a demon who's trying to use magic to gain power."

Sammael's glare fell on Caden.

Caden raised his hands as he took a step backward. "She's not referring to me. Notice, even though the chain she wears is mine, I'm not the one donning it. I've no wish to make enemies. Alistair, on the other hand, has been waiting centuries for a chance to become king of hell." Caden indicated to his boss with a jerk of his thumb.

Alistair slammed his fists against the invisible wall created by the demon trap, testing various points for a weak spot. He found none.

I went on. "Just like I can't break a promise and Caden is bound to honor the deals he makes, Alistair has been given a limited reach." That was why more demons weren't walking around topside and why Alistair had to wait until he could blackmail Caden to make his move for more control over hell and earth. "A demon shouldn't be allowed to control a witch or anyone else, human or otherwise."

"And yet a witch created a talisman that would allow one to do just that," Sammael remarked.

"I'm sure they didn't expect it to fall into the wrong hands." I rubbed the crest that bound him to me. "The rules that govern the supernatural are there to keep any one creature from becoming too powerful. They're checks and balances, aren't they?"

Sammael inclined his head in way of answer.

"You're one of the few beings strong enough to stop a demon that breaks these rules."

"My job is to reap souls, not settle your disputes."

"He'll never stop until he has me and the chain I now wear around my neck." My gaze traveled from Alistair to Sammael. "You could easily become his servant. I can't allow him to have that much power. And I highly doubt you want to become a demon's puppet. Like it or not, you need me as much as I need you. Caden and I are prepared to return your crest to you. All we ask is that you stop Alistair."

Alistair's face drained of color. "An angel has no control in hell."

"Lucky for us, you're no longer hiding in hell," Caden spat.

Sammael's eyes narrowed as he studied me. I wore the binding chain. I could demand he do as I say, but I didn't think it would be a good idea to force the Angel of Death into doing my bidding. So, when Caden had told me his plan, I suggested we ask Sammael for his help instead of using the power of the chain to control him. I reasoned that I would eventually have to release him, and I, for one, didn't want to become his enemy.

I shifted my weight from one foot to the other and fought the urge to run back to my friends. Sammael might follow, and I wouldn't risk putting them in even more danger. I hoped if Caden's plan failed, they'd remain unharmed.

The very air around us seemed poisoned by Sammael's presence, as if he could take the life of those near him at will. I wondered what mystical rule bound him from doing just that, doubting it was the talisman of a witch or his love for the supernatural. I prayed that despite what this creature in front of me was, he preferred to let death come to the living naturally.

If only he looked more like my kind old neighbor. But Sammael was skin and bones, his body worn by a never-ending existence.

"It's a fair deal," Caden said, breaking the uncomfortable silence.

"Very well." Sammael raised a wrinkled hand. "Return my crest, and I will end Alistair's reign."

"End Alistair's reign, and we'll give you the crest," Caden countered.

Sammael's indifferent gaze fell on me. Its weight had me swallowing audibly. "You'll make it so Alistair will never be able to return to cause me or my friends harm?"

"You have my word," Sammael said.

"Madison, you can end your contract with Caden too," Isaac called.

Isaac might have been right. If the Angel of Death took Caden and his boss, I might be free of demons forever, but I'd be no better than Alistair.

Out of the corner of my eye, I saw the flames around Isaac stretch higher.

I reached next to me and wrapped a hand around Caden's wrist. "He means well."

"For who?"

"Please." I jerked my head at the ring of fire that was still growing. "That's not necessary." When Caden didn't lower the wall, I added, "I promise I have no intention of betraying your trust." *And we don't have time for you and Isaac to go at it.*

Caden's shoulders slumped forward. "Fine."

Isaac's cage returned to a waist-high flame.

I frowned at the angel in front of me and hoped I was making the right decision. "Are you a man of your word?"

"I'm not a man at all." Sammael raised his hand. "My crest."

I looked at Caden.

"You know my feelings on this," Caden replied.

Caden didn't like to leave things up to chance. That was why he'd chosen to use Sammael against his boss.

"Know your enemy," he had said while we'd still stood in Irene's bedroom. "Then go into battle with the bigger sword."

He'd known he couldn't beat Alistair in a fair fight. So, Sammael was Caden's sword, metaphorically speaking.

"And I have a weapon no person — human, demon, or otherwise — can beat," he had added just before he'd told me his plan.

I rubbed the crest between my fingers and looked over my shoulder. Kaylee bit the nail of her right thumb. Josh shook his head. Isaac's gaze flashed to Caden before holding mine. "Madison —"

The fire around him flared and crackled, drowning out the rest of his words.

"Caden," I hissed. "Not helping."

Sammael cleared his throat. His hand still held out, waiting for his crest.

I wet my lips and unclipped the crest from the binding chain. "I'm taking you at your word that you will honor our agreement."

The crest fell into his waiting hand. Gingerly, he gripped it in two gnarly fingers and examined it. "I'd given up hope on seeing this again."

Caden had said Sammael would be happy to have it back. The corner of Sammael's lips rose as he snapped the crest into the silver surface of his ring. His eyes closed, and he inhaled deeply. A fine purple light radiated from his pores.

"Shield your eyes," Caden screamed as he jumped in front of me.

The next thing I knew, I was crouched low with Caden hunched over me. I could see a fierce glow through my closed eyelids. I didn't dare look until darkness came, and then I cautiously opened one eye. "Caden?"

He released me. "It's okay now."

My gaze went to my coven first. Kaylee pressed her hands to her face. Isaac and Josh stared open-mouthed at something just past me. I stood and pivoted.

The frail angel was gone, and in his place stood a man who appeared to be in his late forties. He had hair as black as a raven's feathers and an obscene amount of muscles. But that wasn't what took my breath away. Spread wide like an eagle in flight was a pair of dark wings. Sammael's gaze locked on me.

"I can see your soul. You draw upon positive emotions to fuel your powers. So, tell me, how is it that you've become involved with the likes of him." Sammael looked at Caden, not hiding his disdain for what he was.

"It's complicated," I admitted.

"Our choices often are. I've heard of you," he said to Caden. "The crossroad demon with a heart. The two don't go together."

Caden shrugged. "Sometimes people attempt to make a deal for the wrong reasons. When I see that, I simply suggest they ask themselves if what they seek is truly worth the price."

Sammael cocked his head to the side. "An honest soul doing hell's work. Who would have thought it possible?"

"You might be surprised to find I'm not the only one."

"Ah. Yes. You have a brother who I hear likes to stir things up."

Caden rubbed the back of his neck. "Well, I'm never really sure whose side he's on."

"You'd be wise to figure that out." Sammael clapped his hands together once. "Now, I do believe there is a rodent problem I promised to take care of."

Alistair's gaze traveled the width of the demon trap. "Madison, you're an honest witch. Good. Can you live knowing you're responsible for my death?"

I glanced over my shoulder at my coven. They'd never truly be safe with Caden's boss alive. Neither would my father and brother. Nor would my friends. If we let Alistair live, there was no telling what he'd do next. Still, could I live with myself, knowing I'd ordered his execution?

Sammael walked through the demon's trap as if it weren't there. He wrapped his long fingers around Alistair's throat. "Let me make it easy on her conscience. I'm doing this regardless of her reply."

Sammael and Alistair vanished.

"If it makes you feel better, you really didn't order Alistair dead. I did."

I looked at Caden, brow furrowed.

"You were merely following my directions." He smiled, all teeth and dimple. "You are my Beck-and-Call Witch."

"Yeah, well, I think I've earned myself a break. Say a year."

"I'll give you twenty-four hours."

"A month."

"Seven days, and that's my final offer."

One week of demon-free duties. "I'm going to hold you to that."

I rocked from toe to heel, wondering what we'd do now. Then I realized I'd almost forgotten about a promise I had made.

"What about Shane?" I had no idea how to get him back.

A tap on my shoulder startled me. I turned to find Shane smiling.

I flung my arms around him. "I'm sorry I used you like that. I promise I'll never do that again."

He hugged me back. "You can use your seven-day break to find a way to get me home with my parents."

"Deal."

Then Kaylee's arms were around us. "You did it!"

"Thanks to your help," I said.

I caught Caden staring at us, so I let go of my friends and straightened my jacket. "Do you think you can release the guys?"

"Personally, I prefer them caged."

I put my hands on my hips and frowned at him.

He held up his hand and wiggled his fingers. "My chain."

I slipped it over my head and gave it to him.

"Have them help you fix the fissure." Caden glanced at Isaac and Josh, and their fiery prison sank into the ground. He vanished before I could thank him.

Josh and Isaac sprinted over to us.

Isaac pulled me to him, lifting me to my toes. "I thought I was going to lose you."

He might have, had Caden lied to me or had Sammael held a grudge. The familiar scent of Isaac's cologne eased the last of the tension from my muscles. It also made me realize he had tightened his hold on me.

"Can't…breathe," I managed to croak.

"Sorry." He let me slide down the front of his body.

"Don't you ever do something like that again," Josh scolded. He had an arm draped over Kaylee's shoulders and a grin on his face that told me how relieved yet proud he was.

I laughed. "Trust me; I have no intentions to."

Isaac gingerly grabbed my hand. "You're bleeding."

My palm hurt too, but instead of complaining, I said, "It's not as bad as it looks."

Isaac ran his thumb alongside the cut, slowly circling the wound. Vanilla and spearmint enveloped us. His touch was soothing, and my hand tingled as the skin knitted together. When all that was left was a red smear of blood, he tenderly kissed my palm.

"Thank you," I said.

"Madison." He brushed my hair away from my face. "You could have been killed."

"But I wasn't, and I have you, Josh, Kaylee—" I reached next to me and laced my fingers through Shane's "—and Shane to thank for that."

Caden too, I added silently.

Josh rubbed the back of his head. "What do you think the people who run this place are going to say when they see the backyard?"

"Ah, yeah, about that." I crinkled my nose. "We can't leave the hole in the ground."

Isaac and I waved our hands over the cleft. It took an extra push of power before the earth grew back together is if zipped by an unseen hand.

Things weren't quite over, though. Caden still had the chain. Shane still needed a home. And a bunch of ghosts still guarded a coffin that should have been buried six feet underground.

But tonight was a victory—we'd kept Alistair from getting his hands on a binding chain. That was cause for celebration.

Chapter 19

Double Life

After a much-deserved victory dinner at a diner not far from Hammond Castle, we went to the cemetery to take care of Shane's casket. We weren't alone. Jeremy McGregor, Candace Cromwell, and the ghost of the woman we'd met before were there. They had kept their word and made sure no one tripped over the unseen casket. As soon as we put it back where it belonged, Kaylee planned on finding out what they needed from her.

Jeremy and Shane gathered around the gravesite with Isaac and Josh. Kaylee and I leaned against the back of a headstone and watched as our boyfriends did their thing. The ghosts of Candace and the woman — Carrie Nelson, we learned — huddled close to Kaylee and me for a little girl talk.

"Do you think we should help them?" Kaylee asked when Josh let out a disappointed grunt, his most recent spell having failed to accomplish what it was meant to do.

I couldn't lie; I was glad Isaac and Josh didn't walk up, wave a hand over the casket, and *poof*, they were done. It sort of made me feel better about my magic that it was taking them time to figure this one out.

"Probably," I replied to Kaylee's question. At the very least, we'd learn how to properly bury something. If it weren't for the events of the last few weeks, I would have said it was a skill we'd never need, but the truth was, one never knew what spells would come in handy.

"But I'd rather hear more about where Derek took you." I dropped my voice. "Did you kiss him?"

I'd been dying to ask her that since she'd told us she had spent the afternoon as a prisoner in Derek's apartment in Cabo San Lucas. I got the feeling she'd downplayed his hospitality for the guys' sakes, because her cheeks had a little more color to them — as if she'd spent most of her time on the balcony, soaking up the sun — and she had picked at her burger and fries during dinner. Not at all the behavior of a person denied sustenance.

Candace and Carrie moved closer, waiting to hear the answer.

"No." Kaylee glanced at the guys. "It was more of a snatch and grab."

"Did he molest you?" Candace asked.

"No! Jeesh!" Kaylee wrapped her arms around herself. "Derek was upfront with me. He told me that his boss wanted additional leverage, and he knew Madison and I are best friends."

I already knew this from our conversation at dinner. Derek had kidnapped her, brought her back to his place, and given her two options: be a compliant prisoner for a few hours, or be gagged, tied to the bed, and left there until she was needed. Kaylee had chosen option number one.

She kicked her heel into the ground. "I don't think Derek's as bad a person as he wants everyone to believe. I mean, in class he skipped ahead in our books to the molecular structure of various items. It was hard and boring, but I think he realized I knew what he was, and he was counting on me reading every word of that chapter to keep him out of my head. What I learned in his lessons helped me visualize the magical wall I threw up between you and Alistair. I was able to picture the molecules in the air solidifying to create a wall."

"That's how you were able to cast the spell from within the circle." I had known it was her spell that had protected Shane and me from Alistair's fire. But normally we stood in front of the spot where the barrier was to be raised, not half a basketball court away.

"And even though Derek denied it, I think you were right," she said.

"About what?"

"Derek was here to protect his brother. You know what else I think?" When I shook my head, she said, "He helped us because Caden cares about you."

"She's dating the one with the muscles, isn't she?" Candace whispered to Carrie.

"I think so," Carrie replied just as quietly.

I'd almost forgotten they were there.

Kaylee pointed a finger at them. "Not a word of this conversation to anyone, dead or alive, or I'm not helping you."

Candace pretended to zip her lips. Carrie drew an imaginary X over her translucent heart.

"Speaking of that…" Kaylee dug her phone from her purse. "It looks like we're almost done here."

Sure enough, Shane's casket slowly sank into the ground. Isaac and Josh high-fived.

Kaylee looked at Candace. "Tell me how I can help you."

I strolled over to Isaac, leaving Kaylee to gather the details. It was her help they wanted, not mine. She was the necromancer, therefore the one they trusted.

I gave a nod at the vanishing casket. "How'd you do it?"

"Quicksand. It was Shane's idea." Isaac draped an arm around my shoulders, and we watched the last few inches of the casket get swallowed by mushy dirt.

"You'll have to teach me that one."

He pulled away. "Please tell me you're not planning on raising any more dead people."

I swatted his shoulder playfully. "Of course not."

Isaac waited a full minute before he stuck a branch in the soil of the gravesite. Satisfied that the casket was far enough below the surface, he reversed the spell they'd done to cause the ground to become the consistency of quicksand. Then I used my powers to cover it with the same straw-looking grass as the rest of the cemetery.

"Not bad." Isaac wrapped me in a hug.

"Thanks."

Kaylee strolled over to us.

"Ready to get out of here?" Josh asked.

"Yeah."

"What about them?" I glanced at our ghostly friends.

She held up her phone. "I have a list of what they'd like me to do. Nothing too difficult. If it will help them find peace, then it will be worth my time."

"This is why I love you. You have a big heart." Josh kissed her.

Jeremy glided closer. "You know, her aura is like a beacon to us ghosts."

"Stick around much longer, and she's going to have a line of spirits wanting her help," Candace added.

"Right." I looped an arm through Kaylee's. "Maybe we should call it a night."

We thanked Jeremy, Candace, and Carrie for keeping an eye on the casket. Shane left with Josh and Kaylee, and Isaac dropped me off at my house.

I sat cross-legged in the middle of my bed, eyes closed, breathing slow, controlled breaths. The idea was to clear my mind so that I could get a good night's sleep, which would have been a perfect end to the day.

If it had worked.

I woke drenched in sweat, pulse pounding in my ears, and with Caden's hands on my shoulders. I was sitting with one leg over the edge of my bed as if I'd been ready to get up.

I only remembered snippets of the dream: the enchanted forest, Reed with his hand out, waiting for me to take it. I closed my eyes in an effort to still my racing heart, but I heard Reed's voice coaxing me to join him and snapped them open.

"You're trembling." Caden pulled me into an embrace.

"It was only a dream." But I let him hold me. I needed to feel grounded to the here and now until the chill inside me subsided.

"Madison, let me help you."

"I'm fine." My words were muffled by his shoulder.

"You're infuriating, that's what you are." He leaned away and looked me in the eyes. "You do realize that if it weren't for me, you'd probably have opened the door to Sanctus by now. Reed would have won."

I peered at Caden through a curtain of sweat-drenched bangs. "Then I guess it's a good thing that I'm stuck with you for the next twenty-five years."

He brushed my hair away from my eyes with his hands. "What's ten more?"

"Years I don't need to commit to, because I can beat the dreams on my own."

"You're stubborn."

I twitched a shoulder. Maybe I was. "Earlier today, you left before I could thank you. So, thank you…for everything."

"You're welcome."

I twisted my hands around the comforter. I wanted to ask him why he'd risked everything for me. He knew another witch — one who thought highly of him and helped him when he asked. He didn't need me. He could have handed me over to his boss, kept his binding chain safely hidden, and avoided the drama. Deep down, though, I already knew the answer to that question, and I wasn't ready to hear him say it. So, instead, I asked, "Have you talked to your brother?"

"Nope, and don't plan to."

"He helped Kaylee with her powers. He wouldn't have done that if he wanted to hurt you."

"I'm sure there was an ulterior motive."

"Yeah, me too — to keep his little brother alive." When Caden huffed, I said, "Derek told me about your father and why he killed him."

"Then you know why he hates me."

"He wouldn't tell me what happened next." I rested a hand on his knee. "Caden, how'd you guys end up demons?"

He rubbed a hand over his face. "We used to be thick as thieves. Hell, we were thieves. Only stole enough to feed ourselves and our mother and never from those who'd miss it."

Not his father.

"No, not our father. Derek was arrested for his murder. There was no denying he'd done it. Several people saw him ram the knife through his chest. They threw him in jail. Back in the fourteen hundreds, there was no such thing as three square meals. Those imprisoned either died of hunger or died of disease. Either way, it was a death sentence.

"I tried pleading for his life. When that didn't work, I tried to break him out. Not so easy, and I nearly got myself a cell of my own. I lost hope."

"What did you do?"

"I prayed to the heavens. When Derek remained imprisoned, I prayed to whoever would listen." His eyebrows rose and fell as if to say that wasn't his best idea. "Alistair answered. He promised not only to free Derek, but immortality for us both if we agreed to work for him. To tell you the truth, I didn't believe he was a real demon. I pictured him as a rich landowner—a duke or possibly a lord. Figured he overheard me praying."

"And you agreed?"

"Not at first. I had to check with my brother. Alistair was able to arrange a private meeting between Derek and me."

"And Derek didn't like the idea," I guessed.

"He said he'd rather die than sell his soul to the devil." Caden paused. "I couldn't stand the idea of leaving him to die. And I was probably a little selfish. I didn't want to live without my brother. So, I made the deal anyway. Derek swore he'd never forgive me."

"I think he has."

"I doubt it, but I'm glad he didn't hurt Kaylee."

Silence fell around us. It was just before two in the morning, but I didn't want to fall back to sleep.

Caden popped off the bed, pulling me up with him. "Come run an errand with me."

"Caden, it's the middle of the night."

"That didn't stop you before."

I rubbed the goose bumps on my arms. A distraction would help me forget my dreams. "Is it far?"

We ended up at the River of Five Colors. Although, I insisted we make a pit stop in Orlando, Florida, so that we wouldn't have to kiss in order for me to make it there. We landed in front of Cinderella's castle. Remembering his previous request to visit there, I suggested we wander while I caught my breath. I even enchanted a couple of rides so that our trip would be complete.

Now we stood on the banks in Columbia. A few dozen orbs hovered around us, providing light.

"I love this place." I twirled in a circle, absorbing energy.

"I thought it might make you feel better."

"It does." The soft *swoosh* of water cascading over the falls relaxed my jumpy nerves. And, if I were to be honest, so had our stroll through Disney World.

I should have insisted we stay close to my house, but when Caden told me he was coming here, I couldn't resist. I kind of felt like I lived a double life—Teen Madison: daughter, sister, girlfriend, and best friend; and Witch Madison: crossroad demon's assistant, spell-caster extraordinaire, and world traveler. I selfishly wanted to be both those girls.

Caden pulled the blue piece of the binding chain from his pocket.

My mouth fell open. "You broke it apart again!"

I instinctively looked at my palm. Only a faint salmon-color line remained as evidence I'd been cut, but I still remembered how much it had stung.

"Roxie did it for me. I already told you that I agreed with you. No one should have complete control over another being—human or otherwise. Want to do the honors?" He gave a jerk of his head toward the falls.

"You're putting the pieces back where we found them?"

"Most." He took my hand and dropped the chain into my palm. "Maybe you could use your powers to make sure it sinks to the bottom."

I held it up, admiring the ice-blue metal. Even though it had been in Caden's pocket, it was cool to the touch. "This is my favorite link. Is it from Sanctus?"

Caden nodded. "When the binding chain was given to me, there was a blue orchid dangling from that section. I still have it somewhere."

"I bet it's beautiful." I raised my arm over my head and paused. "Are you sure about this?"

"Just make sure it sinks."

I mumbled an incantation and then whipped the chain at the falls. A watery orange hand reached up and grabbed it. Then my wave disappeared into the frothy basin below. I smiled, pleased the spell had worked.

Caden and I sat along the shore and watched the flow of the water. My lights cast a bright hue, making the red and orange of the river even brighter.

"I saw you buried Shane's casket."

I gave him a sidelong glance. "You did?"

"I might have stopped by there earlier today."

"Looking for lost spirits?" I hoped he hadn't run into Jeremy and the others. They were harmless.

He chuckled in lieu of a reply. "So, what are you going to do with Shane?"

"He really wants to stay, and I sort of feel I owe it to him to let him." I'd sent him to the void, after all. And he hadn't complained or held a grudge. "I don't know. I guess we'll try the delusion and aging spells and hope for the best. It will take some work, and we'll have to change the name on his headstone at the cemetery." I tucked my hair behind my ear. "But witches don't have the ability to warp time." I paused. *Omigod!* Or should I have thought *Omidemon?* "Can demons? Can you make it so that people forget he died, have them believe he went away for treatment and his leukemia is in remission?"

Caden had saved my brother's life. He had to be able to do this. I couldn't believe I hadn't thought of it sooner. But then again, a few weeks ago, Caden and I hadn't been this close. Our relationship hadn't fully moved from employer/worker to friends. At least, I hadn't allowed myself to admit it had.

"Madison, you know the rules. A deal has to be made."

"How many years will it cost me?"

"Ten."

The same price he gave for removing the damage caused by the faerie food I'd eaten this past December. "How about a two-for-one?"

"You know I don't do that."

"Now who's being stubborn?" I frowned. "Your rule or Hades'?"

"Hades'."

That meant there was no room for negotiation. But if I had a surefire way to grant Shane's wish, I had to take it. He'd be able to start a new life, even if it was jumping back into his old one. Things could go back to normal for Kaylee and me. Well, as normal as things got these days.

"Will you do it?"

He let out a snort. "I'd rather you let me help you."

"You would be."

He was quiet a minute. I wished I knew what he was thinking. Finally, he said, "If it means that much to you, yeah, I'll do it."

"You're not going to get in trouble with your new boss, are you?" I wanted to help Shane, but not at the expense of putting another friend in the hot seat.

"Miranda's next in line, and she has a witch in her service due to a deal similar to ours."

That was a relief.

A few of my orbs flickered and dimmed, reminding me that my spell wouldn't last forever, nor could I stay at the River of Five Colors all night.

A giggle slipped past my lips, and I shook my head. I should have known I'd end up kissing Caden before the sun rose.

I took a few more minutes to enjoy the beauty around us, then asked, "Shall we seal the deal?"

Caden's fingers caressed my cheek and traveled to the back of my head where they got tangled in my hair. His mouth moved over mine with tenderness, until the first searing prick of hell's unseen quill scratched my skin. He pulled me closer, no longer holding back. Hell did play a cruel joke on its crossroad demons. On the one hand, they held extreme power. They were stronger than Fae and witches. On the other hand, they were destined to walk the earth for all eternity buying souls or services. To watch the people around them grow old and die.

What had Derek called friends? A luxury?

Even as our mouths moved as one and our tongues did a seductive dance, I could feel the scratching on my arm. It no longer hurt. It was more like having a fingernail scrape me from the inside, under my skin.

I breathed in Caden's smoky scent and focused on the way his thumb massaged my neck. His free hand had come to rest on my thigh, and I was all too aware of its warmth. I had one hand wrapped around his bicep and the other at my side, fingers curled into a fist.

It wasn't until he changed the cadence of our kiss back to soft brushes of his tongue and gentle nibbles that I realized we were no longer outside. I opened my eyes. We were in my bedroom.

His irises were red again. "Shane's parents will think he spent the night at a friend's house. When he returns in the morning, he should act as if he was only gone a day." His fingers were still tangled in my hair.

I nodded, needing a moment for my mind to catch up to my body.

"I can't erase time. He's still missed several months of school. He may need help catching up."

"My coven can do that."

"You said we're friends. I'd like to believe that we'll remain so even after you've fulfilled your contract."

"Me too." I liked having Caden in my life, even if our relationship was unconventional. He was like that crazy friend you know you should stay away from, but you just can't because, like it or not, you're drawn to his wacky antics.

"Then why not agree to another ten years and be rid of Reed's magic?"

At the rate I was adding years to my contract, I'd soon owe Caden my services even after I died of old age. But that wasn't the reason I kept refusing his help. I believed there was a way to fight Reed's magic without hell's intervention. I couldn't be the first human to have eaten faerie food and remained in our realm. If I could find a way to send Reed back to Sanctus, then I could find a way to negate the dreams. I just had to keep trying.

There was another reason. One I was willing to voice to Caden. "Like I've said before, I'd rather be your friend who you come to for help than your Beck-and-Call Witch. I'd still help you, Caden. Regardless of *what* you are, you have a good heart." I shook my head in wonder. "I wouldn't have thought that someone could be a demon and kind until I met you."

And Derek. I'd bet money he was one of the good guys too, but I didn't allow myself to think that and let Caden hear it.

Caden's lips were on mine again, moving sensually and screwing with my resolve. My stomach fluttered as my body froze. But he kept the kiss brief. Before my mind could wrap around a way to react, Caden rested his forehead against mine. "Get some rest."

And he was gone, leaving my lips tingling and my heart doing a sprint in my chest.

Thirty-five years of Caden taunting me with what could be if I allowed myself to be his girl.

I lowered myself onto my bed and swept a hand through my hair. "You are definitely going to have to find a way to ignore his charm."

I could have sworn I heard a whisper of a laugh echo through my room.

Chapter 20
The Right Choice

My fingers curled around Dad's car keys. In their place, I left a note letting him know I'd be back before he had to leave for work.

The sun was just beginning to touch the horizon. The air was brisk, but the sky was clear. It would be a nice day — chilly, but that was life in Massachusetts this time of year.

Traffic was light, so it took no time at all to get to my destination. A shade greeted me as I knelt beside Mom's grave. I'd already etched her name into the white taper candle I brought with me.

With a wave of my hand, I cleared the frost off the daisies I'd put there a few weeks ago. Something glistened in the dark red bouquet, though. I reached for it, pulling a small ice-blue orchid charm from within the stems. I ran a finger over the cool metal and knew immediately that it was from the length of chain Caden and I had hidden in the River of Five Colors.

With two fingers wrapped around the charm and two around the candle, I pushed out a little power, lighting the wick. My hand trembled as I recited the spell to call Mom's spirit forth.

The air over her grave grew hazy as if a million microscopic pale-rose dots hovered over the ground. Slowly they began to group. A willowy silhouette of a woman formed. Darker specks formed curly hair that danced on the currents of a non-existent breeze. Her eyelids fluttered open and, upon seeing me, her lips quirked upward into the smile I had missed with all my heart.

"Hi, Mom."

"Maddie." Her translucent figure was slightly paler than Candace's ghost had been. Unlike Candace, Mom's soul was in the afterlife. So, what I'd managed to call forth was Mom's spirit, not her ghost on earth. "It's good to see you."

"You too." Happy tears blurred my vision, so I sniffed and wiped them away with the back of my fingers. "You don't seem surprised to be here."

Mom giggled. The molecules that made up her delicate form scattered and reappeared with her sitting crossed-leg in front of me. "My dear, sweet girl, I never left you, though I know it may seem that way. I've watched you and Dad and Chase. You've grown into a beautiful young lady." She paused. "Or should I say witch?"

"You know?" Of course she knew. I set the candle on the ground next to us. "Did you embrace the powers?"

Mom's eyes widened. "I didn't know magic was real until that day I watched you nearly burn down the house testing yours."

I bit my bottom lip. That was the day I had learned that magic existed and that Isaac and Josh also possessed the powers.

"I'm sorry."

She studied me. "For what?"

I picked at the grass as I spoke. "For being angry with you when you died, for giving Dad such a hard time like it was his fault, and for resenting Chase." After Mom had died, I'd hated the world: Dad for getting Mom pregnant, Mom for not being strong enough to survive childbirth, Chase for being born. I had even been angry with my friends for trying to comfort me. It had taken me a long time to realize the hatred that burned inside me was grief and that the same people I had been pushing away were the ones who were making sure Mom's memory didn't die along with her. I swiped at a tear. "I was pretty hard to live with when you left."

"But you got past that, and you've grown into a wonderful young lady that I'm so very proud of." Her ghostly hand came to rest on my knee. I couldn't feel it. "Madison, it's how a person comes out of a difficult time that counts."

I smiled. It was amazing to have Mom there. I rambled on about the last few years, absentmindedly rubbing the orchid charm. I told her about school, how Dad's handyman business had grown, and how Chase had her eyes. "Chase possesses the powers too."

Mom laughed so hard when I told her about the presents bobbing their way into the kitchen during Chase's birthday party, and I found myself laughing right along with her. "I made him promise not to wish anything into becoming real. Isaac said it should be enough to keep his powers locked down, for now."

"You're father has an open mind. When you're ready to tell him what you and Chase are, he'll be able to accept it."

"I know." Dad had always been supportive of Chase and me.

"So…" Mom's eyes grew to the size of golf balls. "Tell me about Isaac."

A smile stretched across my face. "He's caring and fun, and he gets this sly sort of smirk when he looks at me." I scrunched my nose. "It makes my heart skip a beat." I paused. "I like who I am when I'm with him. I think you'd like him."

"I've seen you with him. He's a good guy, Madison." Her gaze dropped to my hand. "If you're not careful, you're going to lose him."

Just like Dad had said. I palmed the charm, holding it hidden in my grip. "Caden's just a friend." Whom I happened to have a complicated relationship with.

Mom ran a hand over the grass. Her fingers passed through the blades as if they weren't there. "Did I ever tell you about Danny Ireland?"

I shook my head.

"I was a sophomore in college."

"That was the year you met Dad."

She nodded. "Danny was the DJ for the college radio station. He was sweet—" She giggled. "No, he was charming, handsome, and came from money. All the girls at school wanted to be his girlfriend because he had access to some of the finer things in life: fancy charity events, tickets to sporting events, dinner at the best restaurants. They hated that we hung out."

It was weird to hear Mom talk about another guy. "Were you dating him?"

"No. But I wasn't blind, either. Our friendship could have grown into more." I could tell from her smile that she and Danny'd had a good relationship. "But I was a realist. He and I were from two different worlds, and I knew I wouldn't be happy in his, yet I couldn't ask him to give up the big house and lavish lifestyle he was accustomed to for me."

That was the hidden message in her story: I needed to decide what I wanted in life, and I needed to make choices that helped me to achieve those goals. I didn't belong in Caden's world. Heck, he wasn't even human.

"Plus," Mom said, "I had a crush on this guy in my art class. He had the most amazing candy-brown eyes. He was easygoing, spontaneous, and thought cheesy fries were one of life's delicacies."

I smiled. "That guy was Dad."

"Yeah. We started dating later that year."

"What happened to Danny?"

"We remained friends. Even went to each other's weddings. Last I heard, he was living in New York."

Mom was never one to lecture. She'd give me her advice in a roundabout way and let me decide what to do. She didn't ask me about Caden, nor did she say anything else about Danny, but I knew her Danny was my Caden.

We talked awhile longer, and when it came time to say good-bye, I didn't feel as if I was losing her all over again.

Dad had just poured himself a cup of coffee when I got home. "Is my truck still in one piece?"

"Yes." I stared at him, for the first time noticing that his irises were the color of the root beer candy Chase was so fond of.

"What?"

"Nothing." I smiled and bumped him with my hip to get him to move from in front of the cabinet with the coffee mugs.

Later that day, the doorbell rang.

"I got it!" I hollered as I hopped down the stairs.

Isaac waited on the other side of the door with his hands stuck in his jacket pockets and a serious expression stamped across his face. My talk with Mom had helped me to put things in perspective. Caden wasn't going anywhere anytime soon, so it was good that we were friends — the next three-and-a-half decades would be long and torturous if we weren't. But Isaac and I had chemistry. We went well together. And he was the one who got my heart fluttering with just a look.

Ignoring the way his lips formed a straight line and the way his eyes seemed to look everywhere but at me, I grabbed his hand and pulled him inside. A quick glance over my shoulder told me that Dad and Chase couldn't see us. I wrapped my arms around his neck and planted a kiss on his delicious lips. "Hi."

"Hi back at you." He wrapped an arm around my waist and kissed me again. He smelled like a mix of the ocean, which would be his shampoo, and vanilla — his powers. I stifled my giggle as he backed us up a few steps and savored the moment.

"I didn't think I'd see you tonight." I slipped my fingers though his and called to Dad, "It's Isaac. We're going to study upstairs."

"Leave the door open!"

Isaac and I barely made it a step into my room before I threw my arms around his neck again. He picked me up and carried me to the bed. We were being bold, considering Dad and Chase were home, but I thought making out for a few minutes was worth the risk.

He trailed a line of kisses down my neck and along my collarbone. "I can't stay long."

I draped a leg over his and let out a moan of disappointment. "Can't you skip your cousin's party?"

He'd invited me to go with him, but the last time I had attended one of his family functions, the guys ended up watching sports on the big-screen TV in the den while the girls sat around talking about past family events. Seeing as I didn't have much to contribute to the conversation, I'd found myself spending the evening trying not to yawn.

He moved my hair away from my eyes with his fingers. "I can't, but I had to see you before I went." His sober expression was back.

"Is everything okay?"

He kissed me. "Yeah, thanks to your greeting. I needed that."

My eyes narrowed. Isaac sat up and handed me a dark blue bottle he'd taken out of his pocket.

I pushed myself up and accepted it. "What's this?"

"*Somnium Remedium*. It's a sleep elixir."

"Sleep elixir?" I echoed.

"I got it from Anastasia. Put a teaspoon in tea or take it straight and you'll have a dream-free sleep."

Had Anastasia been referring to my dreams when she'd told me Isaac had a right to know? I pulled the cork from the top and inhaled its sweet bouquet. "It smells like strawberries."

"It comes in a couple different flavors. I thought you'd like that one." Isaac scrubbed a hand over his face and raked his fingers through his hair. "Why didn't you tell me you were dreaming about Reed?"

"How'd you find out?"

Something dark passed over his face. "Caden."

I didn't know what to say. *He had no right to tell you* seemed petty, considering if Caden had gone to Isaac, then he had to be worried there'd be a time he'd arrive after I had opened the door to Sanctus. *How much did he tell you?* would have been the same thing as saying I had something to hide. And *You weren't supposed to find out* seemed ungrateful, considering Isaac had found a way to help me. I settled for the same thing I kept telling Caden.

"They were only dreams."

Isaac snorted. "That had you gathering the things you'd need to reopen the door to the faerie realm."

I recapped the bottle. "I didn't want to worry you."

"But you were fine with worrying Caden." Isaac stalked away from me. He looked out the window in a daze. "How do you think I felt when the guy who is supposed to mean nothing to you has to tell me that you need help?"

"I was handling it." More like ignoring the dreams with the hopes they'd stop on their own. "Caden only knows because he can read minds." And because of the connections we shared due to my contract, I wanted to say, but I wasn't sure if Isaac knew that Caden had been the one to wake me from several of the dreams, and there was no way I'd be the one to tell him that.

"And I only know because you refused his assistance." Isaac continued to watch the world through the window.

"I'd have to make a deal with him. I don't want to owe him more than I already do."

"Do you have any idea how hard it is for me to watch my girlfriend leave me to spend time with another guy? I tell myself it's business. That Chase is alive because of Caden, and that I shouldn't get upset, but I do. I hate that I couldn't save Chase—"

"You did save Chase," I said. After the car accident that my brother and I had been in, the doctors couldn't figure out how Chase had hung on. They'd told us it was only a matter of time before his body would give out. They hadn't known that Isaac had been the one keeping Chase's heart beating. Isaac had played as big a part in saving Chase from certain death as Caden had. "If it weren't for your powers, my brother wouldn't have lived long enough to be cured."

"I could only delay his passing. Caden healed his wounds." Isaac heaved out a sigh. "I get why you don't argue with Caden. Why you're doing his bidding. And I see how your relationship with him has changed. How you trust him."

I rubbed a finger over the bottle's smooth glass. I did trust Caden to keep his word, to honor our contract, and to not put me in harm's way. He had risked his existence to protect me from his boss, and he had trusted me with a talisman that could have been used against him.

"He cares about you," Isaac said. "And I know you care about him."

"As a friend." I set the bottle on my dresser. "Isaac, look at me."

When he didn't, I rested a hand on his arm and turned him so that we faced each other. "Yes, Caden and I have become friends. He and I are stuck with each other, and it's better to get along than to despise one another. But at the end of the day, you're the one I look forward to seeing. You're the one I choose to spend time with. That's not going to change."

He nodded.

I ducked down to catch his diverted gaze. "Caden hasn't just shown up to pull me away from you or our friends since I had him amend our contract. I did that for you, so that I wouldn't have to cut our time together short to go on demon duty."

"I know."

I slipped my fingers through his. Relief flooded me when he gripped my hand tight.

"Thanks for the elixir." I planned on trying it tonight. If Isaac believed it would block my dreams, so did I.

"You're welcome."

My arms slid around his waist, and I craned my neck to brush my lips against his. "Are you sure you can't skip that party?" I bit his bottom lip. "Your house will be empty for, what…a few hours," I cooed.

Isaac's mouth pulled upward into the sly grin of a fox. "Maybe you could talk me into skipping it."

I smiled and covered his mouth with mine.

Acknowledgments

This is always a fun part of publishing a book.

I'd like to thank the dedicated and hard-working professionals at Omnific Publishing for believing in me not just once, but three times, and for helping make my dream of sharing this series with readers a reality. Special thanks to my amazing editor, Colleen Keough Wagner, whom I've been blessed to work with on this series. Her enthusiasm and keen eye for detail helped polish *Entwined*, and I couldn't have captured the local color of the British setting in one of the scenes without her knowledge. I'd also like to thank my publicist, Traci Olsen, whose support never wavers. It's great to know she's just an email away.

Thanks to my family, who remain supportive of my writing. I love you guys.

And last but definitely not least, thanks to my readers, whose love of Madison and her friends, their world, and the trouble they get in is the reason *Entwined* exists. You rock.

About the Author

Cherie believes there's a little magic in everyone. She also believes in following her dreams and never giving up. Her books are proof of that.

Besides writing, Cherie enjoys spending time with family and friends, reading, the great outdoors, and she loves a challenge. While she has had many great experiences, what she finds most satisfying is seeing her children and stories grow into their own exciting and distinct entities.

Cherie lives in Illinois with her family. This is her third book for young adults. To learn more about Cherie and her novels, visit CherieColyer.com.

New Adult Romance

Three Daves by Nicki Elson
Streamline by Jennifer Lane
The Shades series: *Shades of Atlantis* & *Shades of Avalon* by Carol Oates
The Heart series: *Beside Your Heart, Disclosure of the Heart* & *Forever Your Heart*
by Mary Whitney
Romancing the Bookworm by Kate Evangelista
Flirting with Chaos by Kenya Wright
The Vice, Virtue & Video series: *Revealed, Captured, Desired* & *Devoted* by Bianca Giovanni
Granton University series: *Loving Lies* by Linda Kage
Missing Pieces by Meredith Tate

Paranormal & Fantasy Romance

The Light series: *Seers of Light, Whisper of Light* & *Circle of Light* by Jennifer DeLucy
The Hanaford Park series: *Eve of Samhain* & *Pleasures Untold* by Lisa Sanchez
Immortal Awakening by KC Randall
The Seraphim series: *Crushed Seraphim* & *Bittersweet Seraphim* by Debra Anastasia
The Guardian's Wild Child by Feather Stone
Grave Refrain by Sarah M. Glover
The Divinity series: *Divinity* & *Entity* by Patricia Leever
The Blood Vine series: *Blood Vine, Blood Entangled* & *Blood Reunited* by Amber Belldene
Divine Temptation by Nicki Elson
The Dead Rapture series: *Love in the Time of the Dead, Love at the End of Days* &
Love Starts with Z by Tera Shanley
The Hidden Races series: *Incandescent* & *Illumination* by M.V. Freeman
Something Wicked by Carol Oates
Chronicles of Midvalen: *Command the Tides* (book 1) by Wren Handman

Romantic Suspense

Whirlwind by Robin DeJarnett
The CONduct series: *With Good Behavior, Bad Behavior* & *On Best Behavior* by Jennifer Lane
Indivisible by Jessica McQuinn
Between the Lies by Alison Oburia
Blind Man's Bargain by Tracy Winegar

Erotic Romance

The Keyhole series: *Becoming sage* (book 1) by Kasi Alexander
The Keyhole series: *Saving sunni* (book 2) by Kasi & Reggie Alexander
The Winemaker's Dinner: *Appetizers* & *Entrée* by Dr. Ivan Rusilko & Everly Drummond
The Winemaker's Dinner: *Dessert* by Dr. Ivan Rusilko
Client N° 5 by Joy Fulcher
The Enclave series: *Closer and Closer* (book 1) by Jenna Barton

Historical Romance

Cat O' Nine Tails by Patricia Leever
Burning Embers by Hannah Fielding
Seven for a Secret by Rumer Haven
The Counterfeit by Tracy Winegar

Anthologies

A Valentine Anthology including short stories by
Alice Clayton ("With a Double Oven"),
Jennifer DeLucy ("Magnus of Pfelt, Conquering Viking Lord"),
Nicki Elson ("I Don't Do Valentine's Day"),
Jessica McQuinn ("Better Than One Dead Rose and a Monkey Card"),
Victoria Michaels ("Home to Jackson"), and
Alison Oburia ("The Bridge")

Taking Liberties including an introduction by Tiffany Reisz and short stories by
Mina Vaughn ("John Hancock-Blocked"),
Linda Cunningham ("A Boston Marriage"),
Joy Fulcher ("Tea for Two"),
KC Holly ("The British Are Coming!"),
Kimberly Jensen & Scott Stark ("E. Pluribus Threesome"), and
Vivian Rider ("M'Lady's Secret Service")

Sets

The Heart Series Box Set (*Beside Your Heart, Disclosure of the Heart* &
Forever Your Heart) by Mary Whitney
The CONduct Series Box Set (*With Good Behavior, Bad Behavior* &
On Best Behavior) by Jennifer Lane
The Light Series Box Set (*Seers of Light, Whisper of Light, Circle of Light* &
Glimpse of Light) by Jennifer DeLucy
The Blood Vine Series Box Set (*Blood Vine, Blood Entangled, Blood Reunited* &
Blood Eternal) by Amber Belldene

Singles, Novellas & Special Editions

It's Only Kinky the First Time (A Keyhole series single) by Kasi Alexander
Learning the Ropes (A Keyhole series single) by Kasi & Reggie Alexander
The Winemaker's Dinner: RSVP by Dr. Ivan Rusilko
The Winemaker's Dinner: No Reservations by Everly Drummond
Big Guns by Jessica McQuinn
Concessions by Robin DeJarnett
Starstruck by Lisa Sanchez

New Flame by BJ Thornton
Shackled by Debra Anastasia
Swim Recruit by Jennifer Lane
Sway by Nicki Elson
Full Speed Ahead by Susan Kaye Quinn
The Second Sunrise by Hannah Downing
The Summer Prince by Carol Oates
Whatever it Takes by Sarah M. Glover
Clarity (A *Divinity* prequel single) by Patricia Leever
A Christmas Wish (A *Cocktails & Dreams* single) by Autumn Markus
Late Night with Andres by Debra Anastasia
Poughkeepsie (enhanced iPad app collector's edition) by Debra Anastasia
Poughkeepsie (audio book edition) by Debra Anastasia
Blood Eternal (A Blood Vine series single, epilogue to series) by Amber Belldene
Carnaval de Amor (*The Winemaker's Dinner*, Spanish edition)
by Dr. Ivan Rusilko & Everly Drummond

coming soon from
OMNIFIC PUBLISHING

The Adventures of Clarissa Hardy by Chloe Gillis
The Hidden Races series: *Illumination* (book 2) by M.V. Freeman
The Ground Rules by Roya Carmen
Trouble Me by Beck Anderson
The Forever series: *Forever Winter* (book 2) by Christopher Scott Wagner

www.ingramcontent.com/pod-product-compliance
Lightning Source LLC
Chambersburg PA
CBHW020512120726
47904CB00003B/807